"**I** am not about to be shackled . . . owned . . . not now . . . not again, and not by you!" Holly cried in desperation.

He was stung by her words. Odd that they penetrated, but they did. He only wanted her body. He only wanted what her body could do for him . . . at this moment. There was no future in that and it was fair enough. He couldn't know that she was still a virgin, an innocent, and that she thought sex, love, and marriage were words that went together. She stared at him a long moment. Her arms came up to cover her nakedness and with a stifled cry she ran from the room. . . .

Fawcett Books
by Claudette Williams:

AFTER THE STORM   23928 $1.75

COTILLION FOR MANDY   23664 $1.75

JEWELENE   50060 $1.75

LACEY   50007 $1.75

LADY BRANDY   50165 $1.75

NAUGHTY LADY NESS   50045 $1.75

PASSION'S PRIDE   24278 $2.50

Buy them at your local bookstore or use this handy coupon for ordering.

COLUMBIA BOOK SERVICE (a CBS Publications Co.)
32275 Mally Road, P.O. Box FB, Madison Heights, MI 48071

Please send me the books I have checked above. Orders for less than 5
books must include 75¢ for the first book and 25¢ for each additional
book to cover postage and handling. Orders for 5 books or more postage
is FREE. Send check or money order only.

Cost $_____	Name _____
Sales tax*_____	Address _____
Postage_____	City _____
Total $_____	State _____ Zip _____

*The government requires us to collect sales tax in all states except AK,
DE, MT, NH and OR.*

This offer expires 1 December 81   8999

DESERT ROSE . . . ENGLISH MOON

Claudette Williams

FAWCETT CREST • NEW YORK

DESERT ROSE . . . ENGLISH MOON

Published by Fawcett Crest Books, a unit of CBS Publications, the Consumer Publishing Division of CBS Inc.

ISBN: 0-449-24388-5

Printed in the United States of America

First Fawcett Crest Printing: April 1981

10 9 8 7 6 5 4 3 2 1

dedicated with appreciation to:

> *My uncle, Dr. Alfred Nissan, who pointed me to genetic manipulation;*
>
> *And to Bob Conn and his wonderful Norwood Farms*

Part One

Chapter One

Spring is a seductive season. Its early rushes of scents and sounds enchant the senses, soothe the soul. It was 1958, it was spring, and London was in a fever, but this time Mustafa came ready to accept the Western World.

It had not been so in his salad days. When he had been a young and studious man at Cambridge he had found things there to be degrading, tastes to appal, but the years had taught him much and he came this time with a mind willing to be enticed.

He looked at the women who wore no *mukhamara aba* to cover their faces and bodies and this time he was not shy about his thoughts. He went to English pubs and studied the Englishmen gulping down their ales in hearty enjoyment and smiled at them. Gone was the diffident young Arab student and in his place stood a mature man who had seen and accepted much change.

It was in this frame of mind and on his fourth day in London that he chose to visit the Tower of London. He strolled past the quaintly garbed attendants to the main causeway. Construction was underway, and he stopped to casually study what was being done to the stone framework.

A voice, feminine, light, and musical, came to his ears and brought his head around. This was his first glimpse of Delia Winslow, and as his lips parted he felt himself stunned.

Mustafa's dark Arabian eyes were mesmerized, his body was held in a spellbound grip, and his thoughts were frozen. Nowhere had he ever seen a woman whose total aura so captivated. Her height seemed perfection, her figure even in its confining gray suit denoted its delectability. Her full waving hair fell to her shoulders in sparkling lights of reddish gold. Her skin glowed in creamy smoothness, and her round aqua-blue eyes held a delightful twinkle as she spoke to the assembled group of tourists,

"The Tower's ravens are protected by law," she was saying brightly. "Once a common thing in London, there are but these six, kept here at the Tower, and it is said that the Tower will fall if it loses its ravens." She was smiling, moving her group of day-trippers onward, answering questions easily as she kept them walking.

Mustafa followed. He couldn't help himself. His feet simply glided in her direction. He had to keep on listening to her voice, looking at her face. She was speaking still about the ravens.

"Yes," she answered someone's query, "they do attain a remarkable age. We have a fellow here known as Mr. James Crow, and he has been a resident of the tower for thirty years." She smiled at their awed response. "And we expect he shall continue to grace us with his presence for still another thirty years. . . ." She moved on to the Bell Tower, all the while answering questions and entertaining her group.

Mustafa followed. He could not help himself, did not wish to try. He only knew that he had to pursue. She was a goddess to be worshiped. She was an angel to be adored. Under the power of such thoughts, what could he do but follow and listen?

However, this was not without its difficulties. He had inched closer to her and to her group at every stop they made, and because of this she gradually became aware of his presence. She glanced sharply his way a few times, subtly warning him off, and then in some consternation she watched him approach.

In a low, pleasant voice she advised him that if he wished a guided tour of the establishment he would have to purchase a ticket at the main gate and join the next tour group.

8

Not at all disturbed by this, he nodded and asked, "This next group . . . it will be conducted by you?"

She put up a brow, and there was disapprobation in the inflection of her tone. "No, sir, but I think you will be pleased to find a satisfactory guide. All our personnel are quite capable, you know."

"Ah, of course. Now, when next do *you* lead a tour?" He was not at all deterred by her coldness. Women were such creatures. Often they had to be pursued. . . .

She stopped herself from retorting harshly. Arrogant, but of course he was. He was living up to the reputation of Arab men. She had heard about their attitude toward women. She knew too that more and more of them were in hot pursuit of English women. Dangerous. They were supposed to be dangerous for the emotions. No. She didn't need that. She could see her group becoming restless; some were wandering off on their own. She moved to collect them, but he followed. There was nothing for it but to dismiss him with the information he required.

"I will next be leading a tour from the first counter in about thirty minutes." She did not smile at him as she moved away with her tour, but she could see the gleam in his dark eyes, and in spite of herself it thrilled her.

Mustafa waited the thirty minutes patiently. He was a determined man. As she came along to collect the small assembled party near the ticket counter she could see him in the crowd. He towered above all the other men. He was not handsome, yet there was something arrestingly attractive in his dark face. His black hair was tinged interestingly with silver at the temples, and the curls that fell over his forehead gleamed with it. Her perusal continued in spite of her self-rebukes, and she discovered that his white continental suit displayed his frame to advantage. She felt her aqua-blue eyes harden against him. Danger . . . detour . . . now! He was from the Middle East. That presented problems, and she didn't need any more problems now. It was too soon. Hastily she yanked her eyes away from him and discovered an elderly American woman tugging at her sleeve.

"Miss . . . miss . . . what I really want to see is Henry VIII's things . . . and where he killed off all those wives of his. . . ."

Delia Winslow smiled kindly. "We will wind up our tour with the White and Bloody Towers, which hold Henry VIII's artifacts." Over the elderly woman's head she could see Mustafa's lips curve and his dark eyes glitter enigmatically. She sucked in breath and addressed her group.

"Ladies and gentlemen, my name is Mrs. Delia Winslow. I am your guide and shall be pleased to answer any questions you may have as we take a tour of the Tower of London." She was again looking at *him*. A sudden giggle tickled her as she realized he had been startled when she introduced herself as a Mrs. She wanted to hide her ungloved hands and did indeed clasp them at her back. Too late. His glance had already discovered that she wore no rings. Well, just let him worry about it anyway, she thought as she led her group onward.

Mustafa took a reclining position at most of their stops, finding a wall or other appropriate structure and leaning into it to listen to her recitals. He watched her, studied her lips as she explained how William the Conqueror had built the Tower and its accompanying edifices for the purpose of protecting and controlling the city. He frowned darkly whenever a tourist interrupted her with a question, and he smiled to discover she was wonderfully even-tempered, with bright, smiling eyes. Aqua-blue, such aqua-blue eyes. Devastating.

At the tour's end he stood back and a frown hovered over his dark features. He watched intently and with some irritability as members of the tour group pressed gratuities into Mrs. Winslow's hand. He felt a wave of agitation and controlled it. This was the West, where such things were done. Things were different here for women. He waited until the group dispersed, and as she started to move away he called her name, softly, gently,

"Mrs. Winslow . . . ?"

She turned. She had expected him to make a move. Now, of course, he would offer to take her to lunch. Well, she would just tell him it was impossible.

"Yes, sir?"

"When next is your tour again, please?"

He looked a veritable boy. Puppy eyes bright with expectation. No. This was impossible. He was an Arab. He was a man brought up to believe women were playthings . . . yet he made no cunning move.

She was taken aback. "When? But surely you do not wish to remain waiting about until I take on another group?"

"Yes, but I do," he answered simply. His dark eyes were somber.

"You cannot mean it. Look . . . perhaps you don't realize. I am going to lunch now. I shan't be back here for another group for at least an hour."

"An hour then." He smiled, pleased enough with this.

She stared at him for a long moment. This was impossible. He didn't seem to want more than table scraps, and that did not fit in with the picture she had formed of Middle Eastern men. She started to move away. Guilt! It waved through her body, taking over completely, and she found herself stopping and turning around.

"Perhaps, sir . . ."

"Mustafa el Zahour," he corrected gently. "It is my name and only fitting that you should use it, as I have dared to use yours."

His manners were charming. She found herself softening toward him. He seemed a helpless being, lost and lonely.

"Well . . . er . . . Mr. Zahour . . . it may be that you are hungry? May I recommend somewhere to eat while you are waiting?"

11

"That is very kind, but as I do not want to miss your next tour, I think I shall remain here."

There was no reason to feel such agitation, but she did. Flooding through her system, pounding at her brain, guilt, guilt, guilt! Damnation, but he was a stranger. Why should she care whether he sat and waited alone for an hour?

With a sigh of resignation she turned back to him once again.

"Mr. Zahour . . . would you like to join me for lunch? I have only a sandwich and an apple . . . but I am a light eater and don't mind sharing with you. . . ."

He grinned wide. "I am honored." He bent his arm and offered it to her.

That's how it began.

Chapter Two

Beautiful women usually play starring roles in the dreams of most men, and Delia Winslow headed the cast that floated about in Miles Eckford's fantasies. He had decided that she would one day be mistress of his bed, and he had diligently worked toward that goal.

He was a wealthy man, powerful both financially and politically. He was also married, but that fact certainly never weighed with him as he pursued Delia. It was a cool evening, and he pulled his gloves on tighter as he took the steps that would bring him to her flat. Damn, but he had wanted her from the first moment he had seen her in that pub near Westminster. He had backed into her and spilled his ale over them both. She had been loaded down with packages, and she had laughed and managed somehow to come up with a napkin.

"Here . . . take these," she said on a light note as she shoved the three small crisply wrapped packages into his open arms. "I don't have a table, so you'll just have

12

to hold them while I dry both of us off." She went about the matter briskly, good-naturedly.

He found his voice. "Please . . . I have a table reserved . . . there." He pointed with his squared chin: "Do allow me to make it up to you . . . won't you join me for a bite of lunch?"

She continued to brush away at the glistening dark ale that covered his rich brown suit. "Oh, that isn't necessary . . . and besides, I've nearly finished drying off your suit."

"Hang my suit . . . never liked it anyway."

She laughed. "No? I can't imagine why. It is very conservative and exactly fits the party you campaign for."

He was flattered. She had recognized him. Damn but she was a stunning bird. "Please," he said with adroit charm, "do allow me to redeem myself. Have lunch with me."

She liked his face—he was ever so handsome—and she was intrigued by his manner. He was already leading her to his booth, and she had to admit that she was a bit impressed with him. "Thank you," she said softly as he seated her.

"What will you have to drink?"

"White wine."

He was gone and when next he returned he was laden down with an assortment of cold cuts, another ale for himself, and an excellent white wine, which he watched her sip for a long moment before he said anything.

That was how they met. She had agreed to see him again, and just as he felt himself progressing with her, she discovered that he was a married man. While he had never allowed his wife and child to interfere with the pursuit of his pleasures, he found that Delia Winslow had principles about such things. Nothing he had done had altered her principles, and he was at a standstill, for he meant to have her, one way or another. . . .

Delia opened her door and stood back, a frown descending over her features. "Miles . . . I rather thought I made it clear . . ."

He smiled apologetically. "You did . . . but it doesn't make it any easier for me." He gave her his most charming smile. "Please . . ." he said on a mournful note. "Won't you let me in for just a bit?"

"There isn't any point. I . . . I like you, Miles . . . but I don't want to get involved with you."

Gently he pushed open the door, and as she stepped back and away from him, he kicked it shut behind him. Quickly he took her into his strong arms and brought her to him. "You want me, Delia . . you know that you do. . . ." His mouth found hers and tried to force the truth of his words.

She fought him. She had found Miles attractive and had been drawn to him, but he was another woman's husband, and it mattered to her. She struggled out of his embrace. "Miles . . . please go . . . I have someone calling for me."

He pulled up straight and glanced over her. She was wearing a soft angora sweater of dark blue and a tight-fitting skirt. She looked marvelous. "With who?" he demanded. His sources had faithfully adviced him that she had been seeing no one.

"That is none of your business," she snapped. He was beginning to worry her.

"Oh, but it is," he said quietly and took her by the arm and pressed her close. "Anything you do is my business, because I make it so!"

She put up her chin and braved him, though his attitude was beginning to make her tremble. "Miles . . . stop this . . . you have no right—" Her door knocker sounded and she jumped toward the door to open it.

Mustafa's smile was bright before it suddenly vanished, for he discovered a man at Delia's back. "Ah . . . I am afraid that I am early . . ."

"No, no, Mustafa . . . you are just in time." She turned to make hasty introductions and then said gently, "Mr. Eckford was just leaving."

Miles Eckford was furious. More than that, he was

14

horrified. Here was a Moslem. She was seeing a Moslem? When had this happened? Damn, but he wasn't about to be cut out by an Arab! He pulled up his self-control and managed to make a creditable departure, but Delia felt a shudder as she watched him go.

Mustafa observed and said on a soothing note, "He worries you?"

She gave him a half-smile and said simply, "He wants me . . . and while it does not worry me, it upsets me."

"Why?"

"I don't know. . . ."

"You do not want him?"

"No." She looked into herself and smiled. "No . . . but what I do want is that dinner you promised." With which she took Mustafa's arm and merrily started forward.

"Ah me," groaned Mustafa mockingly, for he was well pleased, "to be led by a woman . . ."

Morning came through Delia's windows in flooding accents. She groaned pleasurably and rolled to one side and then another before blinking and peeping up at her alarm clock. Seven . . . it was seven in the morning. She still had some time before she had to rouse herself for the daily grind. It wasn't, though, not really. She enjoyed her work. It kept her busy, and what's more it paid the bills, those ever-mounting bills.

Mustafa? Hmmm. So handsome, charming, so boyishly appealing. Involved? No . . . she couldn't risk getting involved with him. He came from a different background, had different notions about the world . . . about love, life, and the way of things. He was by his own words the very opposite of everything that she stood for.

What had he said? Oh yes, how shocked he had been as a young man studying in Cambridge.

"Ah, Delia . . . what did I know of the world . . . of women? Everything about the British shocked me then."

"And now?" she inquired softly, for his dark eyes drew her to him in a way she could not resist.

"And now all that is changed." He laughed. "Look at me ... I am now the Haji. That alone makes me a different being."

"The Haji? What is that? What does that mean?"

"It is a title ... only unlike your aristocracy, one is not born to it. One must make the pilgrimage to Mecca, pray facing the black amber stone ..."

"On foot? Did you make that journey on foot?"

"Ah, so you do know something of our customs?" He smiled, well pleased.

A tinge of color touched her cheek. "Oh ... as to that, I really know so little ... but I did read something once about the pilgrimage to Mecca and its importance."

He smiled ruefully. "Now one has merely to take a plane. But yes, there is a required distance that must be walked ... and then, a man may return honored."

She smiled. "So, now you are the Haji and you are no longer shocked by the free and jolly British?"

"How could I be shocked by the British? I have been to the United States." He was teasing. "A marvelous people ... all of them children." He grew thoughtful, and there was a frown drawing his brows together. "My country suffers upheaval ... they have killed King Faisal and Prime Minister Nouri Pasha. I had great respect for these men, and I am disgusted with the behavior of my mind."

"Politics are beyond sensitive people, Mustafa," she offered gently.

He smiled brightly and said, "So they are. . . . Now tell me about yourself."

"No ... there is something else I want to know first."

"What is it, *fidwa?*" Already the endearment came naturally to his lips.

"Mustafa ... Mustafa ... how is it you are not ..."

"But I am." His features were grave. "I have two wives."

"What?" She scarcely kept it from being a shriek.

He reached out to hold her in her place, keep her

16

from leaving, for she gave every appearance of a woman about to run.

"I am honest with you, Delia . . . so you have no need to go. If you feel you must after you have heard me out, then of course I shall escort you home."

"What is there to explain? You have two wives . . . *two!*" It was an appalling fact to face.

"My family made the arrangements for my first wife. I never saw her until our wedding. She is the mother of my son, and I have great respect for her. You understand?" He waited for Delia to nod and then continued, "There was no passion with my first wife . . . there was not that sort of feeling . . . so I found a pretty woman whom I desired, and because she came from a good family, there was no way of . . . having her without the marriage. It is not an uncommon thing for a Moslem man . . ."

"No . . . but Mustafa . . . it is not something I can cope with."

He smiled. "Then you care for me?"

"No . . . yes . . . I don't know . . . how can I?"

"You are attracted to me?" he pursued.

"Yes . . . and I don't want to let it go any farther, Mustafa. It wouldn't be fair to me."

"Do you want me to take you home?" It was a resigned, dreadful sound.

Delia Winslow surprised herself. "No, I want our evening to end on the pleasant note it started with. Dinner and a show is what you offered me, Mustafa el Zahour, and I still haven't had my dessert!"

Delia stretched and got to her feet. It was time to take her morning shower. Last night had been . . . last night, and from here on she was going to have to force herself to her senses. Oh, but the evening had been wonderful . . . Mustafa's kisses at her door had nearly melted her will. She had almost allowed him to come into her flat . . . to stay. Somehow she had caught herself up. Somehow she had stopped him, but she felt as though his mouth still burned against her own, and what was worse, she wanted more of the same. Wake

17

up! He has two wives . . . two, for God sake! Just what was she going to do? Forget him. You must, she told herself, but could she?

Miles Eckford rolled over in his twin bed and studied the sleeping form of his wife. She was a sweet woman, an excellent wife and mother. She came from good aristocratic stock, and his marriage to her had furthered his career. She was just the sort of wife he needed. She managed to add to his consequence, for he always heard her praised by his political colleagues, and he was well pleased to call her his wife. However, there she was, so very near . . . and he could have her, for she never refused herself to him. He could have her . . . but he just didn't seem to want her, not when all he could think of was possessing Delia.

Damn it! How dare that little bird refuse him? How dare she? Miles Eckford had been brought up to expect many things as his due. He did not in his thirty-two years ever know the experience of rejection, and Delia Winslow's rejection did not go down well. Oh, he wanted her for the pleasure of having her, but that want had little to do with his need to obliterate her rejection.

He knew that Delia was strapped for money, and this knowledge led him to a certain point in his speculations. What would she do if she were without a job and could no longer sustain herself? Just how long would she hold out against his proposal then? Her job? Ha, that was an easy enough thing to handle. Ah, but what of the Arab? Would she turn to the Arab? And then very slowly a sly grin spread over his features, because he knew just how to solve his problem.

He got to his feet, quietly found his slippers, and moved to his adjoining study, where he moved soundlessly over the plush salt-and-pepper carpet to his desk, picked up his telephone, and started his morning.

Helen Eckford listened to him as he got up from bed and moved to his study. What was he up to? Was he calling *her?* Oh yes, she knew all about Delia Winslow. Well, not all about her, for she had only seen them

18

together once. Miles had been indiscreet enough to take the woman to dinner at the Dorchester. . . .

Helen was resigned to such things. She knew what her husband was, what she could expect of him, but somehow Delia Winslow worried her. She had decided to have the Winslow woman investigated, and even this had not turned up very much. She wasn't about to allow Miles to go overboard about this woman . . . risk his career. She was already at her husband's study door, listening. She meant to save him from himself, for in addition to being what Miles thought was a "good wife," she was ambitious for him and, through him, for herself.

Mustafa el Zahour studied himself as he shaved, and his mirrored reflection blurred into a vision of Delia. Red-gold hair of amber lights glistened. Aqua eyes sparkled mischievously, accusingly, laughingly. She was so alive, so real, so very full and many-sided. What was happening to him? Was he changing? Was he becoming a new man after all these years? What had she done to him?

She was an Englishwoman. She was willful, stubborn, frank to a fault, independent, and infinitely desirable in all these aspects. Where did he take it from here?

She would not have him . . . or would she? He had kissed her, and it had sent him into heat. He had never felt that way before. She had responded. He knew it, felt it. She had reacted to him, she wanted him . . . and yet she had sent him off. What to do? He had to have her. Now, one must realize that there was no thought of being unfaithful to either of his two wives as he contemplated Delia. He was a Moslem male, he was Haji, and he was wealthy enough to contemplate four wives had he wished, but it was not marriage with Delia that he was presently considering.

Oh no, that would never do. She was English, and besides, she would never be happy in Iraq, no, no, not Delia. Lovely, bubbling, soft, gracious, and indepen-

19

dent Delia. She just would not mold to Iraq's custom's. What to do? Make her his mistress? And why not? She was no virgin girl. She was a widow, living alone, taking on modern life. It was all very simple, if only she would come around to his way of thinking. If only . . . but she must, she had to, because he found he wanted her more than he had ever wanted a woman before.

Mustafa sighed heavily, for it was a stumbling block from all sides. He couldn't lose her? Well then, one way or another he would woo her, charm her, seduce her, and make her happy. Yes, he wanted her happy. It mattered. An odd thing, that. He had never spent much time wondering whether or not either of his wives was happy; he had always supposed it to be so. It was different with Delia. He wanted to hear her cry out with joy. He wanted to see bliss written in her eyes, and what was more, he wanted to be the cause.

Well then, he would start by leasing a lovely long English Rolls and riding to the Tower at the end of her day. There he would dazzle her and whisk her off to the country. They would dine, they would dance, they would talk, and by Allah, he would win Delia Winslow and make her his own.

As Delia's pump heel caught, bent, and broke on the curb she cursed in exasperation. It was turning out to be one hell of a day! Too many unanswerable questions had been flung at her during the course of her tours, and somehow she had not found her usual patience to cope. Somehow she had managed, but she had known from the looks she received and the small gratuities that she had not given enough to the curious tourists.

She had made it through lunch and floated absently on to her afternoon groups, but all she could think of all this time was Mustafa. Just where was Mustafa? Would he come by for lunch? Would he suddenly appear among the collection of tourists? Where could he be? Didn't he want to see her any more? And of course not, she had told him she couldn't, wouldn't see him.

Where was he? Why hadn't he come by during her lunch hour? Would she never see him again? And why . . . why did it bother her so?

And then the ax fell and she discovered the head that rolled was hers.

Mr. Perkins was a man who had found life hard to deal with. He had achieved none of the things he had set out to do, and so he receded into himself and found an emptiness as depressing as the demeanor he wore. He was stuffy, and aged, and since his only pleasure was eating, gross. He ambled forward in his dark three-piece suit and touched the spectacles as they fell over his snubbed nose,

"Mrs. Winslow." His tone was low but sharp, more than usual. Its effect was to nearly stun Delia into speechlessness, as he rarely addressed her. What could she have done? What was wrong?

"Yes, sir?"

"Come with me to my office . . . at once."

"Yes, sir." She followed obediently. What had happened? Had one of the tourists complained about her? No. She wasn't that bad. A little out of it, surely, but she hadn't been rude to anyone.

She followed him into his rather starkly decorated office and turned to close the door when his voice pierced through her trenchantly,

"Leave it open!" There was no smile, no cordiality, as he moved to his uncluttered and orderly desk and drew forth an envelope. He passed it to her. "Your services here will no longer be required, Mrs. Winslow." Slightly, only slightly, did he hesitate as though to add something, and then he thought better of it. He dismissed her curtly. "Good day, Mrs. Winslow."

She was shaken with disbelief. She picked up the envelope and looked from it to him, "But . . . but why?"

"You dare to ask? You actually have the effrontery to put me in the position of discussing your conduct? Shameless creature." His face flushed with his words.

Had she been somehow transported to another time? Was her skirt too short? Did her gray suit fit her too

21

tightly? "Shameless? I don't understand. What have I done?"

"Mrs. Winslow . . . I find it difficult to have to discuss your behavior with you. I should think you would take this opportunity to leave quietly. After all, charges could be brought up against you."

"Charges? What are you talking about?" She was beginning to get angry. She needed this job, but this was going a bit far.

"Indeed. Soliciting . . . in the guise of tourist guide . . ."

"*Soliciting?*" she interrupted as soon as the meaning of this came through. "You think . . ."

This time he cut her short. "I don't think, I know. A Mr. Mustafa el Zahour from Iraq came to me today . . . but don't think I took his word for it. I asked about discreetly and ascertained that you were seen having lunch with him on the grounds."

"Mr. Zahour?" She repeated the name in disbelief. "He wouldn't have . . . couldn't have accused me . . ."

"Did you or did you not agree to see him after hours?" pursued Mr. Perkins diligently.

"Yes, but . . ."

"Good day, Mrs. Winslow," he said meaningfully, and this time with more softness to his manner, for she was a beautiful woman and he could see genuine distress on her countenance. It did not waver his decision, but it softened his tone.

She mumbled something and withdrew. Outside his office she leaned against the freshly painted walls and drew in breath. Mustafa had done this to her? Why? How could he? She discovered her ex-co-workers gazing at her strangely as she left the grounds and blushed furiously. What were they thinking? Oh, God! How could she ever face any of them again? What had he done to her? She looked up and saw the long silver Rolls. Its convertible top was down, and inside sat Mustafa. He waved.

She turned and walked away from him. How could he? What was he? He lied about her, got her fired, and

22

here he was waving like an old friend! Oh! It was too much!

"Delia . . ." he called as he ran to catch up with her. He had her arm. She tore out of his hold.

"Don't you touch me! You miserable . . . you . . . leave me alone!"

"What is this? Delia?"

She looked up and saw Miles Eckford's limo passing. He was the last man besides Mustafa that she wanted to see right now, but it was an escape. She waved to him frantically, and his chauffeur pulled over to the curb.

"Miles . . . could you drop me off at my flat?"

"Of course, darling. Get in."

Mustafa stood on the sidewalk and watched her disappear out of view. What was this? What had happened? Well, he wasn't about to let this crazy English-woman treat him so shabbily. He would have his explanation, and he would have it tonight! He returned to his Rolls, and a moment later he had peeled out after Miles's limo.

Chapter Three

Helen Eckford pulled the wide brim of her dark-brown silk hat low over her forehead and leaned back against the back seat of the taxi. She watched her husband reach out for Delia Winslow's hand. Oh, God, it hurt. She felt her throat constrict and her gut shaken with pain, but she controlled herself and waited.

How beautiful Mrs. Winslow was . . . and all the more dangerous because of it. The woman appeared to have a certain grace most of the women Miles usually took up with lacked. She calmed herself. Should she wait here? She hadn't expected Miles to be here. She had waited for Delia Winslow to return home so that she could deal with her alone. Miles's presence put an entirely different light on the subject.

"Er . . . 'ow long would ye be wanting to wait 'ere?" questioned the cabby, eyeing her curiously.

"A bit longer," said Mrs. Eckford. Her eyes opened wide as an Arab in a long silver Rolls pulled up near the curb. She watched as Mustafa jumped out and took the steps by twos. Well, what was this?

Mustafa pounded on Delia's door, and she opened it to find that he looked boldly handsome in his rage. It was an incongruous sensation that passed through her. Here was this terrible man. He had gone to Mr. Perkins with terrible lies.

"How dare you come here?"

"How dare I come here?" He ignored Miles. "You will please tell me what all this is about!"

Miles wanted to be rid of Mustafa, but he wasn't confident enough to take on the large Arab by himself. However, he did offer, "Mr. Zahour . . . I think that the lady does not wish for your company just now."

"Please . . ." returned Mustafa, always the gentleman, "I do not wish to be rude, but I must ask you to stay out of this or risk having your face rearranged." He turned back to Delia. "Now, *ayouni,* you will kindly tell me—"

"I can't believe your gall! After what you have done?"

"What am I supposed to have done?"

"Get out, Mustafa! You . . . you . . . oh! There isn't an adjective I could use and still sound a lady!"

He shook his head. "I don't understand . . ." But his temper was already on the rise. He was losing patience.

"Can't you see? I never wish to see you again!" snapped Delia, turning her back on him.

He drew himself up erectly. "It seems I have been much mistaken in you, Mrs. Winslow." He waited, even then hoping for something to change. "Goodbye." It was a final sound.

He was gone. Delia spun around as the door to her

24

flat closed at his back. Tears welled into her eyes, and she had a sudden urge to run after him. Miles called her back to order. His arm went soothingly about her shoulders.

"There, love . . . never mind," he said softly.

She looked up at him. "Thank you, Miles . . . but . . . right now, I really would like to just get into a hot tub . . . and put this day aside."

He was willing enough; after all, his machinations had neatly been carried through, "Of course . . . but may I call on you in the morning?"

"Oh . . . you mean about the job? Yes, yes . . . that would be very nice."

Helen Eckford saw Mustafa tear off in his Rolls. A moment later she watched her husband give directions to his chauffeur and sit back in his limo.

"Driver, I shall return presently. Please wait." She got out of the taxi and hurried down the sidewalk to the steps of Delia's building.

The knocker sounded, and Delia looked up from the tea kettle with a mixture of feelings. Mustafa? Nonsense. Who could it be? She opened wide the door and looked at her caller in some puzzlement, for she had never seen Mrs. Eckford.

"Y-es?"

"Mrs. Winslow?"

"Yes."

"May I come in? I am Miles's wife . . . Mrs. Eckford."

In spite of Delia's innocence, she found herself blushing. "Of course." She stood aside and allowed the woman to enter her drawing room.

Helen Eckford looked around with something of envy. Here was this small room, evidently decorated on a budget, and yet it was warm, alive, and inviting. Plants filled the window in eye-catching array. Lithographs of horses were framed and placed tastefully. The colors were earthy and comfortable. Easy to live with. And here was a woman only another rare woman could compete with. If Delia Winslow wouldn't deal . . .

25

"Please, Mrs. Eckford . . . won't you sit down? I was just making some tea."

"Thank you. It might help to make this . . . less awkward," said Mrs. Eckford, taking up a stiff position on the edge of the creamy patterned sofa.

Delia frowned to herself as she puttered with the tea tray. She could see from the way that Mrs. Eckford held herself that the woman was undergoing a strain, and her heart went out to her. She poured and handed Mrs. Eckford the cup,

"Mrs. Eckford . . ." Delia started.

Helen put up her hand. "No . . . allow me to start this. I am aware that my husband has made you the object of his attentions." She shook her head as Delia began to object. "Please, let us not waste time in denials. I know that he is interested in you and I know that you have not, at least not yet, become his mistress. I wasn't sure about that until this morning."

Delia was leaning forward, her hands clasped together on her knees. "What happened this morning?"

"I managed to overhear his telephone conversation. He contacted someone and requested the services of an actor . . . an actor of Arab demeanor. The man was to go to the Tower to see your superior."

"Oh no . . ." Delia breathed. Mustafa. She had sent Mustafa away.

"He was to have your position there terminated. It was then that I realized Miles was doing this to get you into a position where you would no longer refuse his advances. . . ."

Delia got to her feet and paced. What was she going to do? She had sent Mustafa away. He would never forgive her. Dammit, what could she do? She turned to Helen Eckford, and her eyes searched the woman's face. "Mrs. Eckford, I thank you for telling me this . . . though you never had anything to worry about. I am not interested in Miles . . . and knowing what you know about him, I don't understand how you can be."

Helen cut her off. "I love him and the life we have

26

together. I mean to exert myself and make a push to keep him."

Delia shook her head. "I don't see why. You could do better." She was going to her closet, taking out her handbag. "Mrs. Eckford, again, thank you. I must go out now . . . for there is someone I have to see." Where did Mustafa say he was staying? The Dorchester? Was it the Dorchester? Oh, God, she had to find him.

It took fifteen minutes to get across town to the deluxe hotel. She hurried across its plush lobby to the reception desk and asked if a Mr. Mustafa el Zahour was registered. He was, and she was given his room number. She took the elevator to his suite and knocked on his door. A moment later he had opened it, but his countenance was rigid. Her blue eyes flickered, because at his back were his suitcases, and they appeared fully packed.

"Mustafa . . ." she breathed.

He was standing proudly, angry and hard. "What is it?"

"I . . . want to . . . oh, Mustafa . . . are you leaving?" This was absurd. Why did her heart contract? She had only just met him. He was a stranger to her. What was this?

He turned his back on her and went to a suitcase, snapped the lid shut, and answered her curtly, "I am catching a flight to Paris tonight. London . . . bores me."

"I . . . I see. Well . . ." She bolstered herself. "I am glad I caught you then, for I must tell you how sorry I am."

"Excellent. Your apology is accepted." Stern was his tone.

She hung her head and started to turn, "Well, then . . . goodbye." She began to move away. Her steps were taking her closer to the elevator.

He watched her back and cursed his weakness, for a moment later he was rushing after her, catching her up in the hall, turning her around and taking her into

27

his arms, "By Allah, woman, did you think it would end there?"

Oh, God, but his kiss was good, better than anything she had ever experienced before. His arms were strong and took her off the ground and away. Her hands went to his shoulders, and she laughed and cried with joy as he smothered her with emotion.

"Oh, Mustafa . . . Mustafa . . ." She couldn't say more, and there wasn't any need.

Daffodils and tulips lined the flower beds in Hyde Park. Ducks glided over the Serpentine. Lovers walked hand in hand and contemplated the sweetness of the breezy spring day, and Delia sighed with satisfaction as she leaned against Mustafa.

She took up his large brown hand and pulled him along toward the rowboats, but he was obstinately shaking his head and refusing to participate.

"Oh, but you will enjoy it. Come on, Mustafa . . . you don't want to get fat. It's good exercise," said Delia, laughing.

He pulled her to him and held her close. Two weeks had passed since she had come to him at his hotel and stopped him from leaving. Two perfect weeks, and their relationship had grown so boundlessly that he could no longer contain himself.

"Marry me, Delia, and keep me lean for always. . . ."

She stood back a pace and looked up at his tanned rugged face, and the word faltered from her. "Marry . . . ?"

"But of course, my darling." He frowned, and his hands went to her shoulders, up to her face. "Did you think our passion would make me forget how much I respect you? How much I need you?"

"I . . . I didn't think . . ." She turned away. She had given herself to Mustafa. She had put all considerations aside, and she had given herself totally, joyfully, happily.

"You didn't think? No, I don't believe you, my Delia. You have wondered about marriage with me. I have seen it in your beautiful eyes."

28

"No . . . but oh, Mustafa . . . marriage with you frightens me."

"But why? Are you afraid to be a widow again?" He chuckled. "I am older than you . . . but strong!" He gave his chest a mock Tarzan pound for emphasis. She laughed, and he bent to kiss her nose, "Beloved Delia, I would have you as my wife."

"Mustafa, we come from different worlds . . . I could never, never enter yours. You . . . you have . . . *two wives* already!"

"They are nothing to you!"

"Don't say that. It isn't right," she objected. "You have a son by one of them . . . you owe them something. And if you feel you don't, then perhaps one day . . . it would be the same with me, and I . . . I couldn't face that."

He stroked her red-gold hair. "I was a boy, a decent boy who did what his parents expected of him. They chose a wife for me, and I married her. It was right that I obeyed my father, and I was blessed with a son . . . but, my darling, more than respect for the mother of my son I have never felt."

She looked into his dark eyes and sighed. "And your second wife? Did they also choose her for you?"

He laughed lightly. "So jealous, my beauty? No, by then both my parents were gone, and my first wife . . . as I have said, I respected. I found a girl who was small and pretty. I wanted her. She came from a good family, and the only way I could have her was to marry her." He shrugged his shoulders. "But . . . we were different from one another. . . . Delia, sharing was something that was unknown to us. It is with *you* that I laugh, it is with you that I see things I have never seen before. Delia, I love you . . . and I have never loved before. . . ."

She allowed him to brush her lips with his kiss and then pulled gently out of his arms, "It is hard for me, Mustafa. My husband died only a year after we were married. He'd been drinking . . . he stepped out in front of a car. I was there, and couldn't stop him in time." She turned away.

29

He waved this away. "This is not the point."

"No? Don't you think so? It shaped my life afterward for so long . . . brought me to this moment. Mustafa . . . it would be safer, easier, to leave things as they are now."

"No. I mean to shape your life from here on," he answered simply.

She smiled. "I have certain rules . . . certain principles that cannot bend."

"Such as?"

"I shall never go with you to Iraq . . . to be one of your wives. England is my home. The Western culture is the only one I can thrive in."

"So be it."

"How can you agree to give up your land . . . your customs?"

"I have thought about this, Delia. It is not right that I ask you to come and live in my country, don the *aba* and hide yourself away with . . . with my other wives. You are an Englishwoman . . . it would never work. I will live here with you in England . . . leaving three times a year, each time for a month." He grinned broadly. "You see what a genius you will be marrying? Have I not worked it all out?"

She shook her head. "Mustafa . . . my darling . . . how can you propose such a thing? What of your business, Mustafa? Think . . . what of your son?"

He frowned and then snapped his fingers. "My business? By telephone. Its nature is such that I can work with London as my base."

"Mustafa . . . your son?"

"My son. A delicate matter." He studied her a long moment, "You would not refuse him my affection?"

"Of course not. But . . ."

"Then he will spend his holidays with us here in London. Between his time with us here and my time with him in Iraq, he will do. A fine boy . . . he will do."

Still she shook her head. "I don't know, Mustafa. I think . . ."

30

"I am a wealthy man, my jewel . . . my lands bring in oil . . . my oil brings in new investments . . ."

"What has that to say to anything? Your wealth cannot sway my decision." She was angry now.

He stroked her face. "Then allow my love to do it."

She was frowning still. "My Haji Mustafa . . . you are like a prince from a fairytale . . . and as much as I should like to please you and myself by accepting this extraordinary proposition, I cannot."

He nodded. "So, you say . . . but I am Haji and I know better. . . ."

And he did. Three weeks later in a simple Christian style they were wed. They took a London flat in Kensington and so began their life together.

Chapter Four

The seasons often collide. Temperatures will drop when they should be at their height. Blizzards will trample just when things are running smoothly. Nature is a precarious mistress, and we humans are ever subject to her will.

People rarely live happily ever after, even when they seem to fit the workings of a fairy tale. Even when love prospers, wealth abounds, they are subject to forces without pity. Even when their love seems all-powerful, all-consuming. Even when there is prestige, when there is might, when there is honesty, even then will nature intrude.

Twelve years passed, and the ups for Delia and Mustafa were far greater than their downs. They were judged a happy pair by outsiders, romantics, cynics. Truth was they had found that tenuous aura, that magic, that two people can bring to one another in marriage. Yet, even so, nature plodded unmercifully between them.

Cancer reared its hoary tentacles and ended by taking Delia away from her husband and daughter. The attack was unexpected, the end devastating, and the English house of Mustafa el Zahour felt empty.

He looked out on his garden, and there throwing pebbles into the landscaped pond was his daughter. She was nearly twelve and already displaying signs of great beauty. Her red-gold hair glistened in the sunlight so very much like her mother's. . . .

Mustafa sighed, and purposely he allowed his mind to wander to the day his daughter had been born.

"Khalda . . . I shall call her Khalda," he had announced proudly.

Delia smiled indulgently, but her brow went up all the same.

"Oh, will you, my darling? I think not."

He was taken aback. "But . . . do you dislike it? Beloved, Khalda means 'the eternal, the undying' . . . as is our love."

"As is our love," she repeated sweetly. "Then we shall take from it and she will be Holly, as is the evergreen that grows in England."

"You reject the Arabic name?" He was offended. He stiffened against her, his pride alert on his countenance.

She laughed at his expression and then sobered. "Mustafa, our daughter resides in England. She will play with English children, go to English schools. It will do for her to have an English name."

He was frowning, and he moved away. She would never accept anything Arabic; his Delia resented all that was a part of his heritage. It was a gentle rift between them, ever present, ever lurking, and he always pushed it aside. Such had been his passion for her.

Thus, Holly it had been, but not to him. To him she was Khalda. His Delia was now gone, but there was still his life in Baghdad, there was still his son and his daughter. He called her to him now.

"Khalda . . . come, child."

The elflike countenance turned somberly toward the glass door he held open for her. There was a purpose about him. What she had been dreading was coming to pass. She felt it. She knew it. Her mother was gone and now everything would be different. So hatefully different.

"Yes, *baba?*" It was an affectionate term she always used.

He patted the chair. "Come . . . sit with me. We will talk."

She did as he asked, but her expression was grave, reproachful. He saw it and winked at her, attempting to coax her out of her bad humor. "Come, *ayouni,* do not look so at me."

An endearment to tempt her, she thought stubbornly. *Ayouni?* His eyes. He called her that, but it was not true. It was another part of a culture she had never thought her own. He did not understand. He never would. He wanted to take her away from all that was familiar, all that was dear.

England. England was her home. Her friends were here. Her mother's grave was here. Her mother? No. Her mother would never approve of his plans. Iraq? There were only strangers waiting for her there.

Mustafa sighed at her stern silence. "Khalda . . . we will go home."

Her aqua-blue eyes flashed at him, reminding him again of Delia.

"Home, *baba?* This . . ." Her small hand gestured impressively at her surroundings. "This is my home." She was nearly twelve years old, and at such an age one has all the answers.

He was in fact less than compassionate in this struggle. His jewel, his daughter, was rejecting all that he stood for. She was rejecting all that made him what he was. It was infuriating. He was in pain over his wife's death, but this, this defiance of his daughter's, enraged him in a way no other ever had.

"This is home no more!" He was on his feet now. "Your mother made all . . . acceptable. Even the repug-

33

nant was passed over because of her smile. But I will not tolerate a child's defiance. You are *my blood* . . . therefore you are an Arab, *like me.* You will learn to be proud of it. Our family resides in Baghdad, and *so shall we!*"

She released a gasping sob. "I won't go. My mother wouldn't want me to . . . and I don't want to."

His voice came brokenly. "But . . . your father returns to his home. . . ." His hurt was clearly written in his eyes.

She stopped and stared at him. The tears were streaming down her white cheeks. All at once she was repentant. No longer was he a stranger renting her from all familiar ties and belongings. Here was her father, her *baba,* the *baba* who had always cherished her; and what had she done but insult and hurt him.

She threw herself in anguish upon her knees, for she was sacrificing much. Heaving sobs racked right through her and touched his heart. He stroked her long red-gold hair.

"Don't, *ayouni.* . . ." He lifted her chin. "You will be happy. I promise you. Do you not love your brother, Hassan?"

Hassan. Pleasant memories floated hazily. He was seven years her senior. He had come during summer holidays . . . three, four times over the last few years. They had laughed together. Yes, she cared for her half brother Hassan. She nodded.

Her father grinned broadly. "Then it is settled and we go to Baghdad!"

A dark-haired woman wearing a silk print *meghashaya* moved leisurely away from her terrace and gazed thoughtfully at the dark-eyed, black-haired youth standing in Western-styled clothes for her inspection.

"So, Hassan . . . he brings her, this English flower of his." There was an edge of bitterness to her words.

The tall youth had nearly nineteen years to his credit. In addition to the extensive education he had received and was still receiving, he had traveled to

34

England and acquired Western polish. He had admired his father's English wife. He had found his sister amusing. He was an only son and therefore was not threatened. He had no resentments to air, but his mother was respected, so his response was cautious. "This is true."

His mother fretted with the pleat of her dress. She was still an attractive woman. Perhaps she allowed herself a little fat . . . but then a husband's neglect will do that, and Mustafa had left her too long to her own devices. There was a rash of bitterness in her heart. Only one thing served to give her security. She was the mother of Mustafa's only son. There was safety, comfort, in that fact.

"Hassan, you will not seek this girl's company," she commanded.

He was taken aback, "But . . . she is my father's daughter . . ."

"I will not own it!" She was angry.

He shook his head. "*Imi*, you will honor your husband's daughter." He reached for her hand. "I do not want you put aside as was done with my father's second wife."

She thought of Nahda, Mustafa's pretty little second wife. Nahda had displeased him during his long stay in England. Her favor for another man could have brought about her death, but Mustafa was not that kind of man. He had simply divorced her. An easy procedure accomplished by repeating three times, "*Talqa!*" Nahda no longer shared their great mansion. A pleasant fact.

"I am the mother of his beloved son. He would not divorce me."

"Do not try his patience, *imi* . . . he would not be pleased."

"But she is the daughter of a *Christian!*"

Hassan's black brows drew together. This was something, of course, that he had forgotten. It was not a good thing that his half sister was Christian. His Moslem community would not easily accept this. He waved it aside. "She will give up her Christian beliefs.

After all . . . she must." It was an easy solution. She was a female. She would do what she was told.

The logic simplified whatever concerns he might have had in that regard. She was daughter of Mustafa and therefore was a Moslem just as they were. His mother would adjust to the child. She was a woman and bound to her jealousies, but in the end, she would see that the English daughter of Mustafa must be respected in her husband's home. It was this sort of reasoning that allowed him to continue to pursue the pleasures of the day free of all guilt.

A long black limousine, chauffeur-driven, pulled up to the curb, and Khalda felt herself ushered within its confines by her father's gentle fingers. He sat back and heaved a long sigh. It was good to be home. To hear his native language, to feel familiar with a way of life, to know it as his own.

His daughter, his jewel, his Khalda who thought of herself still as Holly, as English, would come to love his native land even as he did. He was certain of this. How could she not love it? It was a poetic land, a romantic people. Forgotten was Faisal's assassination only thirteen years ago. Put aside were the beatings of Christians and Jews, the cruel prejudices, the inequality of their women. Delia was gone. He was nearing fifty and too tired to look elsewhere or within. He was home, and it eased all pain.

His Khalda, Delia's Holly, pressed her nose to the window of their great long car. She was diverted from her sadness for the moment in wonderment, curiosity. This was Baghdad? This was the land of Ali Baba and his forty thieves? This surely was the wrong place.

Baghdad. Shouldn't there be a carpet or two floating in the sky? Where were the camels? Why were there not tents to charm the sight? Where were the sheer silks and dangling jewels? The cars! Look at the cars. They were all too familiar. Long American cars that she had often seen in films. French squat ones . . .

motorcycles, many motorcycles . . . and faith, the streets! They were paved!

She stared in consternation past green lawns to brick houses. Ordinary! There they sat . . . made of brick? Their roofs were not unlike English roofs . . . not gold-and-bauble-covered. Why weren't they dome-shaped and glittering? What had Scheherazade told of all those nights? Where was the Baghdad of her imagination?

But as they left the airport behind she noted with awe that along with the automobiles they had horse-drawn carriages as well. The horses were being whipped up at a spanking pace, and she cooed with delight. She turned to her father and reminded him of a promise he had made her before they had left England.

"Now, *baba* . . . don't forget. You said I might have my own horse!"

"Yes. Your very own Arabian mare. A chestnut, I think." He smiled.

"No, a black." She spotted a young boy dressed in dirty white robes tied around his waist with a rope. He was leading a basket-laden donkey down a side road. Finally, something to delight the imagination. She aahed out loud over the spectacle. Her father laughed and began pointing out the different type of trees, date trees, palms, juju trees. And then they were entering the city itself and sweeping past the River Tigris.

She was amazed at the glass shops with their fashionables sported in style. She cried with delight over the vendors selling fruit drinks from small cubbyholes in the walls. They passed through a section known as the Eastern Gate, sped past the river boardwalks through New Baghdad, and made their way to the plush suburbia known as Seven Castles. Here resided, in great elegance and state, consulates and the upper echelon of Baghdad society. Here was the home of Mustafa el Zahour!

Holly's home in Kent had been an estate of considerable size. The grounds there had been both extensive and tastefully designed, and she was accustomed to good living. Even so she sucked in her breath with startled awe as she took in the magnificence of the palatial estate laid out before her.

White brick took on gigantic and opulent proportions. Everywhere on the green lawns were objects of art. Dark and richly green, the lawns were spread wide between flower beds filled with exotic blooms. There was the aroma of the blossoms from the fruit orchards. Gazebos of Middle Eastern fancy stood romantically among flowing water fountains. Peacocks strutted. A herd of small deer grazed, and in the midst of all this was a pair of miniature horses Mustafa had imported from Virginia, America. Great were Holly's exclamations of delight. This was not a home but a fantastic showplace, a circus of treasures to be explored.

She followed her father up the wide stone steps, and her head moved in all directions. Servants bowed and murmured a welcome as they moved into the central hall. She recognized only some of the words, all spoken in Arabic. She stood on the deeply veined and highly polished marble floor and caught the dark reflection of herself on the floor just before a woman's voice brought her head up sharply.

Here now was the woman who had recently occupied her thoughts, held a place in her fears, touched a secret resentment. Here was the other woman. . . .

Holly's mother had once told her how her father had another wife in this country, how it was an accepted custom here in Iraq. Even so, it had troubled her then, and it troubled her now. She turned and watched as the tall and graceful woman came across the hall to greet them.

Holly appraised the woman quickly. She was dark. Her eyes were narrow and unsmiling, and her mouth was too large for her oval face. Yet there was something arresting about her presence. Perhaps it was the woman's air of refinement, of quiet submission made altogether intriguing by the distinction of her self-assurance. The woman's black, slightly graying hair was held tightly at the nape of her neck and wound

38

into a shining bun. Over her head was a pretty silk *aba* of brown. It floated elegantly to her shoulders, where she left it untied about her face and neck. Her dress was stylish enough to have been made in Paris. Its lines of brown printed silk were tailored and high-fashioned. She wore gold jewelry at her ears, neck, and wrists. On her fingers were numerous rings of various designs and stones. She smiled widely as she came before her husband and took up his hand to her lips.

"Abu Hassan," she said.

Holly understood. It was a common thing to do. Many of his friends had visited with them over the years and had referred to him in such terms. It meant "father of Hassan." It was another custom to call a man after his firstborn son. It was a title of honor.

"It is good to have you home again," the woman said softly and in English, displaying the degree of her education proudly.

He patted her hand. "Suham . . . *fidwa.* . ." He turned to Holly. "My daughter, Khalda."

Holly felt a welling of bitter resentment. To hear the term of endearment, *fidwa,* spoken for another woman was salt on her raw wounds, and she cringed within. She could not disguise the dismay in her eyes as she attempted to greet her father's first wife.

"Taali hoani," called Suham sweetly, then, remembering her English, "Come here . . . I would give you a kiss, my child."

She stepped forward, accusations coursing through her brain. Her mother was dead, and here was this woman . . . taking over.

"Holly!" cried a male voice cheerfully at their backs.

Saved! Gratefully, delightedly, Holly turned. Here was someone who would use her name as she liked it. Not Khalda, but Holly—to a child's sense of self, to an emerging adolescent, this was symbolically all-important. Here was a friend. The dark-eyed woman, Suham, stirred too many warring emotions, but her son, Hassan, was a friend. She went careening into his arms.

Hassan gave her a bear hug and then held her away.

She had been his pet on the few occasions he stayed with them in England. A cherished plaything. She was seven years his junior and willing to worship him. He teased her then, and did so now. "But," he began in amazement, "you have grown. Are you sure you are my sister Holly? No, it cannot be . . . why, you look all of ten . . . even eleven . . ."

She swatted him with easy comradery. "I am twelve years old, and you know it!" Then she realized by his twinkling eyes that he had been baiting her and smiled, already quite the coquette. "But these things are hard to discern for a boy only . . . what is it, Hassan . . . fifteen . . . sixteen?"

"Sixteen!" he exploded. "Little fool . . . you are not too old for a spanking!" he was giving her shoulders a shake, and then he drew himself up to his full height. "I am nineteen, and you will remember the respect due to me." The playfulness was in his eyes.

She sighed happily and cast him a look of adoration. "It is so good to see you again, Hassan."

"Well, of course it is," he answered promptly.

His mother was frowning impatiently. "Hassan," she objected, "Khalda is tired. I will have her taken to her room."

"But no, *imi*. Tired or no, she will do the grounds with me and then I shall escort her to her quarters." He turned to Holly. "It is, after all, only her just deserts. I remember vividly what tortures she put me through on my arrival, my first arrival in England, and I mean for her to suffer the same."

She clapped her hands gleefully. "Come on, then. See if you don't surrender first . . . *again!*"

He had her hand and they were off. They stopped at the doorway for a moment, for she had tugged at his arm. "Hassan . . ."

"Yes, little one?"

"It's gone, you know . . . *baba* sold my home . . . to strangers. . . ."

Hassan grew momentarily serious, an oddity for him. "So it is, but you are here at Seven Castles, and see if we don't live happily ever after. Now . . . look there, see those miniature horses?"

"Oh yes . . . come on I want to pet them. . . ."

Mustafa's gaze followed them. It seemed to him that his daughter trusted Hassan even more than she did him, and this stirred a feather of jealousy in his breast. Perhaps soon he should find reasons to keep them apart?

Suham's gaze also followed the youthful pair as they loped off, and she thought much the same as her husband, but much, much more determinedly. The dislike she thought she would feel for the English child of Mustafa's English wife was nothing to the loathing she actually felt upon sighting the red-gold hair and the aqua-blue eyes of the girl who promised even now of becoming a ravishing beauty!

Part Two

Chapter One

A peacock spread its iridescent tail of aqua blues and emerald greens and shattered the quiet with his ear-splitting mating call. It was springtime at Seven Castles.

Holly brushed the long tresses of red-gold from her face and studied the bird as it preened not more than twenty feet away. The bird moved about restlessly in the spacious garden courtyard. A prisoner, she thought, he is a prisoner . . . as I am.

Seven years! They had dragged by and brought her to this space in time. She was nineteen, nearly a woman, she was told, a marriage prize. She sighed, heard the melancholy of her own sound, and sighed again. So many hopes had been dashed. She had begged and pleaded to be allowed to go away to a finishing school, but even as her father began to relent, that woman would whisper in his ear. He would throw up his hands. He would walk away from it and leave it to Suham, who seemed to enjoy Holly's misery. So, tutors had been brought in and carefully screened. Khalda had received her education at home.

"So here you are . . . your mother said you would be near this garden." A male voice at her back.

Holly spun around in a fury. This was her own place. A sacred corner all her own. How dare Suham send him here! "She is not my mother, Wahid, and well you know it!"

He frowned. Wahid Ahwaz was a suitor for her hand. His desire for the fair Khalda was such that he was driven nearly to madness. He only knew he had to have her. Why was she so cold? He rather thought himself a handsome fellow. He sat beside her on the gray stone bench.

"Khalda, am I so terrible? What is it about me that makes you so angry?"

She relented. He was Wahid. He was Hassan's friend . . . had been, she thought, a friend to herself, but that was before. That was before he had applied for her hand in marriage against her will. That was before her father had agreed to give her away without her consent. "Wahid . . . I am angry because all of you force me into a marriage I do not want!"

"What do you know of such things?" he asked incredulously. "Ah yes . . . part of your upbringing was English . . . there is the rebel in your nature . . . but is there someone else?"

"No," she said softly, "there is no one else."

His hands were on her shoulders immediately. He should not be so handling her, but he could not help himself. He crushed her to him in an embrace that was far too rough, too inept to stir anything but repulsion from her. She yanked out of his touch.

"How dare you!"

"Indeed!" came a strong voice at their backs. "How dare you indeed, Wahid?" It was Hassan.

Wahid spun around, his face aflame with his shame, his irritation, his frustration. "Hassan!"

"I know that my sister is irresistible." Hassan inclined his head and his dark eyes twinkled. "But still I would expect that you keep your hands off her until the wedding."

An audible growl lit in Wahid's throat, and he tore off in some confusion and embarrassment. Hassan's brow rose as he watched his friend stomp off. He turned to Holly and found her trembling. Immediately he took up her hand. She flung herself into his arms and released a low, long groan from the very pit of her depression.

He stroked her long red-gold hair and sighed. A

predicament indeed. He could feel the soft full swell of her breasts beneath the simple cotton shirt she wore. No! She was his half sister . . . and praise Allah his mother had seen fit to keep him away from Holly all these years.

He put Holly from him. A mistake. Her eyes, their aqua depths, held him captive. Yes. He had not been allowed to be alone with her as she grew. Wise. She was daughter of his father . . . what he felt for her was wrong, indecent.

"Holly . . . what is it? Wahid? Wahid, I know, was clumsy . . . but such unhappiness? Why?"

She wrung her hands. "Oh, it wasn't because he tried to kiss me! Hassan . . . they are forcing me to marry him!" She moved impatiently in her extreme agitation. "Hassan . . . I cannot!" All these years they had been attempting to drain the English out of her. It had not worked. Few friends had been allowed to her, only some movies, some television, and Hassan's company only now and then. Her youth had been hell! Now they wanted to hound her in adulthood as well. *No!* She would not allow it.

Hassan frowned. He was a thoroughly modern fellow, a liberal in his own estimation. However, the Moslem way of life was for a Moslem male far too attractive for him to throw away in the name of progress and an open mind. He touched her cheek, but the words froze on his lips.

"Hassan!" It was his father at their backs.

Mustafa's moods these days were high and low, fierce and soft. Too much was happening too soon. Tradition was the key word. Suham whispered it often. His daughter, she would complain, though beautiful, though an heiress, was a Christian . . . a Christian . . . a word synonymous with danger in this land. Khalda had refused to relinquish her mother's religion. If not for Delia's memory it would have been an insult to his heart.

Thus, instead of sending her to a finishing school outside of Iraq, he kept her home, hoping to instill his

45

culture in her character. Now he found that again Suham was correct. He would have to save Khalda by marrying her off to a Moslem willing to accept the fact that she was a Christian . . . and this would ensure his keeping Khalda near. He didn't want to lose his only daughter, his link to Delia.

"*Baba* . . ." Holly said softly. "What is the matter?"

He did not answer her but directed a hard glance at his son.

"What are you two doing here alone, and why did Wahid leave us so abruptly?"

Hassan grinned. "Wahid is an anxious groom denied a sampling of his bride."

Mustafa's dark eyes opened wide. "Ah . . ." He turned to his daughter. "You are upset, my *gulbi?*"

His *gulbi*, his sweetheart, had all the defiance of her age and nature. "Upset? Yes, I am upset, Father. You are trying to make me marry a man I do not love . . . and I won't." With which she stalked off.

He called after her, but she wouldn't stop, wouldn't look back. In some embarrassment and confusion, he faced his son,

"She is a rebellious child . . . but she will come around in the end. She will do what I wish."

"Will she, *baba?* I wonder," said Hassan thoughtfully.

"Talk to her, Hassan . . . she will listen to you."

Holly stood in her room, a rage keeping her fists clenched at her side. She was near breaking point. What to do? If only she had enough money she would take it and run away, but her only cash was given to her in a small allowance, and even if she had it in her hand now, where could she go? England? She was a natural English citizen. Her mother had seen to that. But even her passport was not in her possession. Where could so go without papers? He would find her and bring her back.

A knock at her door interrupted her desperate thoughts, and she called out in English, "Who is it?" It

46

was an obstinacy against Suham that she continued always to speak in her native tongue and not in Arabic.

"Open the door, *fidwa*." It was Hassan, and his voice was soothingly soft.

She was surprised. Hassan was rarely permitted to attend her in her own quarters. Warily she opened the door wide and stood pouting. "If you have come to plead my father's case I shan't listen."

Hassan discovered her aqua eyes burning through him. She was tantalizing, and not for the first time did he wish she were not his blood relation.

"May I come in?" He was mocking her, exaggerating his politeness.

"Your mother will not approve," she answered, forcing the coldness to remain in her tone. It was hard, though. She cared too much for Hassan to hold back against him.

He was a free-loving bachelor, and though these things were allowed to a young and wealthy man, Hassan's escapades were often the talk of the staid society of his community. He laughed easily,

"And my good mother has excellent reasons for her censure." His eyes were dancing. "Nevertheless, I will enter and be with my . . . sister awhile." He came forward into her room and moved toward her open terrace. He turned halfway toward her. "Close the door, Holly." His voice had softened. He was all too aware of her movements, and again reminded himself out loud of the relationship that existed between them. "*Taali hoani*, sister, and we will talk."

She did what he asked and joined him on her terrace. She cast him a troubled look. "So then, Hassan . . . how will you help me?"

"How do you know that I shall?" He was only half in earnest, for he knew already that he would help her if he could. It was an odd thing, her defiance. It took him some soul-searching to understand. After all, men were beings to be worshiped by women. Men chosen for daughters were worthy creatures to be admired, respected, and loved. How could a woman not want such

47

a man? He expanded upon this in his mind; women, now . . . these were artifacts, jewels, sweethearts to be molded, caressed, cherished, *owned!* But what would he feel if he were forced to take to bed a woman he found repulsive? Terrible. Then no different for Holly!

He studied Holly, his Holly, and imagined Wahid perhaps a little too much impassioned. He had seen Wahid take a woman when they had been on a binge together. His friend was a feisty lover . . . *no!* He couldn't bear the notion of Holly in such a predicament. He didn't want Holly under any man's power but his and his father's. He would speak to Mustafa . . . and even so, he knew Mustafa would not alter his decision. His father's word had been given to Wahid's family. It was a contract, a contract that would not be broken.

"Holly . . . our father plans to take a trip to London in two days. We have business there, and I shall accompany him. I think that you too will join us. There are your brideclothes that must be shopped for. Yes, you will do your shopping in London. Perhaps in England he will see things differently."

She went into his arms. It was always so safe here in the fold of her brother's arms. "Thank you, Hassan."

"So, I have at last made my sister smile," he said, stroking her long red-gold hair and thinking again that fate had ill served them both by putting her out of his reach.

Chapter Two

Things had been running smoothly. Plans were made, ready to be put in action. Now if only he could keep his work secret, if only the press would leave him alone, if only . . . But these were things he believed he had taken care of.

Sir Justin's dark ginger brows were drawn together, and his gray eyes flickered with his thoughts. He ran a casual hand through his thick sweep of ginger hair, pushing it off his forehead, where it strayed more often than not.

"Good evening, Sir Justin." The doorman at the Ritz Casino opened the glass door wide, smiled readily.

"Evening . . ." Sir Justin nodded absently, moved across the hall, down the stairs, smiled again at the man behind the booth, and signed in at the registration desk. Again he was greeted, again wide glass doors were held open for him.

Dim lights, dark, rich elegance, scented air, the sound of chips, the calling of bets, soft, gentle, subtle, alluring. He appraised a nearby female croupier; she looked up, recognized, winked; he smiled and moved forward. The Ritz was one of his more favored casinos. Everything about it spelled quality and an age long ago abandoned. Such was the atmosphere. Sir Justin always felt comfortable here. An odd circumstance, considering that he wasn't really a gambler. His nature was conservative, cautious, yet even so, he liked an evening at the roulette table. He enjoyed playing the game, teasing luck, testing himself. Rarely did he lose, he left that to the beauties he usually brought along with him. Ruefully he thought of women . . . and what they had cost him!

Sir Justin moved leisurely toward the cashier's window, nodding at acquaintances, stopping to chat with an intimate. He cashed five-hundred pounds into chips, smiled provocatively at a well-rounded barmaid as she glided by. He watched her bend to serve her tray of drinks to the players and sighed. (Not tonight, Justin.) He had promised himself no romantic entanglements of any kind. He had this evening to relax, and then it was for Hampshire and his lab.

Tomorrow he would be hidden away in the country. Tomorrow he would put himself fully into his project and its risks, but tonight all he intended to risk was money!

* * *

"Holly . . . the Ritz is famous for its food, yet you will only pick! Shall I order you something else?" Mustafa was exasperated with his daughter. She had seemed so excited, so happy, so ineffably lovely these last few days, and now she sat and pouted. She was spoiled. Yet, was he wrong? Doubts tugged at him, made him feel a strain of guilt, and he reacted defensively.

She poked the filet mignon with her fork. "Please forgive me, *baba* . . . I am just not hungry." Her eyes were downcast. She had to get to him. She had to make him see that she belonged here in England, not Iraq.

Hassan observed the heightened color in his father's cheeks. This was unlike Mustafa. He could see that soon his father would ask him to see Holly to her room. It was a sad thing. He attempted to turn things about. "I know what our girl will like, Father."

Mustafa regarded his son. Hassan looked well in his dark-brown velvet jacket, his ivory silk shirt and brown silk tie. He was a good man, his son. "What, then? For I am tired of this nonsense."

"The casino. I brought Holly by this afternoon and showed her how to place bets. My instincts tell me she will be a winner tonight."

Mustafa considered this as he studied his daughter. "Would you like that?"

"Of course," she answered without spirit. Hassan trod on her bare toe beneath the table, and she glanced at him sharply before adding, "Very much, *baba,* thank you."

Hassan sat back and gazed at her a long moment as his father called for the check. She was so beautiful with her red-gold hair flowing freely in full waves past her shoulders. Her shoulders? White in their exquisite bareness . . . the gown did her justice. Creamy white, the soft crepe crossed at the neck and fell in clinging lines to her ankles, where her toes peeped out of high-heeled French sandals. At her ears, brightly glittering, were the delicate diamonds her father had bought for her from Cartier's that very afternoon. As they rose from the table, he whispered, "My sister outshines all women."

She blushed but averted her gaze. It was infuriating. She hated being pampered like a pet. Here they were, both men who professed to love her, yet they were insensitive to her despondency, offering her trinkets and refusing her what she wanted most, her freedom!

What would she do? Her father flatly refused to discuss her marriage to Wahid. He had made up his mind. Wahid was the son of a beloved friend. It was the match he chose, and he would be shamed if she withdrew. He had even stooped to calling her an ungrateful child!

How could her father think in those terms? How could her father give her away like that? Life was a bitter draft indeed.

"Holly . . ." It was her father, impatient now because she still was not smiling. Hadn't he bought her the loveliest, most expensive gowns in London? Hadn't he allowed her to choose them? Hadn't he taken her to Hyde Park, to Westminster, to . . . damn, she was behaving like a spoiled girl! Wahid was an excellent man, and she had not showed them he was displeasing to her. In fact, for many years he had imagined she liked Wahid very well.

She sent her father a superficial smile. "Yes?" Hassan had one arm; she felt her father take her other. She felt a veritable prisoner. Something inside wanted to scream, scream, scream.

He placed a wad of bills in her hand as the porter opened the wide glass doors for them. She took the money, and her eyes widened in delight. It hadn't been like this in the afternoon. Egad! Everywhere fashionable men and women strolled, laughed softly, moved leisurely to the tune of clinking chips. Every nerve in her body went taut, and for a moment the future was forgotten.

She could see that there were a great many people from the Middle East here and that some of the English resented them. It was not openly displayed, but it was a fact she privately noted all the same. She stood watching the quiet shifting of small fortunes as an Arab sheik lost ten thousand pounds in a matter of moments. A tug at her arm caught her attention.

"*Fidwa* . . . our father goes to play baccarat with his friends. I will take you to an exciting roulette table."

Sir Justin looked up in time to see the new arrivals. He watched as the Moslem men led their fair-haired beauty to one table after another. His brow went up. Exceptionally possessive they appeared. Proud, but no wonder; she was one of the loveliest women he had ever seen, and he assumed she was English. A sigh. It was a common thing these days to find a beautiful English girl on the arm of an Arab. Fair hair, fair skin, it seemed to attract the Middle Eastern male. He frowned. These things usually turned out sadly for the girl involved. He attempted to dismiss it from his mind and returned his attention to the numbers of the board and the spinning ball.

"Hassan . . . this table," she cried excitedly as they did a tour of the various roulette tables in play.

He laughed and pulled out a seat for her. His whisper touched her ear. "Remember, *fidwa* . . . there is only luck . . . no pattern." He took the money her father had given her and purchased her chips in ten-pounds denomination. "There . . . that should do for some time, unless you turn out to be a big gambler." He took her fingers and put them to his lips.

All this Sir Justin watched as Holly was seated beside him. Two hundred pounds the Arab had given her. She must certainly be a new acquisition. From the corner of his eye he could catch her expressions, and reluctantly he found his interest fixed.

"Hassan . . . you are going?" she asked on a note of surprise. She had rather thought her father might have asked him to stand guard over her.

He gave her an apologetic grin. "You know what I am, and at any rate, my game is blackjack . . . where you may find me should you need more money."

She knew full well that he wished to flirt around,

boast with some of his cronies, and enjoy a few drinks. His leaving filled her with tingling sensations. Here she was actually on her own. Frightening but somehow deliciously so. "Good luck," she called after him.

"It is ever with me, *gulbi*." He smiled and was gone.

Gulbi . . . sweetheart, thought Sir Justin. He had been around Arabs in his business long enough to have discovered the meaning of that word. She was therefore certainly mistress to the Moslem. Dammit, why should he care?

Holly turned to the game at hand. A pretty dark-haired croupier was calling for all bets. With a quick decision Holly put down thirty pounds on red. The gentleman beside her received her quick appraisal as he did the same. With some interest she could see that his face was chiseled in hard lines and very handsome. His ginger hair fell over his forehead. His shoulders seemed very broad. She felt herself blush and turned away to hear the ball had landed on the number one, which was red!

She released a small squeak of delight and then covered her cherry lips apologetically with her delicate hand. The dealer put down thirty pounds in chips next to her original bet. She scooped them to her side.

The ball went around again. Bets were called for, and she saw the good-looking, well-dressed gentleman beside her place several chips on a few numbers across the board. He chose among these number five. She liked the number, and her thirty pounds in winnings joined his bet on five.

Sir Justin glanced at her sharply and grinned. She returned his amused glance with one of her own and said on a breathless note, "I don't know why it is, but this is very exciting."

"Is it your first time?"

She nodded enthusiastically.

He released a chuckle. "And already you have the bug."

"The bug?"

"Gambling fever."

"I don't know if that is true," she answered on a thoughtful note. "You see, I haven't lost yet."

He laughed easily. "Quite right, love."

She wasn't sure he should address her in such a manner, but there wasn't time to object, and after all, she was in England. The dealer was placing the glass marker on number five, indicating the winning number. This time, 1,080 English pounds were added to her original bet. She watched in round-eyed awe as the female croupier laid the large rectangular chips next to her thirty pounds, and suddenly Holly knew what she was going to do!

It wasn't a new idea. It had been an all-consuming desire for many weeks now. And now she had the means of doing it. In her purse was the passport her father had felt it necessary for her to carry while they were in England. She had papers. She was an English citizen, and now . . . now she would have the money!

Not enough. In addition to her 200 pounds she now had 1,110 pounds in winnings. She would need more . . . for she would have to hide.

"No more bets . . ." the pretty dealer was calling.

Hurriedly she placed a hundred-pound chip on number thirty-six. She didn't know why. The number had popped into her head. Were the fates aiding her tonight. Was Lady Luck sympathetic to her cause?

The ball spun round, it landed, popped, spun a few numbers more, and landed on thirty-six. She couldn't believe it. She had won! Again rectangular chips totaling 3,600 English pounds were given to her. She now had a total of 4,910 English pounds!

She slipped the various sizes of chips into her white evening bag. She traded in her colored chips for the larger denominations and glanced around. Bets were once again called for, but she wasn't paying attention this time. She looked over her right shoulder and discovered her father deep at play at the baccarat table. He was into his game. His cigarette was held up between fingers which pressed to his forehead. His back was to the glass doors leading out. She looked further, this time for Hassan, and found him standing near the blackjack table with two friends and a pretty blond woman.

Holly slipped off her high cushioned stool and moved toward the cashier's window. Her heart was racing. Impulsive, she accused herself. You have always been impulsive, and you will end in a mess of trouble. Darn .. you could be ruining your life. Your father ... he will worry. She answered the accusation furiously, My father was giving me away! But ... where ... where shall I go? What will I do? How will I manage? What in hell does it matter? *Free!* I will be free!

She placed her chips firmly on the counter, smiled as the young man in the black tuxedo made some small est about her good fortune. She found that her hands were trembling as she scooped up the large bills he counted out. She couldn't meet his gaze but stuffed the cash into her evening purse and once again glanced around. Her brother and father weren't looking her way. They didn't know. . . .

She nearly ran toward the glass doors. Impatiently she waited as the porter opened the door wide. Hurry .. hurry ... down the dimly lit hall, past the coatroom. Her shawl? Leave it. Must escape. Must! Up the flight of stairs ... the next ... another porter ... glass doors .. *air ... air...*

And Billy Joel's music rang out at her back—

> *With some money in her pocket, she's a rocket*
> *on the fourth of July,*
> *And she don't know where she's going, but she*
> *sure knows what she's leaving behind ...*
> *Goodbye ... goodbye ...*

Her father's chauffeur and limousine were just down the block. The chauffeur ... was turning her way. In another moment he would see her! There was a large silver Rolls-Royce limo just in front of her. Its driver and two other chauffeurs who were awaiting the pleasure of their employers were in jolly conversation not far from her, but none of them had her in sight.

Quickly she opened the Rolls door and dived in. She hadn't known what else to do. Her father's chauffeur would have seen her if she hadn't.

On the seat, neatly folded, was a black furry blanket. She took it up, found a corner on the floor behind the bar setup, and hid herself. Just for a few minutes. Just until she could sneak out the street side and vanish out of view. . . .

Sir Justin watched Holly accumulate her winnings. What the devil was the matter with the bird? At first the girl had made delightful little sounds over her winnings, but now . . . now such intensity. Damn if she didn't look frightened. Then he watched her get up with a considerable profit. He noted that she looked anxiously toward the men she had arrived with. He watched her nearly run to the cashier's window and then leave the casino alone. Odd, very odd! A moment later, he found himself cashing in and following her up the stairs and outdoors.

Up on the sidewalk he stopped and glanced around, the frown still pulling at his ginger brows. Where had she slipped off to so hurriedly? He felt a rush of disappointment. Idiot, he began chastising himself.

You came for a little gambling, some relaxation . . . but the little bird is in trouble . . . so? What is it to you?

He sighed and allowed his man, Cal, to open the door to his silver Rolls. Hampshire was nearly two hours' drive, and the old man looked tired. He shouldn't have kept him so late.

"You up to this drive, Cal?" Sir Justin asked solicitously.

The elderly chauffeur had been with Sir Justin nearly eight years now. He would have done anything for his young employer, but that was another story.

"Sure now, Sir Justin. I'm that fit. Just come from a nice round wit' the boys."

Sir Justin grinned. "Well them, we're off for the

cottage." He slid into the back, sat down, opened his dark-blue suit jacket and slipped it off and onto a hanger beside him. As the large car pulled out onto the road he took out a small container of cognac and poured himself a glass. He sipped this slowly and attempted to relax. The beauty's face was recalled. Such red-gold hair, such blue blue eyes . . . provocative . . . what had made her run off?

Holly moved with the dark blanket to the window and peeped. Someone was moving her way! Good God! She scrunched herself back down. The door of the car opened. She heard a strangely familiar male voice. The man was getting into the car! What to do? What to do?

Stay down. Stay down. So she attempted not to breathe and hoped for the best. Holly was nineteen, and she had led her teenage years in a sheltered environment. Her imagination had been fueled by books and some of the movies she had been allowed, but she was at her age a rarity in the year of 1979, an innocent. And here she was on an adventure, for that was exactly how she viewed it.

Sir Justin's hand swept away his ginger waves from his forehead. His home base was London, but he was glad to be getting out of the city for a time. He needed this space alone, and Sophie's Grange was just the place for his retreat. There he could work without interruption. Even as his thoughts came to this point, something caught his attention.

Not a movement, not a sound, but a snip of creamy white. He frowned and focused his vision on the small edge of white material. They were traveling the motorway, taking it southwest, and he could see the signs to Heathrow Airport out of the corner of his eye. For some reason, he tried to ignore the slip of creamy white on the floor. It irritated him. Why was the blanket all piled up on the floor? He bestirred himself and leaned forward. He took up the small quantity of white material and gave it a tug, expecting that it would come up with his hand. Instead, he felt it tug back!

His dark ginger brows went up in mild surprise. Beneath the blanket, Holly raised her eyes heavenward and prayed.

Sir Justin pulled harder, exposing more and more of the creamy white, and as his violent attentions threatened to disrobe her, Holly let go a yelp of annoyance.

"Stop it!"

Sir Justin sat up straight. His eyes were wide gray questioning pools. In one movement he swept aside the blanket.

"Well, lo and behold!" was his comment.

She recognized the friendly gentleman who had been beside her at the roulette table and blushed. "Oh, it's you, sir. Well, that is something, at least."

Sir Justin, where women were concerned, was something of a cynic. After all, he was wealthy, titled, and eligible. Females using all sorts of unorthodox methods to further his acquaintance was not something he was unaccustomed to.

"No doubt you have made a terrible mistake and climbed into the wrong limousine, and fell asleep while waiting for your . . . er . . . escort," he said on a note of dryness.

She caught the sarcasm in his voice and blushed hotly. "I wish I could give you such an easy explanation, sir . . . but that is not the case."

He was intrigued. "It isn't? Perhaps you would like to offer me one, then . . . an explanation, that is."

She sighed sadly. "The trouble is that I can't. I don't wish to lie to you."

"Don't you?" Again the dry note.

She frowned. "No, of course not. You don't know me, and therefore . . . I can understand why you might have some doubts . . . though I don't really understand why you should . . ."

"My dear—" he started, interrupting her.

She cut him off. "Do you think, sir, that you might help me up from the floor? My legs fell asleep, and I'm beginning to feel a bit stiff."

Again his ginger brows moved expressively. He

reached out his hand, caught hers, and lifted her to the seat beside him. She was very near his shoulder, and he regretted having to shift over to allow her to straighten out her gown. She released a long sigh.

"Gosh," said Holly. "If only I could think of something to tell you."

He felt a chuckle tickle him. She was a strange mixture of child and woman. "Why don't you start by telling me the answers to two very important questions that I have."

She returned his look gravely. "I shall try."

"Who were the gentlemen you came into the casino with tonight, and why are you running away from them?"

Here now was the problem. She was starting a new life. Should she start it with a lie? But he was a stranger. He might think it his duty to return her to her father. What to do? Her consternation was clearly evident on her face.

"No doubt the younger of the two men is . . . your lover?" Sir Justin tried to help her along.

She was astonished and glanced up at him sharply. It made her want to laugh. But of course, what a marvelous solution. She looked away from him and took to road-gazing while she assembled her thoughts.

He took this to mean her confession. An irritating wave of regret touched him. He shrugged it off. "And of course the other man was a friend?"

"No . . . his father," she said without looking at him.

"I see," he said digesting this. "And why did you feel you had to collect your winnings and run away from them?"

"Because they are trying to force me into marriage!" she blurted out. A half-truth. She would give him only half a lie. She would use her mother's maiden name. She would search out a job . . .

"How can they do that?"

Fiction came darting into her mind. Romantic novels came into play. "It is very strange . . . and will appear very odd to you . . . but you see, for the last seven years

59

I have been . . . kept . . . by those two men in Baghdad, Iraq . . . where they took me as a child."

He was shocked. "How could they have taken you out of the country?"

"My mother died . . . Hassan's father was my legal guardian. That doesn't matter. What does is that I don't wish to marry and live in Iraq. When I won at the table tonight . . . I thought I would take my winnings and run away . . . hide somewhere in the country. . . ."

This was one of the strangest stories he had ever heard. He studied her a moment. She was a beauty . . . but she had been kept by those two men, by her own admission. God knows what she wasn't admitting to. He reached out and took up her chin.

"What is your name, love?"

"Holly. Holly Winslow," she answered brightly.

He hesitated. He shouldn't be getting involved. What if she was a plant? It could be. Were the Arabs using this girl to get to him? They couldn't know what he was up to. Could they? What if they were using her? Then, keep her within sight?

"Well then, Holly Winslow, I think I know how I can help you."

Chapter Three

"Help me? I don't see how you can." She arched her brow. "And I am sorry . . . I don't even know your name."

That wasn't possible. Some of the finest racing machines and sports cars carried the family name of Laeland. Gossip columns always played with his pictures. The news found ways of involving his name. Everywhere he went in England he was known. He indulged her lie.

"How remiss of me. I am Sir Justin Laeland."

Holly received this piece of information blandly. It

made no impression upon her whatsoever, and as she could see that he meant to continue talking, she waited patiently for him to do so.

He was again taken aback by her. Didn't it matter to her who he was? Damn, but she was something of an actress.

"Now . . . the way I see it, you will need a job. You can use some of your winnings to get yourself some clothes and perhaps a nice little flat."

"Well, of course, but what has that—"

"You see," he cut her short, "as it happens, I am involved in a firm . . . in which I hold a position of authority. I could get you a job."

She brightened at once. "Oh . . . that is wonderful!"

"Which brings us to some questions I must put to you."

"Right," she agreed. "Ask away."

"Do you type?"

She shook her head. "No . . ."

"Steno? Office work?"

Again she shook her head. "Not at all. I could learn . . ."

He pulled a face. "No, I wouldn't like to foist someone inexperienced onto my staff. I make it a rule not to do that sort of thing. Very well, then, why don't you tell me what you can do?"

She hung her head. "I have never worked."

He studied her. "So . . . always the good life?"

"I told you . . . I was taken to Baghdad when I was very young . . . and I have always been . . . looked after."

"By both those men?"

"Yes, by Hassan and his father."

He frowned. She spoke quite easily about her sordid past. To have embarked upon such a career when only a young girl . . . but that was another rumor about Moslems.

"Well, then . . . you must have had some hobbies? Perhaps we could put them to use."

This time she felt like crying. It was one thing to play at being the modern sophisticated English girl; it

61

was quite another having to admit how little you had in accomplishments. She sighed. "My all-consuming interest is horses. I spent all my free time at our stables. I rode well enough to teach"—she was going to say "some of my father's friends" but caught herself—"and . . . and have even been given a number of Arabian horses to train."

He held his breath. Danger! It was all fitting too neatly. Here he was going to his cottage at Sophie's Grange, and Sophie ran a riding academy. If they wanted this girl to spy on him, they were certainly setting him up.

Again his voice came coldly. "How very convenient."

She frowned. "What do you mean?" He was certainly quixotic.

"Never mind. Certain things should be left to the clarity of daylight." He had moved closer to her, he was taking up her hand, pressing it to his lips, caressing her fingers with a lingering and incredibly tantalizingly soft kiss.

"What interests me, sweet thing, is . . . are you going to be . . . grateful?" Why was he doing this? Was he lowering her or himself? Is that why the words tumbled out? Was it easier to reduce all things to a banal level?

As inexperienced as Holly was, she knew what he meant. What a child doesn't learn by practice in this world, she may by observation. "No, I think not, Sir Justin. You see, I did not run away from such a situation only to find myself in another . . . of my own making!"

He couldn't stop the grin. Boyishly it transformed his features.

"Good!" he answered happily.

She was conscious of the light in his gray eyes. "Good?" his reaction surprised her.

His reaction surprised himself. He slipped his arm around her waist. "Ah, love . . . when I get you into my arms"—his voice was low, strangely husky—"I don't want it to be because of gratitude." He dropped a kiss on her bare shoulder.

She felt hot blood course through her veins. Gently she eased out of his hold. "But you already take unfair advantage, Sir Justin. If you wish to help me, then do it freely and don't expect anything in return. Otherwise, you should let me out of this car, now."

He sat bolt upright and considered her. "Now, just a moment, Miss Holly Winslow. I didn't ask you to hide yourself in my car and to keep silent as we drove out of London . . . you do know that we are a good way out of London?"

"Yes, but . . ."

"So, then, what do you take me for? Some kind of monster? What the bloody hell am I to do with you? Let you off in the middle of the motorway in the dark of night for some lorry driver to take you up and perhaps get his kicks?"

"No . . . but . . ."

"But what? Does that put me at your mercy or you at mine?"

"You could take me to some village inn . . . where I could get a room . . ."

"Daft bird!" he ejaculated impatiently. "Without luggage, without protection. A fine spectacle you would make, and if anyone is on your trail, you would be found. Or perhaps you really wish to be found?"

She sank into her thoughts. He was right. He did make sense. She needed his help. But he made it so difficult to accept.

"I think you have involved yourself in my affairs enough. Kindly have your driver pull over. I should like to get out."

"I am afraid I cannot allow you to do that. Look . . . you have my word, I shall keep my hands to myself." (Well, look at you, outmaneuvered.) "I mean to take you to my cottage . . . where you will have your own room. Tomorrow I'll run into town and buy you some clothes. Does that meet with your approval, Miss Holly Winslow?"

"You are very kind," she said carefully. Here was another domineering male. English, but in many ways much like her father. She was not about to get caught up by another such man now when she was finally breaking out.

She put back her head and closed her eyes. So much had happened in the space of moments. She had run away. By now her father and brother would be looking for her. What would they do? Should she send them word that she was safe? No. They would come and find her. They would then be certain that they had been right in attempting to keep her locked up in their country. They would marry her off to Wahid! But her father would worry! Guilt. It pushed through her thoughts, and she smashed it down. She was still angry enough with him to accomplish that feat. And peacefully content with her decision, she dozed.

Sir Justin appraised her from his corner. As delightful a beauty as ever he had come across. Her game? He wasn't quite sure yet, but he knew one thing. For the present, he was willing to play. He saw her head fall and frowned. In the morning she would ache because of it. He reached over and gently guided her over until she was resting in his lap. She sighed pleasurably in her sleep and hugged his flat belly much as she might a pillow. He found it strangely amusing and far too arousing to think about. He reminded himself of another time, another woman, and he hardened his thoughts very well.

He saw the sign indicating Winchester had been passed. They were now on the winding country road that would eventually take them to Brockenhurst in the New Forest. He thought of the quaint little town, the wide green forests, the wild ponies forever munching away at the grazing land. The daffodils would be in bloom. It was good that he was going there. He had loved the place as a boy. It was too bad about Sophie's new husband . . . but never mind, Sophie was strong enough to weather it.

Tudor buildings rich with history and tradition were

passed. A dozen or so deer skipped over the roadway, coming into full view of the headlights. They froze a moment in panic and then flew out of sight into the dark forest. Soon they were passing through the small village and taking a side road that led to a large red-and-white sign, "Laeland Grange and Riding Academy." Sir Justin read the words to himself and smiled. He had only been a boy when his uncle and Aunt Sophie had decided to turn his uncle's inheritance into a riding academy and thus support the growing taxes on a land his uncle would not, could not, part with. Now, his uncle was gone and Sophie carried on. . . .

They turned off and came up on a narrow gravel drive that took them deeper into the forest, past an open field of wildly blooming daffodils, past well-kept gardens, to a thatch-roofed cottage that was in fit condition.

Sir Justin slid his charge into a carrying position and before the presence of his surprised chauffeur, delivered Holly into the house. A set of lights were flicked on, and Sir Justin managed his sleeping burden through the plush living room, past a cozy though modern kitchen, down the hall, to a door diagonally across from his own bedroom door. It was open, and he went through to deposit Holly on the wide bed. He turned to his man, who was advising him in grim terms that he had brought the luggage in from the boot.

"I've set your bags in your room, sir. Shall I unpack for you?"

"No thanks, Cal . . . go on and get some rest. I am certain you must be done in."

"Thank you, sir," returned the older man. He did not always approve of his employer's behavior. Holly in repose looked no more than a babe. Cal didn't know where she came from, didn't know what she was doing here, for his employer's presence in Hampshire was supposed to be a well-guarded secret. However, it was not his place to question Sir Justin's habits. He set this problem aside and made for his own comfortable lodgings over the four-car garage.

Sir Justin listened for the closing of the front door before he turned to the problem of Miss Holly Winslow. He contemplated the ivory crepe covering her body, and started with her sandals. These were slipped off. He straightened. He could clinically disrobe her. After all, it wasn't the first time he had undressed a beautiful woman. No, it wasn't the first time. Damn, how the devil had he gotten into this?

Swiftly, deftly, he undid the hooks at the back of her neck. She made a soft sound and moved cooperatively. Was she asleep? Was she just playing a game? The dress came off easily, and he sighed a breath of relief to find she had a full slip on underneath.

He moved the covers of the bed and folded them over her. He felt the heat rising in his body. (Fool. She is off limits. She is dangerous.) He picked up her dress and sandals and went to the door, where he took a long look before he shut off the lights to her room and proceeded to his own.

Chapter Four

The rays of the sun penetrated the sheer hangings and came gratingly upon Holly's eyelids. Her lashes fluttered and her hand came up to shield off the glare. Warm. Hmm. Comfortable. She rolled over and then all sensations froze into one. She sat up with a jerk. (Where? Oh, God . . . yes . . . she had really run away.)

She looked around her. What was this place? How did she get here? Where was Sir Justin? She discovered suddenly that she was dressed in her slip. Her eyes widened. How?

The last she could recall she was in the back of Sir Justin's Rolls . . . talking to him. Only that came flooding back into focus. She had a hazy recollection of a strong shoulder. She had nodded into it, opened her eyes a moment as she swayed, and then closed them again. He must have carried her in here as she slept. He must have ... ? She looked down at her body. Mortified, she imagined him touching her as he undressed her. No man before had ever seen her in a state of undress.

She scanned the room for her belongings. On the floor near her bed were her stockings. No shoes, no gown. Where were her clothes? On the dresser was her evening bàg. She jumped up to inspect it and breathed a sigh of relief to find her total cash winnings still safely tucked inside. She opened the drawers to the dresser. No clothes there. She crossed the plush dark carpet to the closet. Empty. She felt her ears; the diamonds were still there.

A knock sounded at her door. "Miss Winslow?"

She shrieked, "Wait a moment!" With this she dove toward the bed and grabbed the quilt.

A bit impatient to be on with his business but not unamused by all this, he persisted, "Now, Miss Winslow?"

She eyed herself. "Very well," she allowed reluctantly.

He opened the unlocked door and took a step inside, halting abruptly as he saw her. Gone was the regal, the fashionable beauty of the other night, and what she had been then was nothing to what she was now! She stood in her tousled, flustered glory, and she was magnificent. Her red-gold hair was a fluff of waves all around her face, and her eyes glowed in aqua hues.

A rushing sensation swept over him and took his breath away. He made her a mock bow; it belied his traitorous thoughts.

"Good morning, Miss Winslow. I trust you slept well?"

"Good morning. Where are my clothes?"

"I took the liberty of taking them with me to the village this morning to ascertain your size. . . . I thought you might need something more serviceable today."

She frowned; she was becoming too much in this man's debt.

"I could have done that myself."

"In your evening gown, Miss Winslow?"

She bit her lip. "Oh . . . I suppose I should thank you. . . ."

"Not if you don't wish to. I wouldn't want you to trouble yourself." He was enjoying her momentary discomfiture.

"Don't be absurd. I do thank you. There is something, however, I should like to know. . . ." She hesitated. (Stupid girl . . . you are not in Baghdad. You are here in England . . . men and women are very open here about sex.) Still she had to ask, "How . . . did you get my clothes off me?"

"How do you think, love?" He was teasing now.

"You did it yourself, then?"

"I did. You were most cooperative, though. A nudge was enough to get you to move."

She blushed. "Then I am to understand that you carried me in here and then removed my clothes?"

"Precisely." He was vastly entertained.

"Thank you," she said simply.

He pushed two brown packages at her. "You'll want these after your shower. You'll find a pot of hot coffee in the kitchen. There are some buns there, too—I am afraid you won't have time for more." He started to move away.

"But . . . wait . . ."

"Yes?" He turned.

"What do you mean . . . about my not having time? What are you planning?"

"You will see, love."

She frowned. "And the clothes . . . how much do I owe you?"

"A trivial matter."

"Not to me. I want to know."

He was not pleased by this. "Miss Winslow, you may find the simple clothes in there are not to your taste.

68

After all, I only meant them to get you through the day."

"That is not the point, sir."

"No, of course not. I had quite forgotten. You don't wish to be grateful to me."

"I am already grateful to you. I don't wish to be in debt to you," she returned.

He restrained a retort to this and said only, "I will leave you to shower and breakfast and return in an hour's time."

"I shall be ready . . . though I do wish you would tell me what you have in mind."

"You will find out soon enough. . . . You see, Holly, I have quite made up my mind to keep you within my reach." With this he was gone.

She stared after him a long moment. What did he mean? Was he just flirting again, or was there more to it than that? Never mind, no doubt he wanted to seduce her. That was it, of course.

Sir Justin had looked boyishly attractive in his denim jacket and jeans, so different from his formal attire last night. There was a rugged line to his face that she liked, but he was arrogant and overbearing. There was also no doubt that he had had a long line of women. No, she didn't want a man like that.

She opened the large brown packages and found within a pair of socks, sneakers, a pair of stylish jeans, and a matching jacket. There was a warm and very pretty pale-blue angora sweater, but no bra. Ah well, she would have to do without until later. She totaled their cost, went to her bag, and removed that amount and put it aside.

"Now for my shower," she said out loud and moved down the corridor with the quilt still wrapped around her.

Mustafa grumbled over a loss and turned to his friend with a small jest. He thought of his daughter and turned farther in order to catch a sight of her at the roulette table. The crowd obscured his line of vision, and he stood in order to get a better view. She was not there. He frowned while he considered the possibilities. One must not allow one's fears to rule his actions. Slowly he told his heart this was so, and still he felt a trickle of dread. His Khalda had been in such a mood.

A child. Such a wondrous child she had been. Self-willed and strong. Passionate and idealistic. Rebellious and still gentle. These thoughts came in quick bolting explosions. Something was wrong. He knew it, sensed it. He moved toward his son.

Hassan stood with the blond nestled in his arm. He was laughing with his friends. Mustafa observed this with a heightening sense of displeasure. What was Hassan doing? Why was the boy not watching over Khalda?

He brushed this irritating notion away and stalked his son. Just before he reached him his voice came sharp and clear.

"Hassan!"

Hassan's laughter died suddenly. He turned and felt a streak of uneasiness as he moved toward his father's call. His friends would understand, the pretty English girl would not. But there was no embarrassment in respecting one's parent. It was what he reminded himself when pride threatened. He moved forward and in Arabic responded, *"Eee . . . baba?"*

He was answered in Arabic, and roughly. "Where is your sister?"

Hassan's gaze went immediately to the roulette table where he had deposited her not so very long ago. His brows went up. She was not there. Quickly he scanned the room. He frowned and then almost at once brightened. "What? Cannot the child go unattended to the ladies' room?"

Mustafa's expression relaxed. He had not thought of that. (Why? Such an easy explanation. Because it was not so?)

"We will await her." He led his son across the dark carpet past the milling flocks of nightbirds and gam-

70

blers and took up idle position. After ten minutes they grew restless.

"I will ask after her," said Hassan and went in search of the blond awaiting his return.

It didn't take long to ascertain that Holly was no longer at the casino. Hassan was surprised, perhaps a bit shocked, but certain that she must have returned to their hotel.

"She probably did not want to bother us," he suggested reasonably.

"Mejnoon!" spat his father, calling his first, his only son insane. "She would not have taken her leave without bidding us goodnight . . . she knows we would worry . . ."

"Where, then? Look, *baba* . . . she is unhappy about this marriage you have planned for her. She . . ."

"You are suggesting that she is angry with me. Perhaps that would make her run off without saying goodnight to me . . . but would she not inform *you?*"

"It could be that she is upset with me as well. Holly has a wild streak in her, *baba* . . . she may be showing us that she is fully grown. . . ."

Mustafa considered this. Upon further reflection he felt himself seized with an unnamed fear. "Hassan . . . quickly, you will make discreet inquiries here. I will return to our suite!"

By the next morning Hassan was frantic and Mustafa's fears had given over to anger. She had run away. It had not been hard to come to this conclusion. It was unthinkable, but it was the only explanation.

Unforgivable, and what was worse it hurt to the core. His darling, his babe, his Khalda, daughter of his English heart, and she had fled him. He would have her found, and in his own way he would have her punished!

Wahid? By Allah, his daughter had put him in a precarious situation. There was honor to save. Honor as a Moslem. He, Mustafa, the Haji, had promised his Khalda to Wahid, and to Wahid she must be given!

"Hassan . . . you will hire a private detective!"

71

Hassan considered this. They knew that a beautiful girl with hair the color of burnished gold had cashed in chips for more than 4,500 English pounds. This would make her quite self-sufficient for some time. Carefully he answered, "We will not want this known."

"Of course we don't. You will acquire someone who can be discreet. We will say that Khalda is visiting with some old and dear English friends in the country, and no one need know that she is missing."

Hassan bowed his head. "Very wise . . ."

Sir Justin was backing his little red custom convertible out of the carport and onto the drive. He always kept this car here at Laeland. It had been a gift from his father, especially designed by the company just for him. It flitted through his mind that two years had passed since his father's death. Two years since he had inherited. Damn!

He sighed over it. At least it wasn't as bad as he had imagined it would be when he first attempted to step into his father's well-worn shoes. Justin was a genetic engineer. It was his chosen field. It was the sort of work he enjoyed, felt at home with, wanted to excel at. Even so, unhappily, almost resentfully, he had allowed his father to install him as chief department head of chemical engineering. It was where he had been when his father had suddenly died of a stroke.

He frowned as the memory invaded. He arrived at the fork in the drive and swerved his car around, downshifting and then power-shifting into high gear, taking the private road that would lead to the Grange and the main house. Ironic. He was about to achieve a goal for his father's company, but it would not be because he was its president. And that thought did much to mitigate his present depression.

He came to the cattle grid in the road and downshifted again. The small sleek car rumbled over the metal poles. He was flanked on both sides by paddocks. Their white sparkling fences held back Laeland horses. Two broodmares looked up from their munching, heavy

72

with foals; they watched him warily a moment before they returned to the rich grazing in their field. He stopped to look at the horses in the adjacent pasture. They were all beautiful. Two geldings were at play, bucking and kicking out their high spirits as they ran. He loved watching them.

Horses. He had grown up with them in his mind, in his blood. He had learned to ride before he was six. It was his love of horses that had brought him back here, and Sophie. . . .

He noted with pleasure that little changed here at the Grange. It had remained much the same for over two hundred years. The Georgian mansion stood in regal if mellow splendor, its gray walls nearly covered over in ivy, its paned windows peaking in symmetrical order on each of its three floors. The house had been only one of many belonging to the old Norman name of Laeland, but it was only one of two that had survived time and taxes. The other had belonged to Justin's father and now to Justin, who rarely used it. The cottage he now used and had modernized had been the Grange's dower house in an age when such things had mattered.

He braked and came to a stop before the great stone lions perched on watch on either side of the wide stone steps. Nimbly Justin jumped out of his car without bothering to open its door and took the stone steps two at a time to the glass-and-oak door. There he proceeded to ring and bang upon the portal with overzealous relish.

"Well now . . . just a moment! Who . . . ?" He heard a woman's soft breathless inquiring voice as she hurried to the door.

He smiled to himself to hear his aunt clucking. Her secretary, Maureen, returned that she had no idea but that she would get it. When the door opened he found both women ready to read a lecture.

"Justin! You rogue!" cried his aunt joyfully instead as she threw open her arms to receive him.

He took up her small plump frame and hugged her

73

affectionately as he winked at Maureen. Sophie was somewhere in her late forties, scatterbrained, lively, sweet, often silly, and thoroughly lovely.

He set her from him with a voice and a pair of gray eyes full with genuine pleasure.

"Well now, Sophie love, what have you been up to?"

She wagged a finger at him. "Where have you been all morning? But isn't it just like you to make me wait? I happen to know that you arrived last night, so there is no wheedling out of this."

He chuckled and and took up Maureen's hand and drew the tall middle-aged woman close enough to him to plant a kiss on her cheek. He felt her go hot with pleasure.

"What, don't tell me you two have set spies on me?" He shook his head comically. "Tch, tch, Sophie, not at all the proper thing to be looking through me windows. Just think what you might catch me at!"

His aunt smacked him playfully on the face, which took something of an effort as she stood no more than five feet and he was over six. "Never you mind, Justin. What do you mean coming in so late when I have been looking for you all morning?"

He took her hand and Maureen's. "Come on, then, and we'll have a cup of tea and you can tell me what has been happening at the Grange." He was leading them down the wide bright hall to a small and favorite room at the back of the house. He bent to Maureen and bantered, "How have they been treating you in my absence?"

"Terrible, sir, simply terrible. I have this list of complaints I'd be ever so pleased to have you look at," she teased.

"What's this? Don't they know you are the apple of my eye?"

She nodded. "That's the trouble, sir, indeed they do!"

He bowed his head. "Stabbed down in my prime."

"Speaking of your prime, you look a bit haggard," put in his aunt with something of a frown.

"Do I? Never mind, you will mend me soon enough."

"So I shall. Now . . ." She had allowed him to seat her before a tea tray. She looked up at Maureen, who understood perfectly and cut in on cue.

"I was just about to run an errand, Sir Justin, but I hope I shall see you upon my return."

"I hope so too, Maureen." He watched her through the open door return down the long wide corridor past antique wall-tables, past gothic dark wooden chairs of enormous capacity, past framed photographs. He turned away and looked out the long clear windows onto one of the many riding rings of the Grange. A young, not overly tall but nice-looking lad stood in its center calling out instructions to the group of five girls on school horses. His cousin Gregory.

His aunt was patting the cushioned sofa of yellow damask. "Come and sit, Justin."

He took up a Queen Anne chair near her instead. "Sophie . . ."

There was something in his tone that made her look up from the cup of tea she was pouring. She held the silver pot in midair.

"Yes, dear?"

"Something has happened . . . but I don't know where to begin. . . ."

She put the pot down and handed him his cup. "Begin with this, dear. There is nothing like a strong cup of tea to push away the cobwebs."

He smiled and set it aside. "Sophie . . . there is a reason for what I am going to ask you to do for me . . . but I can't tell you what that is."

"Yes, dear?"

"I should like you to explain that I am here at the cottage . . . getting myself together . . . recovering from the strain of running the business."

She studied him a moment. "But that is not why you are here?"

"I won't lie to you. I never have."

"Are you in trouble, Justin?"

"No . . . but it might be uncomfortable for me if anyone were to discover what I am doing here."

75

"I see."

"I knew that you would . . . so you will put it about that I am here for my health. A rest period."

"Very well, Justin."

"My needs don't end with that, Sophie." He was grinning.

"Oh?" She was smiling now. "Has this now got something to do with why you were so late coming to me this morning?"

"In a way."

"Do spit it out, Justin. You know I am not the sort that can patiently wait forever." She sipped her tea, made a grimace, and reached for the sugar. "I don't know why it is, but I am forever forgetting to add sugar," with which she plopped a cube in her cup, stirred, and returned her attention to her nephew.

He smiled ruefully. "I have been out this morning putting together a young woman's roustabout outfit."

"Have you?" returned his aunt with mild interest. "No doubt, you had good cause?" Her eyes had begun to twinkle.

"Well, I couldn't very well present her to you in her evening frock at this time of day . . . now could I?"

"Certainly not."

"I mean to do just that, you know—present her to you."

"So you said. Does she wish to take riding lessons?"

"No . . . Sophie, I recall that in your last letter you mentioned something about Thomas's having his hands full with group and private lessons since Clare's finishing school for girls opened its new spring programs."

"Yes, it has been a bit of a problem, as Greg has been taking on more than he is willing to handle."

"I may have an answer."

"Oh?"

"Hire someone," he pursued, "to give lessons."

"Well, and so Greg has tried to do, but no one has worked out yet."

"I have someone who might work out," he suggested softly.

76

"Ah, the girl in the evening frock," she zeroed in, happy to have an answer to the question that had been plaguing her.

He smiled. "She needs a job. She tells me she has trained horses and feels she could teach beginners and intermediates. I thought you might like to see what she can do."

Sophie hesitated. "In other words, Justin . . . you would like us to hire one of your cast-offs?"

He looked taken aback. "Sophie, you know better!"

"I thought I did."

"I only met her last night. She has never been a . . . er . . . close friend of mine. She needs work and a place to stay, but if you would rather not interview her . . ."

"Oh, don't be silly. You bring her to me." Sophie was smiling again and wondering what sort of girl had caught her nephew's interest. He usually didn't bother with women past his bedroom.

"Bring who to you?" A male voice from the doorway.

Sophie and Justin looked up to find Greg standing there. Sophie's only son was twenty-two, and good-looking. Beneath his tweed peaked cap was a mass of glistening waves of gold and bright-hazel eyes. It was an interesting combination. He moved across the small room, hand extended, to Justin, where he stood a good deal shorter than his cousin. "Hello, Justin . . . Mother has been expecting you all morning." He was smiling wide.

"You look fit, Greg." Justin had always liked his cousin.

"Greg, shall I pour you a cup? I think it is still hot," said his mother.

"No, I have another lesson in five minutes, and damn, I am not looking forward to it."

"The Baines girl?" This from his mother.

"Hmm, and she is no nearer to sitting properly to the canter than she was four weeks ago. Lord, but she just can't, and I have her on Birdy, and if she can't ride Birdy she can't ride!"

77

"Thomas says she takes lessons simply to moon over you, Greg," teased his mother.

Greg eyed her thoughtfully for a moment. Thomas Martin would say something like that. Greg cordially disliked his stepfather. "Nonsense. Judy Baines is married, and her husband is something of a friend, you know."

"Hmmm . . . but Thomas says—"

"To hell with what Thomas says!" snapped her son, and then sighed. "Oh, look . . . Judy is one of my private pupils. It's bound to look at times as though she is paying an awful lot of attention to me. That's all there is to it."

"Yes, of course," said his mother unhappily. She hadn't meant to upset him. She had only been teasing. She had quite forgotten that Judy Baines was married. Now Greg was irritated, and he was sure to be angry with Thomas about it all.

"Justin here has someone he feels we could hire as an instructor," she put in quickly, hoping to change the mood.

"Oh?" said Greg with interest, "A friend of yours, Justin?"

"She . . . no, rather an acquaintance. A young girl . . . quite pleasant, presentable," Justin said carefully, hoping to convey the impression that there was no romantic interest there.

"May she work out, for I tell you, ever since old Mrs. Jortz left for Cornwall I haven't had a moment to spare." He looked at his mother. "Thomas isn't into group lessons. He likes taking privates over the hunt course . . . which is something we have got to talk about later, Mother."

His mother glanced at her watch. This was a subject better avoided. Thomas had no patience in the ring with a group of children. He accommodated the adults who sought private lessons and until they had lost Mrs. Jortz, their instructor, things had been comfortable enough.

"Greg . . . you are already late for your next class."

78

"It's just Judy . . . she'll wait . . ."

"Yes, but then you will be off schedule. You can spend time with Justin later. Off with you now."

"There is no justice in this world, cuz . . . simply none at all," were Greg's parting words.

Justin turned to his aunt as he rose. "Well then, Sophie, I shall return with Miss Winslow within the hour."

"I look forward to meeting her," she said and watched him go. Now, here was Justin bringing them a girl he claimed was not his mistress. Very intriguing. Why would Justin put himself to so much trouble for a drab of a girl? And she must be that if Justin had kept hands off.

Justin went outdoors. He had promised himself to stay away from the stud paddock. It would only hurt . . . and still his steps brought him closer. He saw him there, grazing on the rich dark-green grass, and stood a moment in admiration. The stallion picked up his neck and stared back a moment. Recognition. Something in the stallion's mind jarred. He sniffed the air and then snorted, but he stood, taking no chances.

Justin went closer and softly said the stallion's name. "Star . . . ?" The dapple-gray snorted again. Flashes of scenes long past flickered in the stud's mind. "Star?" the man called again. Familiar . . . strangely familiar, oddly welcome. He took a step forward. Him. Him. Memories of that voice, strangely authoritative, soothing, affectionate, touched the horse's mind. He made a small whinny in his throat and moved his head up and down with strength. It was the man whose hands had touched when he had been a colt . . . had trained him to dance . . . whose arms had held that night of fear . . . of sweat and pain . . . him? The horse came forward, head extended, nose blowing softly in his show of welcome.

Sir Justin felt tears well up, and he fought them down. He had raised this grand stallion. Seven years ago seemed a lifetime. He had raised him, worked with him day after day, brought him up until he was ready for the Campagne school of dressage . . . and then all

79

that ended with his father's death. That dream was gone, for reality had put him elsewhere. "Hello, Star . . ." His hand played with the stud's nose, went up along the stud's head and touched the ears. The horse nuzzled him a bit, and then in a buck and a whinny raced off to show his stuff. Sir Justin watched him a bit longer, and the horse executed on his own the serpentine they had spent months on . . . but all that was gone.

With a sigh, Sir Justin turned and made for his car. He had work to do, and he couldn't start it until Holly Winslow was out of the way.

Chapter Five

Thomas Martin's hand slipped up Judy Baines's inner thigh as he pressed her against the wall of the pony barn. It was a small building that housed only eight ponies, some of which belonged to the children of nearby neighbors. Judy arched her long youthful body in anticipation of his touch. She heard him whisper something vulgar and yet oddly seductive in her ear, and she shivered with aroused sensations.

He pushed aside her dark-brown velvet blazer and unbuttoned her yellow shirt. He bent as he produced her small pink-tipped breast, and she stroked his graying blond head as he lowered his mouth to her nipple.

He made her feel as no other man before him ever had. It was a fact that made no sense. She was nearly twenty-four, and she was considered quite a beauty. He was short, fifty, and nothing to look at. Still, right in this barn in their first private lesson he had seduced her. She was married to a young man who provided her with most of her needs . . . but she would throw John over in a second if Thomas would leave Sophie.

"Thomas . . . my lesson," she warned. Some time ago they had decided it would be better if she switched her private lessons to Gregory and took them in the ring instead of on the trails.

"Hmmm. Your lesson . . . is progressing." He leered and pinched her taut nipple.

She giggled. "No . . . really, Thomas . . . Greg will be waiting."

"And so will I. This afternoon . . . at Joy Chen's flat."

She pouted. "Will Joy be there again?"

"No, she has had to go into London . . . but what is this? I rather thought you were beginning to enjoy our sessions with Joy."

"I want you for myself . . . I don't get enough of you when Joy is there."

"Remember something, Judy. Joy and I go back a number of years. I don't mean to give her up, and you should feel flattered that she has allowed you to join us."

She said nothing to this. It was a situation that was still unclear in her mind. "But she won't be with us this afternoon?"

He set her clothes back to rights. "No, she won't." He could hear some of the women who boarded their horses at Laeland out in the parking lot. They would soon be coming this way. Jimmy was moving the wheelbarrow outside getting wood shavings, and he would be here as well.

He couldn't afford to take chances. He couldn't afford to allow Greg to become suspicious of his activities. If Sophie found out there would be all hell to pay!

"I like it with Joy . . . but I like it better when we are alone."

"And we will be, this afternoon, but as you said you have your lesson with Greg. Go on . . . I'm going out the back door."

"Don't you always?" She smiled naughtily as she did up her blazer and moved into the bright spring day.

Thomas Martin waited a moment. He could hear the laughter of women . . . the boarders were coming. Quickly he stepped outside and made his way around the barn and toward the house. It was time to go in and brighten

81

Sophie's day. That would give him some free time later. . . .

Justin didn't bother to get out of his car. He honked his horn, and a moment later Holly appeared in the doorway. Her long red-gold hair floated in the breeze. Her blue sweater heightened the color of her aqua eyes, and her smile shook him with a longing to take her in his arms. He frowned and shrugged away the notion. She was trouble. (Oh, really? Then why are you installing her within such easy reach?) To watch her, he answered himself.

"Hop in," he called.

She slipped on the denim jacket and came to his car. He opened the door from inside. She hesitated and then got in. "Where are we going?" she asked.

"To my aunt's place. Laeland Grange," he answered.

"Why?"

"You, my dear, are going to hire yourself out as a riding instructor at a very select riding academy."

She beamed. "Are you joking? Oh, tell me you are not joking."

"I am not joking. However, you get the job only if you prove you can handle it."

"Of course! Oh, tell me all about it!"

"I will leave that to my aunt."

"Tell me about your aunt, then. What is her name? What sort of a place does she have?"

"My Aunt Sophie was married to my father's brother. She was widowed some time back and inherited the Grange, which he had turned into a riding academy. Being a horsewoman herself, she took over. Her son is a certified instructor, as is her new husband, Thomas Martin. They help run the place. In addition to group and private lessons, they take in boarders. Neighborhood people board their horses here and get full use of the facilities . . . the hunt course, the maze of trails, and of course the New Forest trails."

Holly was gazing at the paddocks, at the horses, at the passing scene. In a bubble of gratitude she turned

82

and put her hand on his, which rested on the gearshift. "Thank you . . ." she breathed.

He felt an electric shock rush through him. What nonsense was this? She had only touched his hand, yet the feeling surged through him, and he turned to stare at her a moment. . . .

It wasn't long before Sophie had set Holly at ease with her idle chatter. They walked toward one of the well-cared-for riding rings as Sophie had requested one of the workers to bring out a horse for Holly to ride. Sophie was even at her time in life naive about many things, but when it came to business, she was surprisingly shrewd.

"Now tell me, Miss Winslow, what do you think the *art* of riding is . . . what predominant idea would you try to teach Laeland students?"

Holly considered the question a moment. It was a good question, and from where she stood there were several answers, but only one that consolidated them all.

"I think the art of riding must be associated with the harmony that can be produced between a horse and its rider. That harmony depends primarily on the correct application of leg and rein aids. Horses are not machines . . . they are not without minds of their own, though some people seem to think so. Every horse is different, and therefore a novice must work toward acquiring the correct aids and knowing how and when to apply them."

Sophie smiled, well satisfied. "Your attire is, of course, not the thing. We expect all our instructors to wear breeches and boots."

"No problem," said Holly, smiling anxiously. She wanted this job more than she had imagined she could ever want anything.

"Very well . . . here is Ulysses," said Sophie as a young boy with a shock of unruly brown hair led out a gleaming gray gelding,

"He is well mannered enough, but as you have pointed

83

out, horses do have minds all their own, and Ulysses is high on that list. One of your jobs here will be to train him for our more advanced riders and jumpers. Do you feel up to taking him on?"

Holly moved toward the gelding and raised her hand toward his head sharply. Not head-shy . . . good. She checked the bit. It was a snaffle. Well, if he was headstrong, his bit was not right. She checked the girth, tightened it, and hoisted herself lightly into the saddle. She could see Justin Laeland leaning into the fence. She smiled at Sophie. "Well, I shall give him a go and see if I can give you an answer."

Holly put the gelding into a walk. He hadn't been used in days. Greg had been too busy, and there had been no one about capable of taking him on. The gelding was nervous, and it showed in his eyes, in the flickering of his ears, in the movement of his head and the prance to his walk. Holly talked to him and put him into a rising trot, posting on the correct diagonal. She took him around the ring twice before halting him and turning him on the fores. Excellent. He took her aids easily and without objecting.

Again, she went twice around the ring and then put him into a figure eight at the trot. Here she noted that he definitely favored his right diagonal and attempted to shift her over. She laughed, halted him, patted his neck, and took him into a canter. He responded to her leg beautifully, and she tried a flying lead change.

"Why . . . he is marvelous," she called to Sophie and turned him to the crossbars. "Good Ulysses . . . good boy . . ." They took it at a trot and negotiated the simple height in fine form. However, as she collected him and pointed him at a white spread she could feel his body tense. She almost heard his thoughts and knew instinctively he meant to duck the jump. Instead she took in rein, animated him, paced him, took her two point, gave him rein release, and took him over the spread. He was annoyed, and when they reached the other side he exhibited this by letting out a sharp buck.

She chuckled. "Angry, are you, Ulysses? But why?

84

You took it beautifully you know . . . and you will again, this time at a canter, my friend." She took him around the ring on the correct lead at a canter, set him at the jump, one, then two . . . perfect. They stopped, he snorted, and again she patted his neck. "Good boy, you'll do."

She trotted him toward Sophie, noting that Justin was walking away, Disappointment? Ridiculous. She smiled at Mrs. Martin.

"He is lovely. Such a comfortable canter . . . but he will duck the jumps if he can, especially the spread."

"Precisely. Of course, he hasn't been able to get away with it if one of us is on his back, but he does with our students, and it is a shame, because he certainly can jump beautifully, and some of them are up to his caliber." Sophie was beaming. This was a girl who was an instinctive rider. She could work out wonderfully for them if she could teach. "Well, Miss Winslow . . . do you think you can get across to our students what you seem to feel when you are up there?"

"I can try, Mrs. Martin, and only time will answer your question," answered Holly gravely. She wanted this job; more than that, though, she wanted to be honest with this woman. She liked Sophie Martin.

"Good girl!" said Sophie, taking the reins and putting them into the stableboy's hands as Holly dismounted. "Now, come along and I will show you where you can stay. . . ." She hesitated. "Justin said you would need a flat . . . Mrs. Jontz used to stay in our stable flat . . . loved it, but she has retired to Cornwall."

"It sounds marvelous."

Sophie laughed. "I don't know about that . . . and you know the pay at first will not be all that attractive. . . ."

"I trust you to pay me what is fair," Holly was saying. They were walking past rows and rows of long white stables; the horses hanging their heads out the stable doors were watching them interestedly.

"These are our school horses . . . mixed breeds for the most part. Over there"—she nodded in the direction of a long rambling barn with a wide main aisle—"is

85

where we house the boarders' horses, most of which are turned out every day." They passed the pony barn to yet another, then walked its length to the rear corner, where a door held a sign reading, "Private."

Here Sophie took out a large brass key and opened the door wide, leading Holly up a flight of gray-painted wooden steps to an open doorway above.

The doorway opened into a large bright room with windows front and back. The back overlooked pastures of grazing horses, the front overlooked the parking lot and some of the stables. The room was filled with a mixture of period furniture. A small kitchenette took up the rear corner of the room. Sophie walked around.

"You have a refrigerator . . . a stove . . ." She moved to a door. "Here is your closet." She moved farther down to another door. "Here is the bath . . . fairly modern, you know . . ." She moved back into the center of the room, where a dark print sofa had been set. "This opens into a bed. You will need linens . . ." In her rambling style she continued to a small Sony TV set and flicked it on. "It is color, you know . . . and in fairly good working order . . . we take care of utilities . . . so you needn't worry. There is no fireplace, of course, because of the horses . . . but you have central heat." She looked about her, wondering if there was anything she had missed. "Well, I do hope you will be happy."

"Mrs. Martin . . . it's perfect," cried Holly, beside herself. Here she was. On her own. She had a job, she had a flat, she had money enough to get the things she needed and still put some away for emergencies. God was good!

"Is there anything I can do for you before I leave you to get settled?" Sophie was saying. She was in something of a hurry to get back to her books. With the show coming up in less than four weeks there was so much to do.

"Thank you, no," said Holly. She wanted to be alone. Alone in her own flat.

"Well then, until later, when I hope to introduce you to my son, Gregory, and my husband, Thomas . . . and,

86

oh, I shall have Maureen, our secretary, draw up your schedule for tomorrow's lessons—you can start tomorrow, dear?"

"Oh, yes, of course. Shall I come up to the house for it?"

"No, it will be posted in the main barn. Please feel free to roam about and get acquainted with your surroundings."

"Thank you, I will," said Holly watching the plump and pretty older woman take her leave.

She looked about herself and did a headspin! Fleetingly she thought of her father. He would be going mad with worry? No. He would now be in a rage.

By now he will have discovered that you left the casino with something of a haul. By now he will know that you ran away of your own free will. He will be furious . . . and if he finds you? What will he do? You are not yet twenty-one. He is your father. He can force you to return with him and marry Wahid. But will Wahid want you? Not if I can stay away long enough. Not if he doesn't find me in time. . . .

She would need to buy riding clothes, towels, boots, linens . . . so many things. Money! The money was still at Sir Justin's! She had left her evening bag with all her cash back at Sir Justin's cottage. She would simply have to walk over there, get her purse, and grab a cab into town. She took up the large brass key, gave her room one more loving look, and went out the door. No palatial scene was this. Gone were the luxuries she had been taught to expect. But Holly felt free at last.

Sir Justin descended the long stairs to the lab that had been constructed beneath his four-car garage. Here was everything he needed to continue his research. God, but he was close . . . he could feel it, sense it. There was something he was missing. An element he had not seen. . . .

Oil. It was at the heart of everything these days . . . and here he was taking Professor Calvin's theories and expanding them, rotating them, slicing through them.

He had the plant, Professor Calvin's great discovery, *Euphorbia*, and it produced oil. Peculiar, but there it was, *crude oil*. It was photosynthesis at its ultimate, it was genetic engineering to find a way of implanting the oil-producing gene from that plant into a fungus so that production could be controlled.

He was close, so close to discovering the key. He sat at his table and worked with his formulas. There was so much that still had to be done, and there was danger in it. There was no doubt in Sir Justin's mind that if the oil sheiks discovered what he was at, they would stop at nothing to destroy the formula . . . which would mean they would have to kill him. His discovery, its perfection, would mean an inexhaustible supply of oil could be harvested and at a relatively low cost. No, if they got to him before he made his find, before he managed to patent it . . .

And this girl, Holly . . . was she what she claimed? Had she been planted in his car as bait? Had he made a mistake by installing her at the Grange?

Damn, but she was beautiful. He couldn't get her face out of his mind, and then there she was on his closed-circuit scanner peeping into his garage windows! His brow went up. Well, well . . . now what does this mean?

Holly contemplated her surroundings before she took the woodland path and headed in what she hoped was the cottage's direction. Darn, but she wished she hadn't forgotten her purse at his place. Would he think it very odd? After all . . . all that money, and she hadn't thought to bring it with her. But why should she? It was safe enough with him.

The narrow path opened into a small clearing, and as she scanned it, she noted pleasurably that it would be filled with heather in two months' time. Would she be here to see it? Perhaps. At any rate, she wouldn't be in Baghdad . . . never again would she return to Baghdad. There was not the least bit of sadness in that. Why had

Mustafa never seen? He was her father and she loved him dearly. How could he have never seen?

The cottage loomed into view, and she was struck with its quaint setting, its thatched roof. Lovely, as were the gardens around it. She went to the front door and found it locked. Her lips pursed as she contemplated her next move. The garage? Perhaps someone was in the garage. She crossed the gravel drive and found the door to the garage open and went in.

"Hello?" she called. No answer. Bother! What to do? The Rolls was within, but Justin's little sports job was not. Perhaps Justin's driver? She saw a dark door at the rear corner of the garage and went toward it. Perhaps the chauffeur was on the other side? She knocked. No answer. She looked about. A strange place for a door. Where could it lead? Light flooded over her, and she spun around, feeling guilty, she couldn't think why.

"Looking for something?" Justin's voice was dry.

"Sir Justin . . . I was just wondering where you might be." She felt reduced to a schoolgirl and compensated for this feeling by putting her chin up defiantly. Even so, she felt intimidated by his air of cool sophistication, and something else she could not name.

"Looking for me? Why?" His voice went low, his eyes were wandering, his hands were reaching. He had his arms around her almost immediately, he drew her closer in a swift, deft, easy movement. "Well, well, do you mean to thank me properly after all?" His mouth closed on hers in hungry sweetness, for he tempered his play with caution and the experience born of distrust. Even so, the unexpected bolt of passion that blazed through him at their touch delineated his warier intentions, and he found himself for a moment lost in her kiss.

For Holly, rockets suddenly shot off in her head and their fireworks lit up the sky. Her flesh singed with a heat that was deliciously seductive and all too consuming. She felt her naked breasts beneath her sweater press into Justin's hard chest. She felt his hands moved

89

along her back. She saw his glittering gray eyes as he bent and remembered their look as his mouth closed on hers and his tongue ravaged her into response.

She sensed herself falling. She was falling . . . wasn't she? She put up her hands and held onto him. Strong broad shoulders . . . she felt herself molding to his touch as another kiss followed the first. Every nerve came alive. Every inch of her peaked into desire. No! What are you doing? Holly! A voice from within called her to order. Stop, stop, stop! She put up her fist, somehow she pushed against the heaviness of her arm and found his chest. Somehow she freed herself.

He was breathing hard. She was out of breath. They stared at one another for a long moment, trying to bring the matter into focus.

"I . . . I only came to . . . get . . . my purse," she managed in a meek voice and could no longer meet his eye. She was ashamed of herself. How could she have allowed him to handle her in that manner? She was blushing furiously and attempting to ignore what had just passed.

A good excuse, he told himself. She conveniently leaves a purse with several thousand pounds in it and then comes back when he isn't about. Her style was amateurish and transparent. Perhaps he had not done the right thing, installing her at the Grange. "Of course you thought you left it . . . *here*?" His tone, his smile, mocked her, as he scanned the garage.

"No, no . . . but when I didn't find anyone at the cottage, I thought your driver might be here."

"I see," he said curtly and turned to the door. "Right, then, we'll fetch your purse." He moved away from her abruptly and led the way outside.

Holly followed him, wondering if she had imagined his kisses a moment ago. He seemed now a totally different man. When she had been in his arms, he had been all passion and fire . . . and now? Now, he was cool, mocking, and . . . and . . . dismissing her. She attempted to ease the situation. "I . . . I have some shopping to do, you see, and . . . that's why I came back."

"Shopping? How do you plan to get into town?"

"I thought I would call a taxi," she said quietly, still not meeting his eye.

"Well, that won't be necessary. I am sure Cal will be more than pleased to get away from the cottage for a bit. I'll have him drive you into the village."

"Oh no . . . please don't bother him."

Sir Justin was already moving across the gravel drive to the outside stairs that led to Cal's overhead rooms. He knocked, and a moment later the elderly man appeared.

"Cal, I would appreciate it if you would drive Miss Winslow into town and wait until she has finished her shopping. She will be returning to the Grange."

"Very well, sir."

"And Cal . . . I want to know if she makes any phone calls . . . or if she manages to meet anyone."

"I understand, sir."

Sir Justin thanked him and took the stairs back to Holly, who stood waiting uncomfortably. He would have to be careful of this one. Evidently she had been sent here to investigate his work. She could be spying for the Arabs . . . or for the newspapers. There wasn't any way of telling for the moment, but he would keep her at bay.

A few moments later he was waving her off. Fresh in his mind was the feel of her trembling body pressed so close against him. Burning was the thought of that kiss . . . damn! He had to get to work. At least Holly Winslow was out of his hair for this afternoon . . . and, he hoped, out of his mind.

Chapter Six

"That was well done, ladies." Greg Laeland smiled as he watched his group of fourteen-year-old girls dismount. It was amazing how young some of them seemed, how womanly a couple of them were. Nice ass, he observed of one in particular as she slid out of the saddle and then turned a lovely heart-shaped countenance his way. "Christina, dear . . . if you don't mind, take your horse to Jimmy and go to the tack room. I'd like you to work on some of the tack for me until it's time for you to leave."

"Lovely," she said softly. "I do so like the smell of . . . leather." Her pale-blue eyes glinted as she moved past him.

He walked toward the remaining four girls and felt their horses' flanks. "Hmmm. A little hot. Walk them and then take them in. I want you to untack them yourselves today."

"See you next week, Mr. Laeland," they called as he moved off and out of the ring.

He skirted the boarders' barn, was hailed by Maureen on her way to post the morrow's lesson schedule, hurriedly spoke a few words with her, and rushed on. He had a thirty-minute break before the next group arrived for their lesson. He came up to the long barn's corner door, and out came his key. Up the stable stairs to the flat that had housed Laeland's last instructor. . . .

Christina Penbroke had already removed her clothes. She was proud of her youthful body. She knew that her breasts were high and perky. She knew that her waist was small, her hips well rounded, her legs long and smooth. She smiled as Greg moved toward her. She groaned as he took her in his arms. She helped as she felt him remove his clothing.

Damn, but she was made for this, he thought as she

92

scanned her naked body. He sucked in breath. She was only fourteen, he told himself as his hand closed over her full breast.

"Ah, Chrissy," he whispered as he lowered her to the floor. "Man, are you built," he cried as he undid his own breeches. (Fourteen . . . fourteen . . .)

"Oh, Greg, I do love you . . . take me . . . take me . . ." she begged urgently, already too aroused to wait.

He moved to mount her. (Fourteen, you bastard. She is only fourteen.) "Ah, sweetheart . . ." His voice drowned out his thoughts. Fourteen, his mind repeated, but the meaning of the word faded as his passion rose. Hell, she had been so easy. It wasn't his fault. She was always shoving her body into his. Not his fault. So easy . . . she had been so easy. . . .

Thomas Martin watched as Christina Penbroke raced across the boarders' parking area. If she hadn't been so young he might have considered adding her to his collection. He liked the feel of women . . . lots of women. He liked bringing them down, proving they were all nothing but a bunch of cunts!

This one had her eye on Greg, though. He had seen the girl looking at his stepson . . . and then he saw Christina take out a key to the door that led to the stable flat. His brows rose. What the deuce was *she* doing with a key to that door?

His answer came before he could think of how to handle this. He saw Greg leave the ring, stop to chat with Maureen, and then hurriedly move in the same direction as Christina. Well, well. What an idiot! Fooling around with a fourteen-year-old! Damn, but this could mean trouble. The girl was a Penbroke! Good stock there, and that meant trouble . . . for the school . . . for Sophie.

He smiled to himself. Here was one he had over that precious brat's of Sophie's! Damn if he wasn't going to lord it over the boy . . . but wait, this item could be used advantageously. There were many possibilities to be investigated here.

His position as Sophie's husband had not advanced him financially to any great extent. His earnings as manager and riding instructor at Laeland had increased since his marriage to Sophie, but he was not her beneficiary. Her son was sole heir to Laeland and all its holdings. Everything would go to Gregory . . . unless Gregory managed to prove unfit to inherit?

Perhaps Sophie, naive as she was, might be made to see what lecherous activities her son was engaging in . . . using his mask as riding instructor to seduce children? Yes, Hints would have to be made . . . starting now. He turned and made his way for the house, laughing to himself. Gregory would have to find a new place for his trysting now that a new riding instructor had been acquired . . . and what if she were to come in now and find Gregory with his charming companion? He chuckled out loud. Poor Greg, he had forgotten to tell him that the flat had been taken. . . .

Holly tried setting aside her confusion. She put her head back against the luxurious upholstery of the Rolls and closed her eyes. Sir Justin's kisses were still burning a hole through her logic. He was a playboy, rich, self-assured, arrogant, cold . . . no, not really cold, but somehow aloof. His kiss had been full with passion, and still she had known a part of him was held in check. He was no better than any Moslem man her father could offer. He probably had many women. No, she would keep him at arms' length! It was going to be an easy thing to do. Her shopping was done, but she was sitting in Sir Justin's Rolls, driven by Sir Justin's chauffeur, and she would be working for Sir Justin's aunt. Sticky. Never mind. She would simply stay out of his way in the future.

Cal swerved off the tree-lined drive and pulled up to the rear of the long white stable. He parked the Rolls and came around to open Holly's door,

"I'll bring up your packages, miss," he said going to the boot.

"You must let me help, Cal, or it will take you the rest of the afternoon." Holly chuckled, going with him.

He looked shocked. "I can manage, miss . . . if you would be so good as to get the door to your flat?" he suggested gently.

This, however, was not necessary, for at that moment Greg descended the stairs and opened the stable corner door that led to the flat above. There was a look of astonishment on his countenance as he came face to face with Holly. She was no less surprised and wondered how many keys there were to her rooms.

"Well . . . hello," he said on an appreciative note.

She smiled and wondered. Mrs. Martin's son? "Hello . . . I am Miss Winslow." She offered the hand he was already reaching to take.

"Don't tell me . . . Mother has already signed you on?" he said softly, giving her hand a friendly squeeze before allowing it to retreat.

"Well, yes," she answered doubtfully. (Didn't he know?) "Your mother tried me out on Ulysses earlier today and thought I might have a go at this job."

"I see. Well, then, welcome, Miss Winslow." He looked upward toward the flat for a fleeting moment. "I hope you are going to be happy here."

She smiled. "I hope so too, thank you."

"Look . . . I have to run off now . . . have one more group lesson before I call it a day . . . but I'd like to get better acquainted later." He hesitated. "Would it be too presumptuous of me to hope you might join me for a drink at a local pub after dinner tonight?"

Without thinking, without knowing more than that she needed a friend and he seemed awfully nice, she warmed to him. "I should like that very much."

"Right, then . . . I'll come by for you about seven, as we will be dining early tonight. Is that okay with you?"

"Lovely," she said and watched him saunter happily off. She had only a moment, though, for Cal was already weaving toward her with his burden of bags and boxes. Hurriedly she ran up the stairs before him to pave the way.

The Red Hart was located in Soho, and Andrew Benton was fairly certain he would not be found out by a chance acquaintance while there. It was important. He was a married man, an ambitious man, and he didn't mean to have any trouble now, no, not just now. He stood at the pub's counter and ordered the two dark ales and two plates of cheese and sweet relish.

Joy Chen watched him from her table and felt a wave of irritation. This seedy pub, this slinking about . . . what did she do it for? She didn't love Andrew Benton, and he certainly didn't provide for her in any way. Why, then? Because of Justin?

Justin, tall and good-looking, affluent and generous, hot-blooded and skilled, yet always aloof. She had met him eight months ago at the Grange, where she had been riding with Thomas. Thomas had been furious and jealous, but what could he do? She hadn't realized to what lengths Thomas might go to stop her association with Justin.

Now Justin would have no more of her, and she had taken up with one of his fair-haired boys at the plant. But Justin's sneer when he had seen her with Benton last month had not assuaged her bitterness, and it had only served to make Benton more cautious about their meetings.

Benton served her from the tray he carried and slid the empty tray beneath his chair. Joy watched from her dark oriental eyes and said nothing as he smiled at her.

"Come on, love . . . it won't be like this forever," he said, attempting to win her over.

"No, it won't." It was a warning.

He wasn't ready to give Joy up. Her body delighted him, the mystery of her mind intrigued him. She made him feel very much a man.

"Joy, listen to me—"

"No. You are beneath contempt. You want me to slide back into bed with Justin."

"Don't be a fool! All I want is for you to visit him at the cottage. It wouldn't be so odd, after all . . . you two were close . . . you still live in the area . . ."

"What good would it do? He won't tell me anything," she snapped.

"He might, without realizing it . . . and you might find something lying about his place."

"You want me to break in?"

"I want you to discover whether or not he has set up a lab at that cottage. The rest you may leave to me."

"How much are they paying you, Andrew? Is it enough? You could lose your job."

"I'm not such an idiot. There are precautions I am taking."

"In whose pay are you, Andrew?"

"Never mind that."

She pushed her plate away untouched. "I don't know why I came today."

He put out a restraining hand. "You know why." His eyes were intent on her lovely face.

She brushed her long silky black hair away from her cheeks.

"You take too much for granted, Andrew," she said softly. Again the threat was there.

He frowned. "Joy . . . don't think you won't be rewarded. I will take care of you."

"Why don't you just hire some lowlife to break into Justin's place and do the job properly?"

"Because he might not be on to something yet. If I did that now, he would pack it up and move into hiding. Justin is capable of covering his tracks very well. . . . No, this has to be done in careful stages." He stroked her fingers, "Joy . . . do you have to get right back?"

She looked at him. "Don't you?"

"No . . . I have a room booked."

She smiled softly, pleased enough with this. "Do you, Andrew?"

He got to his feet and took up her arm. Willingly she allowed him to lead her out of the pub. Why? Dammit, why? She had no answer to her question, at least no answer that satisfied. It was just one more scene to add to her list of many. It was just one more thing she would do for lack of anything better.

* * *

Sir Justin rubbed his closed eyes and pushed his ginger locks away from his forehead. He opened his eyes and sighed. Papers were strewn all over his black Formica laboratory counter. Something was missing. He had to get things into proper perspective or this was never going to work.

He brought up his wrist and focused his gray eyes on his gold Corum watch. Past seven. Hell, he had been glued to his wooden stool for hours. Perhaps he should call it quits for one day. Wash up and drive into the village . . . have a bite and an ale at the King's Head.

Without meaning to he thought of Holly. A vision of her red-gold hair and her sparkling aqua eyes taunted him. A vivid recollection of the feel of her body in his arms sent a hot rush of blood racing through him, which in turn caught his imagination and charged his manhood. Absurd!

Ah, pretty Holly. What would she be doing now? Would she be alone? Of course she would. Why not drive over and have a look? Like bloody hell he would! Damn, but no one woman was going to make him lose control. He would have her, but on his terms. He would have her, but only after she wanted to be had!

Never mind this folly! Come on, he said to himself, off with you to the King's Head, a small repast, and home for a solid night's sleep before tackling the formula again in the morning.

Holly turned more than a few heads. Her long hair glistened in the light of the blazing fire. Her body cast off alluring invitations with its well-shaped curves so advantageously displayed in the soft blue angora sweater and tight Britannia jeans. She sipped the gin and tonic Gregory had procured for her and felt a certain giddiness. She had nothing but a biscuit for dinner, having forgotten to do any grocery shopping that afternoon. Between sips, she munched on peanuts.

"Well, Holly, there I was on this New Forest pony and Lord could that devil move out. We were charging about the woods in all different directions after this poor fox not one of us had spotted when the master calls out. What must I do but turn my head to have a look. Mistake. When next I looked there was this branch right in my path, my pony was racing for it, and there was nothing I could do but catch hold of it, you see. Well, what a fool I felt, hanging onto this limb while my pony raced on with the hunt!" He was chuckling over the memory.

"Gracious!" Holly laughed. "But what did you do?"

"Dropped to the ground with only my dignity done in, and off I went in search of my pony."

"Did you find him?"

"About two hours later." He was grinning. "But never mind, there were nearly eighty of us on that hunt, and not a one ever caught sight of a fox . . . don't think the master ever did either, as a matter of fact."

She smiled warmly. "It sounds very exciting. I have always wanted to dash about on a hunt . . . but I do so feel for the poor little fox. Only think how terrified it must be."

"Sly little things forever getting your chickens and stirring up the farmers. There are too many of them, you see . . ."

She could hear Gregory go on about fox hunting, defending it, but it was only background for the sudden resounding thudding of her heart. Something caught in her throat and she felt breathless, nervous, and slightly flushed. All this because she had looked up to see Sir Justin walk into the King's Head.

She watched him move from the wide doorway through the dimly lit, oak-beamed, dark-raftered old pub to the counter. He seemed a giant of a man. Tall and ever so broad-shouldered in his dark-blue corduroy blazer and his sleek denim slacks. His ginger hair fell in glistening waves across his handsome head, and she could see the ladies were already turning to smile provocatively his way. Well, not she. Oh no, just look at him. Conceited, arrogant . . . oh gosh, he was waving to them. Oh no . . . would he come over?

Justin Laeland had scanned the room just as a matter

of course, and his eyes lit with surprise when he discovered Holly and his cousin Greg huddled at a corner table. He felt a range of emotions. Anticipation, irritation, and excitement all at once. The fire in the great stone hearth blazed and cast off enough light to center his gaze on her face. Damn, but she was beautiful!

He took up his drink, gave over an order for a mincemeat pie, and ambled leisurely toward them. Gregory called out amicably enough, "Justin, you dog! Where were you at dinner?" He was grinning wide.

"Sorry about that . . . rang up your mother, told her I couldn't make it."

"Yes, so she told me. What she didn't tell me was why." Half jesting, half with serious curiosity.

"I was waiting for a call," said Justin easily and then gave a warm smile to Miss Winslow. "Holly . . . I see Greg has not wasted his time."

Holly blushed. Stupid, girlish thing to do, she chastised herself as she felt the heat rush into her cheeks. "Greg has been most kind."

"I've been telling her about some of my adventures as an equestrian. Sit down, Justin, and tell us some of yours." Greg turned to Holly. "I've always thought myself pretty top-notch in the saddle, but there isn't a man in all Hampshire that has hands or seat next to Justin's!"

Justin pulled up a chair and smiled ruefully at his young cousin. "You mustn't listen to Greg. He is too puffed up about the Laelands and our horses."

"But Justin, you should be entering the Stoney Cross Show!" Gregory sighed.

"Thank you, my showing days are over, for the present at least," said Justin firmly. He turned again to Holly. "So . . . Miss Winslow . . ." There was an unidentifiable tone underlining her name. "What sort of schedule has Greg here given you for tomorrow?"

"I don't know," said Holly, relenting toward him long enough to allow him the glimmer of a smile.

"Not me, Justin . . . Maureen made it up with Mother,

you know, though I know she will be taking over most of my beginner classes. Damn good thing, too. What with the show coming up I have just got to get some time in on Napoleon."

"Napoleon?" This from Holly.

"Ah, Holly, you haven't seen a horse till you've seen my Napoleon," bragged Gregory proudly.

"You're right. That bay of yours is a sure winner," agreed Justin, "but next to Star . . ." His voice trailed off with the memory of Star and their last performance together. Now Star was out to pasture.

"Oh, of course, nothing could come next or near that stud." He turned to Holly. "Justin was preparing him for Haut Ecole, you know!"

"Goodness . . . what happened?"

Gregory coughed into his hand and looked up at Justin hestitatingly. "Well, er . . ."

"That was two years ago, and my time was more my own," said Justin curtly. "Now, tell me more about Napoleon and the upcoming show. It's only a local, isn't it? Why all this excitement?"

"Well, it's the first show of the season in the district, and Laeland has to do well . . . bring home the rosettes, you know. So our classes have to be ready for it and our students have to do well in it to keep up the Laeland reputation . . . and Laeland's instructors will be expected to bring home a trophy or two."

Holly's eyes widened. "Oh no . . . don't tell me I will be expected to . . . ?"

Greg laughed. "Indeed you shall."

"But I have never . . . I won't know . . ."

Justin smiled at her. "You will love it. What you should do is have a go with Tinker in the Advanced Hunter Hacks."

"Hold a moment, Justin." This from Greg, frowning. 'He is not your ordinary hunter."

"That's why I think Holly here should use him. He could do with some of the training she has to give him."

"Well, I don't know. I haven't seen her ride yet, and Tinker is the devil of a black, full of tricks and temperament."

101

"Precisely why Holly should start on him right away. You see, Greg, I *have* seen her ride. She took Ulysses in hand as though she had been riding all her life . . . got him to jump over the spread, which we both know he hates. Took it flying, changed his leads, turned and collected for her, and over the next he went. Didn't your mother tell you?"

Greg looked impressed. "She said something about Miss Winslow's being an accomplished rider, but we didn't go into details. Well then, looks like we have an entry for the Hunter Hack class . . . with Tinker, you know, we could even enter her into the Conformation Hunter Hack," he said thoughtfully.

"Look, you two . . . may I say something here?" put in Holly, taking advantage of the pause.

Both men turned her way and waited. She cleared her throat lightly with a small gulp. "As it happens, I have never been in a show. When I was younger and living in Kent, I was fortunate enough to attend a few . . . but I don't know enough about them . . ."

"Nonsense. All you need know is how to ride and how to bring yourself to the attention of the judges," said Greg.

"What do you mean, bring myself to the attention of the judges?"

"Well, Holly, the sad truth is that professionals in the field play games in the ring, such as riding down and trying to break the gaits of the other horse while passing. They are old tricks. You needn't participate in such doings, but you should be aware of them and also know that you must find a suitable way of jockeying for position."

"Jockey for what position?" she inquired. It all sounded very unethical to her.

"Either to cut a competitor out of the judges' view or get out of the way of a rider who is out to ride another entry down," said Greg grimly. "It happens, and you have to be ready."

They were interrupted at that moment by a pretty dark-haired barmaid in a white tight sweater and straight-legged black high-sheen pants. Holly watched

102

as Sir Justin's eyes went over the girl appreciatively. She put his mincemeat pie in front of him and smiled. He thanked her, and she turned to leave. Both men watched her sway off a moment before turning their attention once again to Holly. However, by now the aroma of Justin's food made her gently lick her lips slightly. She was starved.

Justin noted this at once. "Holly . . . take this. I can order another for myself." He was frowning. Hadn't she eaten all day?

"Oh, no, I couldn't. That must be your dinner," she returned staunchly.

"Good Lord, girl . . . are you hungry? Why didn't you say so? I should have realized you hadn't had dinner . . . thought when you came in with Justin's chauffeur and all those packages . . ." cried Gregory.

She pulled a face. "I forgot to buy food."

"Well, that settles it," said Justin pushing the plate and fork her way. "I'll just order another for myself. Greg . . . you?"

The pretty barmaid appeared again, and Justin turned around, surprised, for he hadn't called for her yet. However, she was looking toward Greg.

"Mr. Gregory . . . there is a call from your mother. She says to have you come up with the vet real quick. Your mare has gone into labor."

Gregory jumped to his feet. "She isn't due yet!" He turned around to Holly, who was pushing the food away, ready to follow him. "Look . . . Holly . . . I am sorry. Please finish your meal here . . . Justin will bring you around later. Won't you, old boy?"

"Of course. It will be a pleasure. Which mare is this, Greg? Studio?"

"Yes . . . and the foal is bound to be a beauty. You know we mated her with your stud, Justin."

"But I will come with you . . . I should like to be there," cried Holly.

"It will take me some time just to fetch old Doc. You come up with Justin later." He squeezed her arm. "Sorry, love, I'll make it up to you." With this he was already making for the door.

Chapter Seven

Holly watched Gregory's hasty departure with a frown while Justin watched her. She was visibly uneasy. Had she wanted to return with Gregory? Had they planned on an evening up in her flat? This thought irritated him.

"Go on, eat," he said softly and signaled the barmaid that he required another order. He picked up his dark ale and sipped it, watching her through lazy eyes.

Ill at ease, feeling his scrutiny, she picked at the food. She was hungry, though, and this soon won out. She avoided his eye and applied herself to her plate. "You seem to have hit it off with my cousin," he said idly.

She put up her chin. "He is very nice."

"So he is, but it wouldn't do for you just now to get caught up there."

He was warning her off. Why? And how dare he? She would do what she pleased. She was finished with arrogant men telling her what she could and couldn't do. "I am quite capable of choosing my own friends and handling my own social life. I don't need a director." And then she added, looking straight into his gray eyes, "I think you have been amply rewarded for your help."

He was amused. "Do you think so? You put a high price on your kisses."

"As a matter of fact, I do," she said quietly.

He took it to mean something altogether different, and his voice took on that dry quality so peculiarly his own. "I'll just bet you do."

She was puzzled by him. "You don't like me. I don't know why, and it doesn't really matter very much to me because I don't think I like you either, but what does interest me is why, just why, have you helped set me up here?"

"Why should that have anything to do with whether I like you or not?"

"Why should you help someone you neither like nor approve of?"

"I haven't said I don't like you and I haven't said I don't approve of you."

She ignored this. "Why have you helped me?"

"There was nothing else to do at the time," he answered vaguely and then asked himself the same question.

She pushed away the remains of the pie and sat back with some impatience. He was deliberately provoking and not quite honest.

His dinner arrived, with another gin and tonic for her, an ale for him. He pushed her drink at her, and she took it up for lack of anything else to do. She sipped at it quietly a moment while he ate. Holly had always been a bubbling girl. Impulsive, merry, forever diving into situations, embracing people. She couldn't sit back and pout at this stranger's rudeness. It wasn't like her. So she plunged in where others hesitated.

"If you were training toward Haut Ecole, you must have worked that horse of yours constantly. Why did you give it up?"

He stopped and stared hard at her for a moment. "It was a frivolous adventure." His voice was cold; it demanded that she drop the subject.

"I don't agree. It is dressage in its highest form."

"If you don't mind I would rather not—" he started on a hard note.

She cut in, ignoring his coldness, "Why give up what you had evidently worked so hard to achieve? Wasn't your horse good enough in the long run?" A challenge. Would he jump to it?

He did, but only for a moment. "Star was fit to compete with the best of them! I would have taken him to Vienna . . ." He caught himself in time and smiled at her skill. Well, well, so the pretty bird knew how to pull strings. He sighed, once again in control.

"If you must know, my father died two years ago, and

105

his death put an end to my work with Star." He was irritated with her, with himself for allowing her to maneuver him this far.

She pursued gently, "I am sorry . . . I didn't realize . . . you must have loved your father very much."

Flashes went through his mind. Love, hate, frustration. He snapped, "No! What I mean is . . . I didn't suffer a decline if that is what you think. My father had extracted a promise from me . . . I was compelled to take on the responsibilities of my inheritance."

"And your responsibilities took up all your time?" A note of doubt.

"Dammit, Holly . . . Laeland Motors is not your small village garage!"

Laeland Motors. Holy Gosh! He was that Laeland. It made it worse, so much worse. Her father did business with one of Laeland's subsidiary companies. She blanched.

"Look, if you are done, let's go on up to the Grange. I'd like to see how that mare of Greg's is doing." He was dealing out some bills onto the table, pushing out his chair. Mutely, she followed.

Sophie met them at the barn door. "Something is wrong, Justin." She was frantic; she was never any good in this sort of an emergency.

Justin took command. It was a natural thing for him, and Holly could not help but notice.

"What about the vet, Sophie?"

"Greg telephoned that Dr. Haley is away from home. Greg should be here soon." She wrung her hands. "Thomas went over to Bournemouth to visit with some of his friends."

Already Justin's blazer was off and he was rolling up his shirt sleeves, his expression grave as he studied the gray mare. She was moving around and around restlessly. He watched as she went down and a moment later was getting up again.

"Sophie . . . how long has she been at it?"

"Twenty minutes. . . . Justin, shouldn't she be down?

106

Why hasn't she gone down? Greg loves this mare . . . he raised her . . . it's her first foal. Oh, Justin . . ."

"Hush, Sophie. Don't work yourself up." He watched as Holly put a comforting arm around his aunt, and then he was moving toward the mare.

This time the mare went down and stayed there. Her body broke out into a full sweat. Justin called anxiously to have towels and iodine ready, and Sophie responded that all was on hand. Minutes ticked by, and the mare appeared to be going through an ordeal. She grunted, flayed her legs, whinnied painfully as the foal would not be expelled.

"Time, Sophie . . . how long has she been down?" cried Justin.

"Just over twenty-five minutes," said Holly, who had been watching the clock.

"I am no good at this . . . I get too upset," apologized Sophie, who was trembling.

Greg appeared, in a flushed state. "Thank God you are here, Justin. How long has she been down?"

"Twenty-five minutes, lad . . . don't worry," replied Justin, himself very much concerned. There was something wrong. He felt it in his gut, but he was no vet. They stood waiting helplessly as the time tortured and gave them nothing.

"How long now?" This from Greg, his voice high with his tension.

"Forty minutes," said Holly as calmly as she could muster.

"Damn!" cursed Justin softly. "Greg . . . look . . . the foal is going to suffocate if we don't go in and break the sac."

"Right, Justin. Do what you have to," agreed Greg. More than the foal was at stake here. His mare . . .

Sophie covered her face with her hands. Holly held her and watched and felt a flash of admiration for Justin.

Front feet and head first came a dark fluff of magic. Holly squealed with delight, and Sophie emerged from her hands to glow with relief and happiness. A filly had been born.

Greg moved into the stall to assist. "What can I do, Justin?"

"The cord . . . it's not breaking. You'll have to cut it, Greg, just six inches away from the foal's body . . . that's the lad . . . and paint it with the iodine." He was cooing to the newborn, wiping it dry with the fresh towels.

He had moved away to help Holly, who was removing the sullied straw bedding, when Greg called him to attention again,

"Justin!" The voice was nearly a shriek. "The filly, she isn't breathing . . . something is wrong."

Justin moved in immediately, bent, and discovered that this was true. He began applying artificial respiration. Holly watched open-mouthed. He was so capable, so very much in charge, so knowing. A moment later the filly was breathing well enough on her own and the mare was getting up.

Sophie was carrying a pail of soapy water, and Holly took it from her. "Just tell me what to do."

"Oh, thank you, dear . . . she needs to be cleaned, you know," and she indicated with her eyes exactly what she meant.

Holly smiled to herself and began washing the mare's genital parts. Some moments later they were all backing off, waiting to see mother and daughter get acquainted. The foal lifted its head and then in some exhaustion dropped it again.

"What's the matter?" Holly was touching Sir Justin's hand in concern.

Greg answered, "Nothing to worry about . . . she'll start to suckle soon."

Justin was frowning, and he noted that Holly's hand was still very much in his own. He dropped it. "We'll give them a little time."

The mare nibbled at her filly, groomed her, gently blew into her nose, and still the filly seemed disinclined to suckle. Justin shook his head and went into the stall again. This time all he had to do was lift the filly's head toward her mother's teats. Immediately the

108

filly got the idea and began sucking away. This set up a cheer!

"Hello!" said a male voice at their backs. "What have I missed?"

Holly turned around to get her first good look at Sophie's husband, and something inside of her recoiled. Stupid girl. You are just tired.

It was some minutes later when Holly found Justin walking her to her flat. She wasn't sure how it had come about. Greg had said something about opening a bottle of champagne, but Justin had declined joining them, and she too said she had to turn in for her big day tomorrow, and here she was, walking beside this man again.

It was brisk, and Holly's arms went around herself. She saw him glance her way. "Cold, Holly? I could offer you my coat or my arm . . . your choice?" He was teasing, though, still in a festive mood over the filly.

"I'm fine," she answered a little too sharply. Why? To tone it down she said, "Your aunt is a lovely woman. Imagine, she told me she has been through countless foalings and has never watched a one."

"That's Sophie . . . always hiding her eyes," he said, but the tease had left his voice and his gray eyes troubled over. He added after a moment, "You were a help tonight, Holly . . . I hope for Sophie's sake you prove out here at the Grange."

"But you don't expect me to?" They had reached her door, and she stopped to glare at him. Why did he always manage to get her fists up?

His voice dropped and his head was low, for he was bending her way. She had pushed back against her locked door, his arm was out, his hand was pressed on the door, and she felt her entire body come alive with anticipation. "I don't know what I expect from you, Holly." His mouth sought and found hers. In that moment it was inevitable for both of them.

She was growing, emerging from her rosebud existence into full flower. She had been wilting in the desert, and here she was blossoming beneath the English moon. She responded to his kiss because she was a woman, because he was awakening new depths, sowing new emotions.

He groaned, "Open the door, Holly . . . let's go up . . ."

She went cold all over. What was she doing? This was too soon. She didn't even like him. What kind of a girl was she becoming?

"No," she answered, and her tone was too cold for him to take it as anything but calculating.

His brow went up. "Oh, I see. There is Greg . . . an interesting prospect . . . and you would like to play both hands before folding."

What was he suggesting? He was despicable! "Goodnight, Sir Justin," she answered. She wouldn't even dignify his remark with a response.

He pulled himself up. "Goodnight, Miss Winslow." There was a sneer curving his sensuous lips as he left her.

Sir Justin got into his red sports car and zoomed down the drive. This one was getting to him. Why? Large innocent eyes. Damn, no innocent. She had lived with that Moslem . . . and who knew how many others? She had already begun working on Greg . . . if he and the filly hadn't come along tonight, who knew how far she would have progressed?

It took him back in time. He'd been young enough to think he was in love. There he was, working on his experiments, working with Star and refusing to go into his father's business. She had been beautiful . . . and she wanted it all. So she married his father.

The pain was gone now and only a dull ache remained. He had written her off by finding her over and over again in the women he took. All of them scheming, sly creatures. Not a one was honest . . . but his father? It wasn't so easy to write his father off. His father had known how he felt about her . . . and then he was off with her and his fiancée became his father's bride.

It was all over. She hadn't even lived to enjoy the Laeland money. She had died in a plane crash . . . and damn, why was he thinking about all that now? He was now twenty-eight, it was four years later, his experiments were forming an answer, finally he was close enough to look upon his work as a sure thing. He was president of his father's firm, and even Star was a thing of the past. . . .

He frowned, but here was this aqua-eyed girl very much on his mind. What was her game? All of them always had a purpose . . . not a one was different. Even sweet Joy . . . but that was something else altogether. He had never been in love with Joy, and then when he discovered that she was one of Thomas Martin's mistresses . . .

Chapter Eight

Holly turned away from Judy Baines and scanned the passing scene as Judy tooled her little Fiat over the country road.

"Do you know, Holly, I have this absurd feeling you really don't know what is going on at the Grange," Judy was saying, looking across at the smaller girl with the long amber hair.

"All right, Judy . . . that was bait, I'll bite." Two weeks, more, had passed. She was amused by Judy Baines, not quite certain she approved of her, but who was she to judge Judy? At any rate they enjoyed one another's company.

"No, but it's odd, really, sometimes you seem so . . . intuitive, knowing, and other times you seem such a naive little puss. We are totally different, you know." She chuckled. "You are like a little mother—no, Judy, don't, Judy . . ." She remembered the first time she had seen Holly. She had just had a fight with Thomas and she had been full with rage and tears, stomping off, and around the barn she plowed right into Holly. Holly still didn't know who had been at the root of her misery, she had only known it was a man, and not Judy's husband.

Holly smiled. "I'm younger than you . . . *puss.*" She mimicked the word and the accent. "So, not your mother . . . let us say your conscience, and just what are you going to do about John? If he can't make you happy . . . why hang in there? In the end, it will only hurt him more."

"He pays the bills . . . and it's only what he deserves. Look, Holly, he thinks marriage means the end of romance. . . ."

"You can't expect a man to bring home roses every night," said Holly wisely.

"I don't want roses. I want some action. Holly . . . he doesn't touch me any more," wailed Judy.

Holly looked her friend over with surprise. Judy Baines was tall, well built, and very attractive. "That is not easy to believe," she said doubtfully. She suspected like everyone else at the Grange that Judy Baines was infatuated with Gregory Laeland. It was what Judy wanted everyone else to think . . . but Judy needed someone to talk to, and she had chosen Holly.

"It's the truth, Holly. He just rolls over and goes to sleep. If I didn't know better, I'd think he was having an affair, but he isn't."

"There are ways, I believe, to spark a man's desire," suggested Holly softly. She was not the one to give advice here . . . just what did she know?

"Yes . . . but now I don't want to. It's too late . . . now I can't stand the feel of him near me," said Judy, her tone inviting Holly to delve further.

Holly stared at her in some shock. "But . . . you are forever telling me how hot-blooded you are, Judy . . . and he is your husband!"

"Come on, Holly . . . you know you can be hot for someone . . . it doesn't mean you are for everybody."

"You don't love John any more?" Holly had met Judy's husband once. He was a large, pleasant-looking, jolly sort, and she had liked him.

112

"I don't know if I ever did . . . and now, as you know, there is someone else." Judy got a faraway look in her eyes.

Holly thought of Gregory Laeland. She had gone out with him only once since the night the foal was birthed. It had been a pleasant evening, simple and enjoyable. They had taken in a movie in Southampton and afterward he had tried no more than to kiss her. She had let him. Thinking of that now engaged a sigh from her. She liked Greg . . . and what was more, she rather thought Greg liked Judy's husband. She had seen them jesting about on occasion. It was all so complicated.

The thought of Judy and Greg together brought a frown to her brows. "That's just it . . . if you are in love with some man and he with you, why do you hang onto John?" There was a touch of impatience in her voice.

Judy looked at her sideways. "You don't approve. Little prude. There is so much you are going to have to learn. I'm surprised that El Gorgeous hasn't been teaching you yet."

Holly flushed. "I don't know what you mean."

"Yes you do." Judy giggled. "You can't say you haven't noticed the way he looks at you when he comes around." She put up an expressive brow. "Hmm . . . would I love to have him look at me like that!"

Holly laughed. "What a dreadful hussy you are! And if you are referring to Sir Justin, I believe he does look at you like that!"

Judy said nothing to this, for they had entered the bustling traffic of Lymington and she was weaving her way in and out of cars. "I hope I find a space near the pub. You'll love it, Holly. It's old-world . . . like you." Again she gave off a tinkle of laughter as her friend struck out at her.

Lymington. Sir Justin had chosen the humming seaport with good reason. It was a yachtman's haven. A seaman's paradise. A thriving, lovely, quaint, and well-appointed resort village of a goodly size. Its stores

113

looked as though they belonged in Tudor times and were bustling with trade at this time of year.

Since he had given out the story that he was in Hampshire taking a breather and a much-needed holiday, it would be appropriate for him to be seen from time to time in Lymington. That's why he had chosen to have his mail sent to its post office in care of general delivery. Certainly its close proximity to Brockenhurst made it a convenient trip.

Thank God for Melvin Calvin, he thought absently as he moved down the street. His work in photosynthesis was the key, the basic structure of all he was now creating. If Calvin hadn't rediscovered the *Euphorbia* plant he might never have gotten this close, and he was close to an answer. It was somewhere in the plant's DNA molecule, and eventually he would hit the right formula.

Justin stopped at a quaintly decorated store with wooden toys displayed in its Tudor front window. They were still there, those two, across the street, now standing insouciantly about. He watched them while they took long pulls on their cigarettes. Who were they? Arabs? They had the look, dark-haired, dark-skinned . . . but business suits? Was he being followed? What could they hope to discover with this nonsense?

He moved toward the post office steps and glanced around idly as he opened the door wide. They crossed over, passed the post office, and went next door to Ye Olde Inn. Just what were they up to? And was it possible he was overreacting, that he was wrong? No. Too many odd things were happening, like Joy's suddenly turning up at his cottage one night. What had that been about? He was all too aware that Joy had switched her attention to Andrew. Yes, Joy was a busy girl, what with Thomas and Andrew. Then what did it mean? Had someone gotten to Joy? Was she being paid to spy on him? Jesus. Was he being paranoid? Wasn't it just possible the girl found him attractive and wanted some action? No. Joy got plenty of action.

* * *

114

Holly looked up as she laughed at something atrocious Judy had said and she saw them. Two well-dressed Arabs, taking a table not so very far from her own. What was worse, she recognized one of them. She had seen him once with Hassan. What to do? What to do? She pulled her chair so that her back was to them and said lightly as she pushed her plate of cold cuts and salad away, "Hmm. Not hungry. Look, Judy . . . would you mind if I took off now? I've got some shopping to do, and I thought I'd start."

"Of course, poppet, go on. I'm only sorry I won't be here long enough to take you back. Will you be all right?"

"Of course, I'll just grab a cab." She stood up. "See you . . . and try to be good in the meantime."

"Uh, no, don't think I shall go that route . . . too boring." Judy smiled her away. She looked up and saw the two Arab men stare as Holly passed by. She saw Holly avert her face, and she saw one of the Arabs gaze thoughtfully after her. However, she was due to meet her husband in ten minutes . . . dull, but then he had promised to buy her that gold piece she fancied. . . .

As Holly came rushing out of the pub she didn't see the tall broad-shouldered man right in her path and went barreling into his arms. He felt his heartbeat increase rapidly and chided himself mentally.

"Miss Winslow . . . what's the rush?" He was smiling but his thoughts were colliding into one another. What was she doing in that pub with those two Arabs? And of course she must have been with them—why else would she be in Lymington? Had she met with them purposely? Was this proof against her? And why did it irritate him so? Then he looked into her aqua eyes. Frightened? Why did she look so frightened?

She was caught off guard. She stared up into his handsome face and stammered lamely, "Sir Justin . . . how . . . how nice . . ." Why did the nearness of him cause her blood to race? Why were her knees melting? What was it he moved in her?

He was taking her arm. She was pulling away. Not

115

from him but with him, taking him away from the pub. He felt himself harden. She wanted him away. She didn't want him to see her Arab friends. He allowed her to take a step across the street and fell in beside her. "How did you manage to discover pretty Lymington so soon, Holly? Or are you here on a special . . . errand?"

What was in his tone? She studied him a moment before replying. Why was he always digging at her? "I worked for Greg Sunday afternoon and he gave me this afternoon off in exchange. Judy was coming into town to meet with her husband to have a look at some jewelry . . . and thought I might like to spend some time shopping here." They were moving down the hilly street to the harbor below. She could see the ships and the traffic moving toward the ferry.

"Judy?" He frowned thoughtfully. Judy Baines, of course. An odd twosome . . . or was it?

"You know, Judy Baines . . . she is one of Greg's students, you must have seen her." She was studying his face.

"Ah yes, of course." Noncommittal.

"Look . . . a ferry." She pointed enthusiastically. "Where does it go?"

"To Yarmouth . . . the Isle of Wight," he answered with a smile. At times, she looked no more than a child. It was dangerously engaging.

"I have always wanted to visit Wight . . ." she stopped suddenly, realizing she was leaving herself open.

He picked up on it at once. His packages had not arrived. He needed some time off, and he needed to get into this bird's head.

"Holly . . . let's hop a ferry and explore the island now."

"Oh no, I couldn't . . ."

"Why not?" he demanded.

She couldn't find a reason, and she did so want to go. "I . . . I . . . don't think we should."

"What, share a ferry ride? Nothing to fear in that!" he teased. "Come on. I am abducting you." He pulled her along toward the ticket office.

116

"Sir Justin . . ." she objected.

He stopped and spun around to face her, "Holly Winslow, we have shared a ride as strangers in my car from London to Hampshire. We have shared a cottage overnight, and I mean for us to share this afternoon!"

Without another word she found herself allowing him to pull her along and was pleased enough in this instance that his strong will, his arrogant air, his self-assurance, and his determination had won out. She wanted to take this ferry ride to the Isle of Wight, and what was more to the point and far too agitating to her sense of peace was the fact that she wanted to be with him.

In the pub she had left sat the two Middle Eastern gentlemen. They were not from Iraq but from Saudi Arabia, and their dialect denoted this to anyone familiar with the intricacies of the Middle East. Their business was not with Holly but with the doings of Sir Justin Laeland. It had been rumored that he was working on a fuel, a new fuel, that would not depend on oil, and that he would have his company's cars reconstructed to make use of it. That was not to their organization's liking. Too many car manufacturers might wish to convert their automobiles as well. This their organization found deplorable. Their job was to ascertain the truth and present their findings to the board. Nothing more . . . at this point. However, one of these gentlemen had an eye for pretty women. He had not missed Holly's exit. He had watched her thoughtfully and then after her departure he continued to sit in meditative contemplation.

His friend frowned and said in low Arabic, "Eh . . . Saeed . . . you are most pensive."

"Am I? I don't know . . . it is a waste of time, is it not, to follow this man. . . ." But he was not thinking of Sir Justin right then, he was thinking of the beautiful girl with the long red-gold hair.

Selim, his friend, shook his head. "I don't know . . . you are probably right, for no one will ever be able to

117

replace the oil these heathens need from our country
... but the board wants to raise their prices next
quarter, and if word of this Laeland's discovery leaks
out ..."

"Hmmm. Yes, that is true." Then in another, more
intense tone, "Did you see that woman who just left?"

"Fair, yes, she was fair and very pretty ... but you
pay too much attention to these things." They had
learned nothing from following Sir Justin that morning, and they were certain that Justin had seen them.
Hence they had taken refuge in the pub. They would
stay in the area overnight and try again in the morning. Selim was planning his move. It was what his
friend should be helping with, not looking after beautiful women.

"Yes, but did she seem familiar to you?"

"No ... I don't know ... look, Saeed, we must decide
how next we shall approach—"

"That's it! Selim ... now I remember. That one is
Hassan's sister."

"Hassan ... Hassan?" This impatiently.

"Zahour's son. He has much influence with the board
... and I happen to know that Hassan is looking for
this half-English sister of his. Come, we are going to
London!"

"But Saeed ..."

"There will be some money in it, and we can be back
in Hampshire tomorrow. *Come!*"

Chapter Nine

Lymington was left behind as the ferry plowed its way
through the narrow Solent toward the Isle of Wight.
They left Sir Justin's little red sports job in the belly of
the boat with the other cars and made their way above
and out to the rail.

It was cold and damp, with the sea wind pelting at

hem. It gently embraced Holly's long hair and blew it
around her neck. Sir Justin was caught for a moment
with the vision of her ethereal beauty and frowned as he
mentally chided himself again.

"Everything is just so glorious!" declared Holly as
she stared at the sea-green Solent waters and past
them to the village left behind. She was shivering for
her lightweight denim jacket was not made for a trip
on a ferry in May.

He slipped off his dark-brown suede blazer and put it
around her shoulders. His camel turtleneck and her
nearness, he discovered, was enough to keep him warm.
She objected, however.

"Oh no . . . I couldn't . . . what about you?"

Easily, casually, his arm went around her. "Stay
close and I'll do."

She couldn't pull away. His touch thrilled and fevered her all at once and far too startlingly. He looked
so boyish, standing above her, smiling happily at some
long-ago memory.

"What are you thinking?" she asked shyly. "You look
a million miles away."

He had been thinking about his last trip to the Isle of
Wight. Then too a girl had been sweetly held in his
arms, but when they returned she had gone off with his
father. Oddly enough, only the pain of the memory
lingered; her face was scarcely recalled.

"Nothing," he said shortly. "Look at Wight's coast-
line . . . it's magnificent," he said, taking up her attention and pointing toward the colored cliffs. "We will be
pulling into Yarmouth. It's a nice little village with a
lovely teahouse. If you are hungry we could stop there."

"Oh, I'm not hungry at all yet . . . maybe later." She
looked up at him. "Talk to me, Sir Justin. Tell me
things about yourself."

"Like what?"

"Like . . . how did you know just what to do that
night when Greg's mare was foaling? Dr. Jakes came
by the next day and said you had handled everything
expertly . . ."

119

"Dr. Jakes, eh? It seems old Doc has a replacement?" he inquired, brow up.

"No, Dr. Jakes is assisting Dr. Haley, who wants to retire," she explained.

He eyed her. "You seem to know a great deal. No doubt our Dr. Jakes is young and good-looking?" There was a slight edge to his question.

"As a matter of fact, he is, but that still does not answer *my* question, sir, though I have answered all of yours!"

He grinned. "I'm the devil, Holly, I warn you of that from the start. Now, *your* question. Its simple enough, really, when you think about it. I grew up around the Grange. All my summers were spent there. My parents had their socializing and I had my horses . . . my uncle and Sophie never minded one more boy about the place."

"Yes, but Greg grew up there as well . . . and he didn't seem to know about breaking the sac."

"He could have done it if he had to . . . has seen it done often enough. After all, that's a very big part of the Grange's operation, breeding horses. But as to my practical experience, I got it going about the countryside with Dr. Haley. At that time I was determined to become a country vet one day."

"And what changed your mind? Though truthfully I can't see you as a country vet." There was a tease in her eyes, in her tone.

He tweaked her nose. "Would you mind if I skipped over that? I have a feeling I'd be happier *not* knowing what role you see me in." He put up his hands, because he could see she was going to repeat her question. "Tenacious puss, hold a moment and you'll have an answer." He was smiling broadly. "At Cambridge I became fascinated with genetics."

"Genetics? What has that got to do with your automobile company?"

"The company was my father's and his father's before him. It was destined to be mine . . . not chosen."

120

"Oh, poor little rich boy," she said on a note of irony. Weren't they both such cases? Absurd.

He frowned. "Come on, brat, we'll be docking soon."

Thomas Martin fidgeted nervously as he waited on the phone for his bookie to answer. He was in over his head, and he was in serious trouble. He had looked for yesterday's race to pull him out of the mire, but instead he had lost another five thousand pounds. What was worse, he didn't have the money.

"Well now, Thomas," said the voice on the other end in heavy cockney, "what would ye be calling for? Another bet? Naw . . . I think not. We'll be 'aving our money now, we will. No more stalling."

"Look, Jarvis . . . I haven't got it. You'll have to give me time."

"No, I don't 'ave to give ye anything atoll, I don't. But I tell ye whot . . . 'ave the money to me in two days and maybe I won't 'ave yer 'ead bashed in."

"Jarvis . . . I'm not a wealthy man . . . I just can't come up with it all . . ."

"Can't ye? It's said yer wife has money enough."

"It's in her name . . . the account is all in her name. . ."

"I don't care about the details, Thomas . . . just get it!" The receiver hummed with its finality.

Thomas looked around and felt himself quiver. Sophie was coming toward him. She had paid off his debts in the past, but she had said she would see him in prison before she did so again. There was just so much that Sophie would stand. She had a troubled look as she approached him.

"Thomas . . . who was that?"

"Business, dear."

"Your stockbroker?" she pursued. "I thought we agreed not to invest any more school funds in stocks just now . . . what we have already is quite enough." He worried her. When they had first gotten married she had made him a ten-percent partner in the Laeland School Corporation, and she had added his name to the company checking account. He had immediately used that power

121

to invest large amounts in the stock exchange. She had discovered then that he had little investment acumen. While she had never been a wit, and her friends often lovingly teased her about her naiveté she was considered to be quite a businesswoman.

"Look, Sophie . . . it doesn't concern you, so don't be forever after me like some haranguing fishwife!" He was off immediately. He couldn't stand it. Here she was with all that money and he was groveling for his life! Damn her and her reproachful eyes. He would make her beg for his favors now . . . beg. Yes, and she would, too . . . later, much later, he would tease her until she begged for it, hot-blooded bitch!

"Give me the key, Chrissy!" demanded Greg as he moved into Holly's flat. His hand was extended. He hadn't been alone with Chrissy Penbroke since Holly moved in. It just hadn't been possible, and he had been glad of it. He had even heard rumors from the stablehands that she had been messing around with the local blood. Good, it let him off the hook if anything was ever said in the future.

"She has gone into town, Greg . . . I saw her leave with Judy Baines." Chrissy flung her bright-yellow hair over her shoulder and undid the buttons of her blouse to her midriff. "I didn't wear a bra, Greg . . . did you notice during the lesson?" She was smiling invitingly. "Come on, Greg . . . come on over here and show me that you noticed."

He felt his temperature rising. Holly was off for the afternoon, but what if she came in unexpectedly? Somehow, instead of putting him off, it stimulated him further. He moved in on Chrissy and wrestled with her for the key. She was on the floor and beneath him before he had it in firm grip.

She quivered beneath his lean hard body. "Greg . . . don't you want me?"

His hand found her breast, and he fondled a moment as he contemplated her face. She was so young, so tempting. Yes, he wanted her. He remembered the first time . . . five months ago when she had exposed herself to him behind the barn. Suddenly she had his hand, and she put it to her breast, naked before his scrutiny. He hadn't been her first . . . so there was no guilt in this. No guilt? He bent now and kissed her hard. The key slipped out of his hand and onto the uncarpeted floor. She ground her body well against his as he kissed her.

"Come on, Greg . . . give it to me," she whispered huskily as his hand teased. "Your friend George says I'm great in bed . . . don't *you* think so?" It was a chastisement for not coming near her in two weeks.

He looked at her a moment. Her face was drawn in passion, hungry and raw. Damn, she was only fourteen, but look at her! "You know, Chrissy . . . you are nothing but a little whore." He was unzippering her breeches.

"Hmmm. So I am . . . and you love it, don't you, Greg?" She was helping him with her breeches, spreading her legs. So he didn't approve? She thought this funny.

"Well enough," he answered on a hoarse whisper and bit her lip. "Well enough . . ." And he groaned as he eased himself into her.

The night was cloudless and clear. The sky was full with its white, bright moon, its glittering jewels, its promise to lovers. Sir Justin shifted into first gear and tooled his car out of the ferry's deep belly, over the ramp, and onto the paved road ahead. Lights from Lymington invited, but he bypassed them as he took the road home. He and Holly were both quiet as they mused on their day.

She looked at him, at his strong handsome profile, and then lest he see, quickly she looked away at the passing scenes through the window. It had been marvelous. He had driven them over to West Wight, saying lightly, almost like a youth on an adventure, that he meant to take her to spots normally missed by the tourists and he hoped she would approve.

"For example?" she bantered.

"Tennyson Down," he answered at once and grinned at her, "What? Did you think I meant to scurry you off to some cave dwelling and ravish you?" He shook his head sadly. "A lovely notion, but alas, I'm too much the coward!"

"I doubt that!" she retorted at once.

"Then too much the gentleman, if you will allow."

"I might."

They laughed easily together and then he was parking the car, taking her hand, pulling her along to the chalk cliff's edge.

"Imagine, Holly, a hundred years ago the Poet Laureate walked here, along these cliffs."

She looked down the white chalk cliffs. They were steep in their fall to the sea, lovely in their quiet glory, mysterious in their silence. "Did Tennyson live near here? I had no idea . . ."

"That he did, in Farringford . . . we can drive through there if you like."

"Oh yes, let's," she answered enthusiastically.

She looked like a woman-child. It was again the first impression he had had of her that night in the casino. A bird escaping. What eyes she had . . . he could lose himself in their depths if he wasn't careful. To temper his rising passion, to soften and restrain it, he took up her hand and kissed it gently, and then immediately gave over to light mirth, for she actually blushed, and hotly so.

> "I kissed her slender hand,
> She took the kiss sedately . . ."

And then his voice shifted, his gray eyes grew darker with his purpose, as he proceeded,

> " 'One is come to woo her.' "

She attempted to steer him onto safer ground, though her voice came shakily. "Tennyson?"

He allowed her to digress. She was warming to him, and he would go slowly.

"Indeed. I've stolen it from his *Maud*." He was looking out to sea, thinking again of another time.

124

She returned him to the present with her soft voice, her wild aqua eyes. *"Maud?"*

He surveyed her. "When you get back, pick it up and read it. Sophie has Tennyson all over the house."

"Tell me about it anyway. Then I can better understand it when I read it," she persisted.

"Let's see. Briefly it is about a young man who is heir to madness, he is morbidly sensitive in an age when money is everything and his sensitivity is not understood. He falls in love and is rescued by that love."

"Oh, good," said Holly with satisfaction.

He laughed. "Ah, so you are a romantic, eh? Well, well." He flicked her nose. "But I am sorry to say, life is never so easy, and Tennyson knew this, so it does not end there. The young man loses his love . . . and he goes insane."

"How dreadful," cried Holly.

"But never mind, he finds redemption in the end, which is what Tennyson was after all along."

"Redemption? How do you mean?"

"In the unselfishness of true love." There was a touch of sarcasm to Sir Justin's voice.

"Oh?" she sounded doubtful.

"Let us see . . . ah yes, there are lines from 'Locksley Hall' which serve here."

"Love took up the harp of Life, and smote on
all the chords with might;
Smote the chord of Self, that, trembling, pass'd
in music out of sight.'"

He shrugged. "Some lucky few might find truth there."

"But not you?" She cocked her head.

He brushed this aside. "Have you never read Tennyson?"

"Only some . . . not often enough to remember. I am a Byron nut." She was smiling.

"Of course you are." He studied her a moment. "I should have guessed." His finger traced her full cherry lips. "All sensitive women have a fling with Byron."

It had been like that all day, beautiful, and she came away all too conscious of his masculinity and of a sudden need within her. She could feel him looking at her. A light drizzle was fogging the window, and she attempted to dispel the fever in the air with bantering. "Can you see through the raindrops, sir?"

He flicked on the windshield wipers. "Happy?"

"Happier," she answered. "And yes, happy. I had a wonderful day and I do thank you."

They were pulling up to her door. He had his hand on the ignition key. They had dined earlier, but he turned to ask her gently, "Would you invite me up for a cup of coffee?"

She hesitated. "It is the very least I can do . . ." As an afterthought she turned with a beaming smile and said, "But it is also *all* I will do!"

He laughed out loud and followed her up the stairs to her flat, where she flicked on the switch to her table lamp. She had a distinct impression when she first walked into the room that something was different. It was the couch. It was off center. Somehow it had been shifted. She frowned.

"What is it, Holly? What's wrong?" He saw her troubled expression at once.

"I don't know . . . you know, I wonder if anyone else has a key to my flat," she said, thinking out loud.

His brows drew together, and he thought of Greg. "Well, maybe you should have your locks changed. You know, anyone at the Grange could have a key to this flat."

"Even you?" Now why did she do that? She could see him stiffen.

He was close to her now, and his voice was low and full with desire. "Holly, when I come on, it won't be a sneak attack."

She wanted him to kiss her, but something inside of her balked. It would mean the loss of her newfound freedom. Warning, warning. He was another strong man. He would hold her down, pen her up. She moved away from him. "I can't give you what you expect," she

126

said, and her voice was broken with her own mixed emotions.

"I don't know what I expect from you, Holly . . . but coffee no longer seems adequate."

He had her in his arms then, and his mouth came down hard and demanding on hers. His body was full with his passion, with the excitement her own fevered body instilled within him. His kiss touched her soul, demanded truth, and her truth was responsible for the arch in her back as her hands went to his shoulders. His tongue commanded her sensations. His hand went to her breast and found it full but confined.

"Holly, Holly . . . I want you . . ."

She could only groan. This was so good. It felt so right. Danger, danger. He will box you in. He will take other women. He makes you no promise. Danger, danger. She tried to pull away and found only that her clothes were dropping around her, that she was nearly naked.

Sir Justin's mouth closed over the rose-tipped nipple; his arm held her to him as his bent head taught her some of what it was all about. He was lowering her to the sofa. Her groan excited him. She was exquisite. Her breasts were high, and so well rounded. He was unzippering her jeans, kissing her midriff, bringing his mouth lower still as he parted her jeans. . . .

"Stop . . . please stop . . ." She had to get control. Look what was happening. He was going too far. It was like a cup of cold water being splashed onto her face. She had never been touched in this way, and it was too much too soon. She pushed at him. "Go away . . . go away . . . you are confusing me . . ."

He felt dazed. He was still fully dressed but for his blazer, which had somehow come off. He stared at her for a moment and shook his head. "I don't understand you, Holly."

"I am not about to be shackled . . . owned . . . not now . . . not again, and not by you!" she cried in desperation. Was it true? Was it? Or did she want to be his? More to the point, did she want him to be hers?

127

He was stung by her words. Odd that they penetrated, but they did. Quietly he returned, "But Holly . . . I haven't asked you to be mine." The words echoed in the still room.

That's right. He only wanted her body. He only wanted what her body could do for him . . . at this moment. There was no future in that, and it was fair enough. He couldn't know the war of East and West in her head. He couldn't know that her values were lashing at her. He couldn't know that she was still a virgin, an innocent, and that she rather thought sex, love, and marriage were words that went together. He couldn't know. So she stared at him a long moment. No answer. She had no answer as her arms came up to cover her nakedness, and with a stifled cry she turned and ran to the bathroom, where she locked herself in.

Justin stood for a long moment staring after her. What a childlike thing to do. Here was a beautiful woman, an experienced woman who had been mistress to at least one Arab and God knew how many others, and what was she doing? Locking herself up in a bathroom. Just what was going on here? What game was she playing? He sighed, collected his jacket, and himself, and descended the stairs to his car.

The day had started out as an investigation for him. He wanted to get into her head. Was she working for the Arabs? Was she doing it willingly? Had they something they were holding over her? That might in part explain her air of innocence . . . if she was a reluctant spy. But if she was a spy, why hadn't she been around his cottage? Why hadn't she tried to seduce him? Why hadn't she allowed him to take her tonight? Just what was this pretty little bird up to? And damn, he had wanted her, wanted her still, and hell, how could he? What is the matter with you, Justin Laeland? How could you want a girl like that?

Holly listened for his motor to start up. She opened her bathroom door and switched the light off. She went to her window, taking up her shirt and holding it to

128

herself as she came to stand by the sheer curtains. She
had ruined everything with her prudishness! She could
have been made a woman tonight . . . and by such a
man! She could have been totally freed of her Arabian
upbringing. She could have flung herself to the winds
and taken yet another step in making her life all her
own. Something inside of her wanted to cry. Oh, God,
she had wanted him to go on touching her . . . kissing
her. He doesn't love you. So what? He could hurt you,
she answered herself. No . . . not if I don't let him. You
will be just another woman to him. . . .

With a sigh of dejection she turned around, and
something glinted on the floor. She went to it and
picked it up. A brass key. Just like her own. How?
Who? What was it doing here on the floor? And why
had her sofa been out of place?

She frowned over this for a moment, for that was all
it took for Sir Justin's face to come back to haunt her.
The sensation of his fevered kisses, his deft hands, his
wonderful hard body . . . stop it! Had she done the right
thing? Would she regret it all the rest of her days? Her
mind, whispered, Maybe, her body cried, Yes, fool.

Chapter Ten

Saeed stepped into the living room of the suite that
Hassan shared with his father and turned to indicate
with his head that his associate should follow. Selim
did not look pleased but did as he was bid. He found
Hassan and Mustafa el Zahour coming forward. He
found them looking at him curiously, and he felt uncomfortable.

"Saeed? How goes it with you?" This from Hassan,
his hand outstretched to take that of his friend's. He
was leading him toward the long plush velvet sofa,
turning to introduce his father, waiting to get an
introduction to the man with Saeed.

129

This done, they took up positions on various pieces of furniture. Selim looked about in a fidgety manner. Mustafa offered refreshment. He smiled amicably. "Shall we sin, gentlemen and take some arak?"

Moslem religion forbade the drinking of alcoholic beverages. Arak was made from dates and was potent alcohol indeed. They all agreed to sin. The arak was passed round, enjoyed, the weather and the pleasures of London remarked upon, before Saeed dared to bring up the subject that had brought him to his friend's quarters.

"Hassan . . . forgive me, but what news of your sister?" He had been present at the casino the night that Khalda had vanished. He had been there looking after Sir Justin.

Mustafa frowned. He had not been sleeping well. The detectives they had hired had not brought him anything to satisfy. All they could tell him was that she was not in any of the hospitals they had investigated. It was something. At least hope had it that she was well. Defiant as ever, but well. He turned to his son. Her disappearance was supposed to be a secret. Wahid was here in London and did not yet know. . . .

"Hassan . . ." His voice was sharp with his annoyance. "What does he mean?"

Hassan pulled a face at Saeed. "Indeed . . ." His teeth gritted; his friend should know better than to speak in front of this stranger. "I don't quite understand you, Saeed. My sister is well."

"Ah. I had wondered when I saw her today . . . so far from London." It was said gently.

Mustafa jumped to his feet. "You saw her? Where?"

"We returned here to London . . . to accommodate you with this information . . . at some cost. . . ." Saeed was studying his hands. His nails were polished and well groomed. He rubbed at them.

Hassan said on a sneer, "Of course." He rose, drew out a hefty wad of English pounds, and put it on the coffee table between them.

Saeed sighed, and his eyes moved toward his friend.

Selim did what was expected of him and picked up the wad of bills and pocketed them. This out of the way, Saeed proceeded.

"She is very beautiful, you know . . . one could not help but notice."

"Come to the point, man!" This from Hassan, impatient and determined that his father would not be moved to strike Saeed, for Mustafa looked as though the thought might become a reality.

"We were in Lymington . . . in a pub . . . she walked past us. When we got into our car I thought she was gone, out of sight, but as we passed the ferry docks, we saw her with a gentleman well known to us. They were driving the car onto the ferry to the Isle of Wight."

Mustafa's voice was a growl. "This gentleman's name?"

"His name is Laeland . . . Sir Justin Laeland."

Hassan frowned. He knew the name. Too often it had been in the gossip columns he was fond of perusing. "She was with him, you say? But how would Holly know such a man?"

Saeed looked at his feet. "It is possible she met him at the casino . . . the night she disappeared. It is possible he—"

"Enough!" This a cry from an anguished father.

Hassan took his friend's arm and urged him to his feet. Selim hastened toward the door before them. "I think, Saeed, that you had better go . . . and, my friend, you know, of course, what will happen to both of you if I hear talk!" There was a dangerous underlining to his voice.

Saeed nodded. "A warning is not needed between friends."

"No, neither is the exchange of money. You now have both!"

They were gone, and Hassan turned to find his father, hands to head, pacing. "Hassan . . . what has she done? She has ruined her life."

"She is English . . . she does what the West does . . . she lives," said Hassan quietly.

"This Laeland . . . if he has taken her for mistress, he is a dead man!"

131

"Wahid will not want her if Laeland has had her, Father," said Hassan practically. He had to do what was best for Holly. Why did his father not think in such terms? Why was pride ever the first consideration?

"Two things you will do, immediately. You will discover how far from Lymington this Laeland is residing. The other will be to procure the necessary documents for a marriage."

"Wahid?"

"We will take Wahid with us, and he will be married to Khalda immediately."

"You will not tell him about Laeland?" What was his father thinking of?

"I will tell him, and he will want her anyway . . . depend upon it, Wahid will save my daughter. I will make it worth his while. And you are forgetting, Holly has beauty to make a man forget. . . ."

No, Hassan was not forgetting. Too often her beauty had nearly made him forget. He sighed and moved to do his father's bidding. There were bound to be repercussions from this. They couldn't destroy a man like Laeland and walk away unscarred, and honor, tradition, religion, all that they were taught, meant that Laeland must be killed. May Allah see them through this.

Sir Justin ran his hand through his ginger-colored hair and grimaced as he studied the *Euphorbia* plant on his counter. Somewhere in the genes of this plant was his answer. An outstanding plant genus, really. From it was cultivated the home remedy for many a child's ills, castor oil. From another of the plant's relatives came rubber . . . and from yet another, the plant in front of him, came oil, crude and nearly perfect. . . .

He stood up and stretched. Yes, somewhere the answer to his experiment was floating about, and one of these afternoons or nights he would light upon it. But not now. No, not now. He moved across the polished lab floor and opened the door, carefully locking it at his back before he took the cellar steps to the garage above. And there he nearly collided with a small and graceful body.

Sir Justin's strong hands went out and held Joy's shoulders. Dusk had not settled in, but the sun was lower and the inside of the garage was but dimly lit. He was surprised, and it was expressed in his tone and on his face.

"Joy? Well . . . what are you doing here?"

She smiled warmly up at him. "And you, my sweet Justin, what are you doing? Poking about in your silly engines?" She knew full well that he had not been working on that old custom job he kept in the garage. She had been up here long enough, and she had heard him locking up below. Until today she hadn't been aware that the garage housed a cellar . . . it was an uncommon asset. Just what was he doing?

"That's the ticket." He put his arm about her waist and led her toward the driveway door, opened it, and gently ushered her outside. Joy Chen had been a responsive and satisfactory lover, but that had been before he had know about her and Sophie's husband.

She had been honest enough about it. She hadn't tried to conceal it at the time. Why should she? They owed nothing to one another, it hadn't been that sort of thing . . . and now she had added to her collection his assistant, Andrew Benton. It was like Joy. She would always need more than one man.

"So tell me, pretty girl, what have you been up to?" He was surveying her face. Were those lines beneath her eyes? Was she still Thomas's woman?

Her oriental eyes moved slyly. "Now, Justin . . . I don't ask you to tell me your secrets."

"No, you never did . . . but is everything you do a secret?" He was quizzing her, not really interested. He was at his front door. "Come in for a drink?"

"Hmm. Yes and no . . . not everything I do is a secret, but the things that are not are too boring to relate." She watched as he moved across the earth shades of carpet to his wet bar. He was as cold as he had been six

133

months ago when he had said it was over. How to get to him? She moved toward him.

"Scotch."

"Yes, I remember . . . on the rocks." Damn, why was he still thinking of aqua eyes and cherry lips and long, long gold-red hair?

Tracy brushed a wayward yellow band of hair away from her forehead, fixed her hard hat atop her small head, kept the chin of her pixy face upward as she aimed her bay gelding at the crossbars. There was a mischievous glint in her green eyes.

Holly had been talking with Tracy's mother, Lynn Patterson, along the fence. The lesson was over, and they had been discussing Tracy's progress. She turned in time to catch the ten-year-old doing what she had not yet been taught. It was too late to stop her, so she called out hasty instructions,

"Two point, Trace . . . two point, heels down, get those elbows in . . . grip mane . . . that's right, good, good!" She watched as the ten-year-old took the bay gelding over the crossbars, easily and in perfect form. A sigh of relief. There was less than two weeks to show time, which meant whipping all their top students into proper shape. But Tracy Patterson was going to outshine them all.

Tracy was an American, and she was Holly's only private student. She was the best in her age class that the Grange would offer up to the local show. Her parents had moved into the area when her father had been transferred to his company's English branch. The child was spunky and with a wit that came from surviving and loving New York. She laughed after she completed the jump and brought her gelding around to do it again.

Holly smiled and leaned into the fence. Jumping was not part of Tracy's lesson. She turned to find Lynn Patterson holding a hand to her heart. She liked Tracy's young American mother and beamed at her. "She is quite a girl, your Tracy."

134

"Watch, Ma!" called Tracy as she took the jump again. "Oh, yeah, she's something all right." Lynn groaned, and her hand went from her heart to the ash-blond afro-fashioned hair atop her well-shaped head.

Holly chuckled. "This is no place for you, Mother."

"No kidding." She shook her head, her eyes closed. "Why is she doing this? She hasn't learned how to jump yet . . . she's too little."

Holly had been drawn to Lynn Patterson almost immediately after their introduction. She liked the warmth of Lynn's chocolate-brown eyes. She sensed a kindred spirit, someone who would understand. She hadn't found that in Judy Baines. Judy was only interested in a good time.

"Never mind, the crossbars are low, and her form is really very good, Lynn. I'd wager she is going to take a ribbon in her class."

"Hmmm . . . but she has her heart set on a blue, and I don't know if she is that good." She sighed. "I don't know . . . maybe we should prepare her to lose?"

"She must be ready for that possibility, but it's slim. She has her mother's seat and hands, you know." She was smiling brightly, waiting for Lynn's expression.

Lynn had a wealth of facial expressions, and each told a short story. Holly found them priceless. Lynn used one of them now, and Holly cracked up.

"Stop it!" cried Holly on a laugh. "You know you are *both* good." And then, turning, she called out to Tracy. "Come on down, now, love, you and Prince need a rest." She walked over to the horse and felt him. "Oh, yes, dear, he is hot. Walk him out."

Tracy patted her mother's bay gelding proudly. "Wasn't he the best, Miss Winslow? Wasn't he great?"

"He certainly was." She returned to Lynn, who was studying Holly thoughtfully.

"So, Holly . . . are you happy at the Grange?"

"Hmm. I love it."

"No kidding? Where were you before . . . also at a riding stable?"

"Well, that's hard to explain."

135

"Oh?" She hesitated before asking, careful not to pry. "How is the love life here?"

Holly blushed. "So far, nonexistent."

Lynn had seen Holly riding through the New Forest the evening before in a car she had noted was Sir Justin Laeland's, There was also talk about the barn that Greg had a thing for the new riding instructor. "It's hard in a small place." Lynn sighed.

Holly had been thinking of Sir Justin all day. She had been trying to make a decision. All resolves, all principles, shook now, for it was the end of her workday, it was the beginning of her free time, and she wanted to see him. She shook this thought aside. She needed someone to talk to. Judy Baines's notions were amusing, but Judy Baines was not the sort to trust with a confidence. Lynn was offering friendship.

"I am going to tell you something, Lynn . . . but it is something no one else must know."

"Oh? Are you sure you want to do that? Maybe you shouldn't."

"Well . . . it's my situation . . . you see . . ."

"Hello there!" A male voice, pleasant and almost boyishly shy in its approach. "Holly . . . Lynn."

It was Dr. Jim Jakes. He was greeted with open friendliness by both females as he stepped up to them. His height was average, and while he was not outstandingly handsome, there was something most attractive about his outdoorsy face.

"Hi, Dr. Jakes. I'm so glad you are here. I wonder if you could have a look at Prince later."

"What's wrong, Lynn?"

"Oh, nothing, I just thought it might be time to have his teeth floated."

"Right, then." He turned to Holly. His blue eyes were smiling, and she liked the way they crinkled up at the corners. "And how is the new Laeland instructor getting on?"

"Just fine, thank you. But tell me . . . have you been here to see that filly? Isn't she a special little wonder?"

Tracy appeared with Prince in tow. "Come on, Mom . . . I'm hungry."

136

Lynn pulled another one of her special faces, which set off Holly's giggle, and off went mother and daughter to the boarders' barn to untack their animal.

"Special indeed. Yes, both mother and filly are doing fine, and so are the Grange's two pregnant mares in the first paddock. They are due any day now, you know. Star was a very busy stud last year."

She smiled and started walking toward her flat. She wanted a shower and a quick change, for she meant to visit Justin. She had to explain the way she had left things last night. What must he think of her?

"You weren't here then, were you?"

"No, I am new to the area. Old Doc Haley wants to retire, and I am slowly taking over his practice."

This is what she had been told by Greg, but she listened with interest, stopping at her door to bid him goodbye. He looked down at the ground before bringing his eyes to her face.

"Holly . . . would you like to have dinner some evening?"

"I should love to," she said.

"Right, then." He beamed. "I'll ring you up and give you advance notice."

"Hmmm. Call at the house and tell Maureen. I haven't my phone yet."

He agreed to this, and a moment later he was happily ambling off. It occurred to her that there was something familiar about him, and she tried for a moment to pinpoint that something. However, this proved useless, and she set it aside as she showered.

Some moments later, her decision made, she was slipping on a blue print cotton skirt and a blue cotton blouse and wrapping a matching shawl about her shoulders. Stockings and sandals were on, and she gave herself a final glance in her mirror. Her long red-gold hair glistened as it waved over her forehead and fell to her trim waist. She had touched her long curling lashes with some mascara but other than that wore no makeup, and she was stunning. She thought only that she would do, and with some excitement she skipped down the steps. She was going to pay Justin a visit and explain herself, perhaps even apologize and hope that they would go on as they had started on the Isle of Wight. . . .

Thomas Martin met her just as she made for the woodland path that would take her to Justin's cottage. She smiled and waited a moment politely, though she was itching to be off.

"Good Lord, girl, you shouldn't be allowed out looking like that!"

In some confusion she glanced over herself. "But . . . why?" She hadn't worn a bra—she wasn't asking herself why—but now she worried that it was too obvious. She wrapped the shawl tighter around herself.

"Because you are a definite candidate for rape." He moved closer toward her and touched her cheek. "Lovely, simply lovely."

She had been out riding with Judy and Thomas recently, and nothing had prepared her for this sort of behavior from him. She blushed hotly. "I think you mean that as a compliment, Thomas . . . though I am sure I don't take it for one."

He chuckled. "But why not?"

"Well, I *know* I don't want to be a candidate for rape." She was bantering now as she started to leave him.

"But where are you off to, love?" he shouted after her.

"Never mind, Thomas, I am on my own time now," she returned good-naturedly and hoped he would not think to follow her.

He did think to follow her. He knew that Judy liked her, and the three of them were getting on well together . . . but that would have to wait. Besides, he wasn't sure how Joy would feel about it. Well, well. So she was going off to Justin's? Where else would she be walking to all prettied up? He sighed and moved toward the parking lot.

Judy waited for him in Joy's flat. He wished Joy were going to be there. Afterward he would come home

138

to Sophie, and he would tell her all about Greg and Chrissy. Damn, he was going to make her suffer before he was through!

Joy did not appear to be watching when Justin threw down his set of keys onto the sitting room's Italian Provincial desk. Instead she centered her attention on Justin. What she needed was to get him to bed . . . and later, she had just what she needed to make a mold of his keys.

She threw a long shining black tress of hair back over her shoulder, and her slender arm traveled to Sir Justin's chest. Her other arm went around his neck, and she brought herself up to her toes. "Why, Justin, are you making it so difficult for me?" She was attempting to tease him out of his stiffness.

Joy had two obstacles to get past. Foremost in Justin's mind was the memory of riding along a backwoods New Forest trail to find two horses from the Grange grazing at the end of their ground anchors. Beside them, rolling between the bushes, were two lovers. They heard him coming and would have been better off remaining where they were, for he was gentleman enough to quickly move off, but they didn't. They popped up, and he saw their faces full. Joy Chen and Thomas Martin. Joy and Thomas. He didn't understand it and didn't care enough to want to. It turned him off to her at once. But more than this was against Joy now, for men can forget when passion sways tenaciously. However, there was Holly.

He had not been able to get Holly out of his mind since yesterday. The time they had spent on the Isle of Wight had been almost idyllic. Dinner together had filled him with a sense of comfort and excitement, an excitement that had been building steadily. He had been sure she wanted him as much as he wanted her . . . and then that sudden strange retreat. While his blood was burning for Holly, Joy stood no chance.

"Come on, Joy . . . you know better. Let's leave it as it was, shall we?" he said gently.

139

"But Justin . . . am I asking for so much? I'm down . . . really down."

His brow went up. Joy took barbiturates for her highs, another fact that set them apart. "I've never been able to help you there, Joy. You don't like advice."

"I'm not asking for advice," she said coyly. She raised her face to him and bent his head down toward her. Forgotten now was the fact that Andrew had promised to pay her a handsome fee for this piece of work. Justin was presenting a challenge she suddenly found tantalizing. "A kiss for Joy . . ." she whispered huskily. "Please, Justin . . . am I no longer beautiful? Show me . . ."

"You have enough admirers, Joy. You don't need me." He was pulling away now, somewhat disgusted with her and totally turned off. He moved to the door. She came after him.

She took his hand and forced him around with a cry in her voice.

"Don't do this to me, Justin . . . don't hurt me . . ."

That caught him, and he turned just at the half-opened door he had in his hand. He took both her shoulders in his grip. "Stop this, Joy."

"Then kiss me, at least," she begged, still clutching at straws. Perhaps a kiss would get things started.

He bent and took her up, saying on a low note, "A goodbye kiss . . ." And then he heard a soft, sweet voice call his name, and the voice was not Joy's but *Holly's*.

Holly came up on the cottage a little out of breath. She saw the door open partially, and she could see Sir Justin's back. She started down the stone pathway toward the front door. His broad back blocked all vision of Joy until she had said his name. Then she saw, and she froze.

Stupid girl, she shouted at herself. Look what you have let yourself in for. When will you grow up? She went rigid with embarrassment as she berated herself, her clumsiness. She went sick with a sudden engulfing gulp of jealousy. It overpowered. She felt her breath

140

seized, and she took a step backward in reflex action. It dawned on her that she must get away. No, said her mind. Be cool. Pretend you haven't seen. Say hello. Say your business can wait and then, with composure and pride, leave.

Instead, she did what had developed into a pattern for her. She turned and ran. Fool! Baby! Her mind raged at her furiously. Running away. It was proving to be the only answer to crisis for Holly, but this time it did not serve. The hurt, the sick churning of her heart, open now to attack, was a feeling that followed her. There was no release as she put distance between herself and Sir Justin, no relief whatsoever.

He heard Holly's voice, and there wasn't any time to question himself. His heart sank. He saw Holly's eyes and for a moment froze with indecision. What to do? And then she was running. "I want you gone when I get back, Joy." And he was charging after Holly.

Joy Chen watched this little scene with interest. Who was that girl? What was she to Sir Justin? Faith! *Justin had left the keys!* Quickly she went to her bag, took out the contents of a plastic container, and proceeded to make a mold of the four keys on his key chain. One of them must lead to his lab.

In the growing dark outside, Holly went dashing down the woodland path, not even sure she had taken the right one. A bramble vine caught her sleeve and made a long slash. She could hear him chasing after her. What was he doing? Why was he running her to earth?

"Holly!" he shouted, for he could just see her take a bend on the path. There was some treacherous ground in this area, for it opened onto the moors and there were bogs up ahead. He had to get to her. "Holly . . . hold for just a moment!" He was gaining on her now. She was just ahead.

Oh no . . . she wouldn't stop . . . couldn't let him see her now . . . not with silly tears staining her cheek. She felt so foolish. And then suddenly he was on her, swinging her around by her arm.

141

"Damm it, Holly . . . what in thunder?" But as she pounded at his chest for release, he brought her to him in one sweeping movement and silenced her with his kiss born of exasperation, stirred by fever, tempered with tenderness.

Without realizing what she was doing, her arms went around him. He was here with her. He had cared enough to come after her. She whispered his name into his ear, and he was stirred as never before.

"Ah . . . Holly . . ." he said, lowering her to the ground with him, kissing her neck, opening her blouse to find her full young breasts. He felt her stiffen, and he groaned, "No, babe . . . no, don't run away again . . . not again . . ." He was kissing her mouth sweetly, almost begging her to submit. He was experienced enough to allow instinct to take over.

It was just the right thing. His words worked on her as no others could. Suddenly he was a boy, begging for her favor, and she wanted to please him. Here was this sophisticated, this fantastic lover of women, and he wanted her. . . .

She returned his kisses in high-pitched fever. Was that a skyrocket in the black velvet sky? Reds, blues, and golds burst into flame. *Burning.* She was on fire. Her body scorched wherever his hand strayed . . and his hands, how they strayed. They worked her pleasure points, taunting, teasing, arousing. Her skirt was up, his pants were unzipped. Oh, Lord . . . she could see his rod hard and pulsating before her. It was thrilling, terrifying, and she stiffened in sudden fright.

He sensed it at once and stroked her head lovingly, assuaging her fears, bringing her back into readiness with words that smothered thought.

"Ah, sweet beauty, how you move me . . . how your body moves me. Give it to me, sunshine . . . give it to me . . ."

She wanted to do whatever he asked at that moment. His touch commanded, his voice seduced, and his eyes, God, his gray eyes had darkened with his passion, and this brought her further into heat. She held onto him, and then his hand was fondling the gold fluff between her thighs. He was spreading her legs with his knees, his finger was dividing the lips of her sweetbun, soothing, moving erotically, circling, tipping inward but not quite. She thrust herself at him.

"Oh, yes, Justin . . . yes . . ." she cried, wild now with ecstasy. There was nothing else but this moment.

He had no way of knowing she was a virgin. He had good reason to suppose this was a game she knew well enough. She was taut, but he felt her ready for his plunge. He had no reason at that point to bridle his passion. In his heat he thrust into her. In his shock he stopped dead. There was no denying that he felt as though he had ripped her apart. She was small, and she was virgin. She had cried out at that moment and stiffened with pain and fright. He raised himself enough to look at her face.

"Damnation, Holly . . . a virgin?"

She nodded her head. He frowned, but already he could feel the tightness of her pulse around his penis. Already he could feel her throbbing for more.

"Don't worry, sunshine . . . it will get much better presently."

He started to rotate gently until he worked her mood again. He touched her nipple until it was teased into pertness. His kiss warmed her lips, his tongue took her to new realms. She started to pitch toward his thrusts, manipulate her body to his beats.

Holly was again in his hands and in a passion. A moment ago she had been rigid with the shock of that first pain, but now with his ministrations and his magic words . . .

"That's the way of it, sunshine . . . give it to me . . . ah, babe, sweet babe, you're perfect . . . so perfect . . ."

He built her up until he felt her climax beneath him, until he felt her relax into dreamy sweetness, and then quickly, hastily, and with a long groan he withdrew to give his seed to the grass.

After a moment he looked long at her and pulled her into his arm. "Well, Holly . . . I think you owe me an explanation."

"No, no, I have paid enough dues for one night," she said softly and shyly dived into the crook of his arm. His chest was so hard and firm, so wonderful.

He smiled absently and stroked her head. "We'll see about that. For now . . . I'm taking you home."

He was already up, pulling her to her feet, brushing her skirt down around her. "Home?" Her face fell ludicrously. Was he done with her? Was that what men did after they had their pleasure?

He grinned broadly and chucked her beneath the chin. "To *my* home, sunshine . . ." And then he was bending, kissing her lightly until he felt the thrill of touching her. He folded her into his arms and his kiss grew into another, more insistent, calculated.

"Well, then," she gasped as she pulled away, "take me home, or do you mean to make me suffer second-class accommodations all night?"

Chapter Eleven

London had the sweet smell of spring that same night. Wahid felt it flutter against his cheeks, awaken his senses. If Mustafa had not taken Khalda to London, she would now be his. . . .

He was angry and he was ashamed. The two emotions did not mix well. He stopped Hassan with a rough jerk of his friend's arm.

"It may be, Hassan, that I no longer want this sister of yours!"

Hassan's dark brow went up. He would allow no one, not even this Wahid, his friend, to speak ill of Holly. He turned and faced him fully, and his thin sensuous lips drew into a sneer.

"You want her. You will always want her."

Wahid looked sullen. Yes, he wanted Holly even though she was sleeping with this English nobleman. At least she had chosen high, but it infuriated him. He

144

would have himself avenged. "Hassan, it is not so simple. Would you take a woman after such an insult?"

Hassan studied him. "If that woman was Holly, I would take her. Perhaps you have never realized, Wahid, if Holly were not Mustafa's daughter, today she would be my wife . . . perhaps the only wife I would ever care to take."

Wahid was not surprised by this admission. He had often suspected that Hassan's love was more than brotherly for Khalda. However, he was taken aback by Hassan's open declaration. He considered this thoughtfully.

"Yes . . . but this man Laeland . . . *I want him dead.*" He spoke quietly, but his words were chilling with their intensity.

Hassan sighed. It was already in the works. Honor had to be maintained . . . and thus a Kabadhai had been sent for. No hoodlum was a Kabadhai. No paid assassin, though this was his work. His particular field, his business, dated back to the days of the Ottoman Empire. He was a Moslem strongman, a brave and courageous creature who took his work proudly. Such was the Kabadhai Mustafa had called to defend the honor of his house.

Wahid grunted his approval. "This is good. The license?"

He referred to the marriage license. Again Hassan sighed. "It is in order, though we had to pay an exorbitant fee to have it drawn up so quickly. You will be married by an English official who will join us in Brockenhurst tomorrow."

"We will know exactly where to take her?"

Hassan looked away from him. Distasteful, that he should be such a strong arm in his Holly's downfall, and he could only think of tomorrow's plans in that light. She would never forgive him.

"Father has sent the private detective to Brockenhurst to search out this Laeland's whereabouts. No doubt she will be in his house. We will take her there."

Again Wahid grunted. "May Allah guide us."

* * *

Joy Chen was a complicated lady. This was her own opinion of herself and it was her excuse for the things she did. It was what she reminded herself of as she took the steps of her building to her modest but comfortably appointed flat.

She was pleased with herself. She had done what she had set out to do. She frowned when the fleeting memory of Justin turning her away came to haunt. He didn't want her . . . but never mind, Andrew did, and Andrew kept her, if not in sable and diamonds, at least with the means to get by until something better came along. It flashed through her mind that she could have had sable by now. Her ex-husband, she was told, was doing very well. . . . A sigh. That was over. Five years had passed, and that was gone. Jimmy Chen had nearly killed her . . . but why was she thinking of that now? Because Thomas is in your flat with Judy by now, and if it hadn't been for Thomas you would still be with Jimmy. . . . Another sigh. Thomas. She had been eighteen and newly wed. She hadn't loved Jimmy, but he was good to her, and then she had started taking riding lessons at the Grange. Thomas was an instructor there, and Sophie was not yet widowed from her husband, William Laeland.

Thomas had never been a good-looking man, though he had been a sight more dashing five years ago. He was short and stocky. His hair then was more blond then gray. Perhaps it was something about his authority in the saddle. She took her lessons on the trail, progressing rapidly, and they grew close, closer still. She hadn't even realize she was thinking of him romantically until that one day out on the trail. She had torn a leather and they had dismounted while he went to work on it.

She watched him as he made another hole in the leather, and then he turned to give her a leg up. Instead she went into his arms, easily, automatically, as though she had always belonged there. He didn't do more than kiss her, but it was their beginning. He was to teach her more than riding skills over the years. He

146

was to introduce her to a new and stimulating world where pleasure reigned supreme.

She could hear hard rock within her flat, and she smiled to herself. Would Judy never learn? Thomas did not appreciate that sort of music. She inserted the key just as she heard the tape die out and another, Frank Sinatra, go on. Ah, now that was Thomas.

Her door opened into a warm large room whose dominating colors were rich browns and soft greens. The brown velvet drapes were drawn, and the room glowed with candlelight. Judy sat on the long heavily cushioned print velvet sofa. Thomas was across the room at the dark oak bar. His blue shirt was undone to his waist, and Joy smiled to see he was really putting on weight. Why did she continue with him? Why?

He looked up and smiled warmly. "Joy? You made it after all." He went toward her, the loving husband in his eyes. "Come to me, angel." He held his arms open for her. It was their ritual.

She went into his embrace at once. She would always go to him. Somehow she was tied to this man. He had probably ruined her life. He had probably been the cause of events that would never allow her to enjoy a "normal" way of life, but she would always go to him. His mouth covered hers, and he kissed her long and hard as his hands undid her blouse and fondled her small soft breast. Judy Baines watched from the couch and pouted. She ran a hand through her short gold hair and felt a mixture of excitement and jealousy. She liked Joy. She was even beginning to desire Joy. The oriental woman had skin that felt like satin to the touch, and this thought momentarily filled her with a sudden urgency. But overriding this still was her jealousy. Joy held a special part of Thomas, and this irritated her.

"Hmmm . . . that was nice," said Thomas softly. He was already undoing Joy's skirt, sliding it off. She stood beneath his appreciative glance, her blouse open and exposing her bare breasts above pink bikini underpants. Joy pushed him toward the bar.

"Go and pour me a scotch, Thomas." Her voice was scarcely audible and yet it was a command.

He understood at once. Joy knew best in these matters, and he could see Judy's face. Better leave her to Joy. And as it turned out the oriental girl knew just what to do.

"Ah, pouting, darling?" Joy touched Judy Baines's cheek and then slid farther to the neck. Thomas had long ago taught her just how to enjoy a woman's body, and she was now teaching Judy. Her hand went farther and undid the short-sleeved mohair sweater, pausing momentarily to fondle one of Judy's breasts. "You must not mind watching Thomas and me play . . . we always get to you, don't we?" She saw Judy begin to relax, and her voice purred on. "Ah, my pet, your breasts are too small for a bra . . . you should never wear one . . . I don't . . ." She had separated Judy's legs beneath her soft suede skirt. "Now . . . help me, love . . ." She was pulling Judy's clothes away, and Judy did as the oriental woman wanted. She helped remove her own clothes.

Naked now and wondering how she had started allowing such things, Judy went onto her back on the sofa. Joy was on her knees, and Judy could see Thomas position himself at Joy's back. Somehow all impeding clothing had been discarded. She raised her hand against her will and took Joy's small taut breast in her hand. Was she doing this? Did someone pull strings to make her do this? What was happening to her?

Thomas groaned. Damn, but he would use these cunts . . . not Joy, no, she was more to him than that, but look at Judy, stretched out, her eyes begging for more, more. All of 'em bitches, grasping, taunting . . . but not him, not any more. He had learned the secret. He had learned how to make them beg. He gloated on this as he released his rod. It was hard and pulsating, waiting, waiting for Joy to ask. . . .

Joy reveled in her ministrations. She could feel Thomas's penis at her butt, and she smiled to herself. Why? Why did she let him do this to her? He didn't want to use her in the ordinary way. . . .

Judy knew what Thomas would do to Joy. How could

148

she let him? Didn't that hurt? She had seen him do that to Joy only once before, and Joy had seemed to like it ... Oh, God ... Joy's hands were manipulating her into a frenzy of desire. She couldn't think any more, couldn't think ...

Joy used her hands with sweet experience. She tantalized, her tongue teased, promised, her fingers sent Judy into wriggling helpless passion.

"Do you want me to bring you to it, Judy?" It was Joy's voice, husky almost cruel. "Do you?"

"Yes, yes ..."

"I can, you know ..." She could feel Thomas begin his entry. It made her jerk with a slight measure of pain. "And maybe I will"—her voice dropped as she kissed Judy's ear—"if you please me, Judy ..."

Judy didn't like touching Joy's vagina. It was the only part of this play that turned her off. She stiffened in the oriental's hands.

"Don't you want me to finish, pet?" It was Joy, taunting. "I can make Thomas roll me over and take me as I wish instead ... we could leave you to yourself ..." Her hands worked Judy as she spoke.

"No ... no ... please, Joy ... do it to me ... finish ..." Judy begged as she pushed herself toward Joy's fingers, which had not quite entered their goal. She took Joy's sweet-smelling body closer to herself, aware, all too aware, of Thomas grunting with pleasure. She inserted the two fingers as Joy wished and did what she was told. Moments later they had their release, nearly all three at the same time, but not quite. Thomas took a bit longer, and he and Joy finished together and Judy looked on.

Judy watched in growing horror. What was she becoming? She must stop this. But she couldn't stop seeing Thomas. She couldn't. She needed Thomas, and what was more terrifying was the faintly growing knowledge that she was beginning to really enjoy this sort of experience.

Joy raised herself to the sofa and put a hand to Judy's arm and stroked. "Oh, lovely bitch ... whatever

149

is wrong now?" She liked baiting Judy, degrading her, reducing her to her own level, for she meant in that manner to keep her . . . and she wanted to keep her.

"It's me . . . and you and Thomas . . . it's not normal, is it?"

Joy laughed. Thomas had moved off toward the bar and was pouring them some scotch. "Normal? What is normal? Getting married, having children, and dying? What is so normal about that? That's dull, Judy, and why should we spend our lives being dull?"

"But . . ." Judy's own philosophy had brought her to the edge, and now Joy's had taken her over.

"But nothing. Who do we hurt with our little stab at fun?"

"My husband," Judy said softly. (Myself?)

"Your husband is a pompous ass! Did you know I had lunch with him last week in London? We met quite by accident . . . and we went on from there to his office, where he locked the door and tried, Judy, he tried very hard to get it up . . ."

"You are lying!"

"Yes, as a matter of fact I am." Joy laughed, not at all abashed. "But that is probably what would have happened if I had made a pass at him. If he can't satisfy you, Judy . . . you don't owe him."

Judy went sullen, and Joy released a sigh, got up, and went over to Thomas at the bar. She reached for her glass of scotch, and he reached over and fondled her naked breast. "Ah, Joy . . . I'm up to my ears in trouble."

She frowned. "In what way, love?"

"They threatened me, you know."

"Oh, God, Thomas . . . you can't play fast and loose with that set." Joy's dark eyes opened wide.

"Don't worry, I am not about to put my head on the block. I did what I had to do."

"Which was . . . ?"

He lowered his voice and spoke only to her. "I forged her signature. Paid them off with some of her personal funds."

Joy laughed. "Good boy!"

150

He sighed. "You don't understand . . . she could have me put away for it."

"She won't."

"No, she won't . . . but she could make my life miserable."

"Fuck her!" snapped Joy. She hadn't wanted Thomas to marry the woman. He had insisted he would end by getting her to sign a will in his favor. She hadn't done that yet, and Joy hated her.

"I don't mean to do that unless she rewrites her will." He chuckled, but it was not a pleasant sound.

"She might not do that, because of her precious son . . . but, Thomas, you could insist on a larger percentage of the firm."

He appraised her a long moment and then bent and kissed the nipple of her left breast. "Brilliant little cunt . . . that's what you are. And so I shall."

"What are you two talking about?" It was Judy. She had risen to her feet and was gliding toward them. She hated feeling left out.

Joy surveyed the tall nicely shaped girl with her white skin and her long legs, and she chuckled long and low. "Thomas . . . let's play with Judy."

"Hmmm. What did you have in mind?" Thomas was grinning.

"I'll show you," she said on a low note. She took Judy's hand and brought her to the floor. Gently, easily, she laid her down. "Oh, will I show you . . ."

Greg Laeland parked his car beneath an overhanging tree full with its lush green spring blooms. The top of his convertible Laeland sports job was down, and if he looked up he could see a clear sky bright with its luminous stars, its milky-hued moon. He wasn't looking up and he wasn't contemplating the night's lush beauty and the moon was not romantic.

"What in hell do you want me to do?" he ranted as he ran his hand through his fair hair.

Chrissy Penbroke was not disturbed by his manner. She was even to some extent amused. "I want you to own it." Her tone was quiet but firm.

151

"You want me to own it? Bloody hell, Chrissy . . ."

She cut him off. "I want you to call it yours."

"Will you tell me what difference that would make?" He was astonished, horrified. "Listen to me, Chrissy . . . I am taking you over to Bournemouth tomorrow and you are going to have an abortion!"

"The hell I will!" she snapped. She was angry now for the first time.

"What? What are you saying? You want the baby?" he was incredulous.

Her voice softened. "Of course I do. I want it. It's my baby."

"Chrissy . . . you don't know what you are saying. You are too young."

"Oh? I wasn't too young to conceive and I am not too young to give birth."

"Chrissy . . ." He was shaking his head. "Damn!"

She smiled. "I want you to claim the child, give it a name."

"Oh, no . . . you don't even know if it's mine!"

"Truth is, I don't . . . but you have got the best name and so you will father the child. We can be divorced right after the baby is born."

He took her shoulders. "I am not going to marry you. There is no way . . . *understand that!*" Why did she seem so much older, surer? Have the baby? Mad . . . the poor girl was mad. "No, you had better take a better look at what I am telling you, Greg. I mean for my child to carry the Laeland name. I am a Penbroke and I had always meant to marry well. If you don't agree to this, I shall have to go to your mother." She put a finger to his spluttering lips. "Yes, she would believe me. She already has her suspicions. You see, in the last few weeks, I made certain of that, and Greg . . . if I tell how you seduced poor young innocent me . . . well, she won't think you fit to run your father's Grange. Will she? No, your mother has her doubts about you . . . and then what would happen? She will sign everything over to that sexy stepfather of yours!" The threat was clear in her tone.

He lost control of his temper. Away went his ready sympathy, his understanding. This bitch was threatening his life. He slapped her face hard and then took up her shoulders to give them a vicious shake. "Slut! I'll see you dead first!"

"No, you won't, Greg. You haven't the stomach for that!" She sneered at him as one hand came up to her reddened cheek.

He turned away from her and stared out into the New Forest stretching before him. A herd of deer skipped across the trail, and he had a sudden urge to run with them. What was he going to do? "I am not going to marry you, Chrissy. I am not going to ruin my life just because you want to ruin yours!"

"I'll give you a day to think about it, Greg . . . you can have all of tomorrow, but tomorrow night I want my answer, and remember, Greg, if you don't marry me I shall go to your mother."

"Then you might as well tell her tonight, Chrissy. I am not going to marry you." What was he going to do? Lose the Grange to Thomas? Hell, no! Sophie held the purse strings . . . she could force him to marry Chrissy Penbroke.

"Take me home now, Greg. I'm tired."

"I'll take you back to the cinema. You'll call a cab from there, Chrissy." She wasn't tricking him into her games. He had picked her up at the Southampton Cinema and that was where he would return her.

She laughed, and every now and then as he caught her glancing at him she would peal off into mirth again. He wanted to wring her neck.

Chapter Twelve

Justin raised himself on his elbow and bent over the sleeping form of Holly. There was a frown drawing his dark ginger brows together. His gray eyes softened as

153

the morning light touched her face. Just what was this creature called Holly Winslow?

She stirred and in her drowsiness turned to snuggle against him. She found the hard line of his strong arm, and her lashes fluttered. She saw his face above her and smiled, warmly, openly. She should have felt ashamed, embarrassed, shy, she told herself; instead she felt wonderfully comfortable and absurdly happy. "Hello . . ." she said softly.

He bent to kiss her pert nose. "Hello . . ." His voice too was a delicate sound, a welcome to wakefulness, but as her arms went around him and he felt her naked body press against his, all softer feelings hid in the sudden wave of passion that flooded his veins. His mouth sought her own, his hands went immediately to her breasts, he groaned joyfully to her response. What was she doing to him?

All through the night they had laughed over nothing, made love in feverish swells. No commitments were asked for, none were given, and yet Holly had felt herself giving more than her body to Sir Justin. He moved her in a way no other man had ever done, but rationality invaded here and reminded her that she hadn't known enough men. No, she hadn't, but she knew that at this moment only Sir Justin mattered. At this moment . . . but she would not tender her life to him, submit to his will. She was here with him because she wanted to be, because she was a free woman . . . yes, woman. . . .

He had been taken aback to find Holly an innocent. He was moved to tenderness by her inexperience, but he had been hurt too badly in the past to break down his barrier in the course of a night's lovemaking. He was in no way promising this woman anything. He would make that clear . . . but not now . . . not just now. . . .

Dawn. A drizzle had started, and Sophie stood at her bedroom window looking outside. If the rain continued there would be no lessons this morning. She turned

154

and looked at her husband sleeping in their bed. Sometimes she thought she was married to a stranger. Did she know him? Was he two people? Where had he been last night?

Thomas Martin had come home late. She had been sitting up watching the last program sign off the air, and he had stood in their bedroom doorway with a sneer on his lips. He looked so cruel, and then he was smiling, moving toward her, saying her name.

"Where were you, Thomas?" she interrupted.

"Out with the lads having a pint." He was standing above her, and it occurred to him that he was married to William Laeland's widow. He had always admired Laeland . . . wondered about Sophie in those days. She had such a nice full body . . . none of his girls had ever been plump and so well endowed as Sophie. His hand went down to her nightgown, and he pulled it away from her body so that he was staring at her enormous breasts. His hand dove and grabbed hard. "Did he like to play with you, Sophie? I'll bet he did. . . ."

"Stop it, Thomas . . ." But her command was weakly said.

He smiled to himself as he saw her relax, as he watched her face and saw a trace of passion engage her senses. He pulled the bodice of her nightgown until her breasts were free, and he put his thumb to her nipple. "And what about Greg? When he was a babe, did he suckle at your tits, Sophie?" And then his voice shifted into cruelty. *"Does he still?"*

Her eyes snapped, and she jumped away as though she had been stung, but he was on the bed throwing her onto her back, grabbing roughly at her breasts. "I'm not done yet, Sophie. . . ."

She pulled away again and raised her nightdress back in place.

"Thomas . . . what are you saying? What is wrong with you? How dare you speak of Greg to me in that manner?"

He feigned innocence. "Sophie . . . listen, I am sorry . . . but it just infuriates me to watch him . . . know what he has been doing and then find him doing you up sweet. . . ."

"What do you mean? What has he been doing?" She had a sickly feeling that she already knew.

"Look, Sophie . . . you are the only one who doesn't realize . . . but he is messing around with some of his students. Young Chrissy Penbroke, for one, and it will end with our school in a great deal of trouble!"

She gasped. "You are wrong . . . he wouldn't . . ."

"He has. Look, Sophie, I will tell you something. I don't think Greg is fit to run this school. The way things are set up now, well, that is what may happen in the end. . . ."

"What are you asking me to do?"

"I want more than the ten percent we settled on."

"How much more?"

"For now, I want equal shares. . . ."

She had slept with that statement on her mind. Equal shares! Now in the morning's gray light she would have to come to some kind of a decision. Thomas. He was the man in her bed, he was her husband, but somehow they shared little. He was nothing to William. He could never know what being a Laeland meant . . . and God, she didn't even carry the name any more. How could she have sold out to Thomas? And that was what she had done. She had given up the name of Laeland in the turmoil of Thomas Martin's courtship and in the misery of her loneliness after William's death. But now, now everything was different. Thomas was different. Her world was hazed, and Greg, what was Greg becoming?

She didn't want Thomas to have equal shares, but if Greg wasn't responsible for himself . . . how could he be responsible for Laeland? Thomas had always taken care of Laeland . . . but there was his gambling. Oh, God, what to do?

The land, the house, the funds, the stocks would all still be Greg's property when he reached twenty-five. However, the academy, the breeding business, the boarding business, all that was in her hands . . . all but ten percent which she had signed over to Thomas on the occasion of their wedding. Her shares in the business she had always intended to go to Greg.

What to do? Could Greg be the man Thomas said he was? Was Greg fooling around with his young students? William would be heartbroken to see his academy so tainted. She had heard some talk, but she had just assumed it was one-sided . . . that Greg did not allow it to go farther than a student's crush. But that Chrissy, she had seen Chrissy touch Greg's hand once or twice.

Well, she was just not going to make a decision based on Thomas's accusation. She didn't quite trust Thomas enough to do that. She would, however, have a talk with Greg. He would not like it, but it was necessary. She would give her son the opportunity to defend himself.

Mustafa's windowshade was drawn down, but he could see through his driver's windshield that they had approached the Laeland drive. He thought of Delia. She stood over him, her hands on her hips in that way she had, and she accused, "You drove your child to do this. She is English and you want her to adopt a foreign way of life. I couldn't . . . why should she? Mustafa . . . you are breaking my heart."

He closed his eyes. If Delia were here, this would never have happened. She was dead, though . . . dead, and all he had left of her was Holly. He wanted Holly to go back with him to Baghdad and bear him grandchildren. It was his dream. There too he was committed. His pride was involved. She, his only daughter, had challenged him, and she must be answered! He would see her safely wedded to Wahid and returned to Iraq with him.

Hassan's dark eyes moved sadly from his father's face to Wahid's set mouth. He could see no difference between the two men. They came from different generations, but both had a goal in mind that would forever kill his Holly's wild spirit. And he? He was standing by and allowing, even making, this thing happen.

Conflicting emotions almost strangled all logical thought. He glanced at the nervous little man beside him, an Englishman hired at some cost to perform the ceremony. Mustafa wanted Holly married in England to Wahid and then again in Iraq. He wanted the marriage legal in Holly's eyes. The English official would wait in the car until he was called for.

In the front seat with their driver—one of their own men carefully selected for the morning's work—sat the Kabadhai. After Holly's lover witnessed her marriage to Wahid, he would be ushered away to a lonely spot and the Kabadhai would end Sir Justin's life without killing him. The punishment was prescribed by tradition. Mustafa wanted in his towering wrath to have the Englishman castrated.

Hassan closed his eyes. Was it all happening? Was this England? Was this 1979? Was all this really happening? Stop! Stop! He wanted it to stop . . . but he was Mustafa's son, and there was family honor involved.

Holly laughed and pulled at the blue silk pajama top Justin had clasped in his hands. He grinned wide as he yanked and watched her come away from her covers. Stunning. She took his breath away.

"Give over, do, Justin . . . you have the bottoms on after all . . ."

"I'll make a deal with you," he bantered. It was good to wake up happy.

"A deal?" she asked warily, still holding a piece of the prize.

"Hmmm. Since it's raining and you don't have to report to lessons, spend the day with me."

"Done," she answered readily and felt the top in question float onto her naked body. "What's more . . . while you are showering, I shall go prepare you some tea and orange juice. I'm good at that." She was buttoning up, moving across the room.

He reached out and held her arm a moment. "It is amazing the assortment of good qualities I am finding out about you. . . ." His voice was a low seductive tone.

158

"Ah, for that I might even butter you a piece of toast!" she announced.

"Right, then," he responded. "And for lunch I mean to drive you over to Burley . . . there is a marvelous little teahouse there. . . ." His voice trailed off as he turned on the shower.

Holly stopped dead. She stood facing the front door as it opened in the Kabadhai's hand, and she would have screamed but for the fact that the Kabadhai stood aside and in walked Mustafa.

"Baba!" He was her father. She loved him. But she was not pleased to see him, and her voice expressed this.

Mustafa closed his eyes a moment. It was true. Somewhere in his heart a hope died. Gone. His little girl was gone, and instead here stood a brazen woman. Brazen . . . hadn't his own dear beloved looked just so when he possessed her? No. This was something he could never forgive! Here was his child, her childhood over. He would consign her to Wahid and think of this no more after today. "Here, Khalda . . . at once!" He called her to heel, to order, to a sense of what was due to him as her father.

Instinct sent her toward him. Independence, new, determined, and strong, kept her stock still. Shame and guilt swept over her, rebellion broke those forces down. Defiantly she glared at him. She had chosen to live her own life, not his. She might make mistakes, but they would be her own . . . *and then she saw the Kabadhai.*

It was a word known to her, and she was quick to recognize the tall, athletic man in a suit that ill fitted his hulking body for what he was. She was quick to note that Wahid was there beside Hassan. What did this mean? A Kabadhai? A strong man? Did they mean to have her whipped? What?

"Baba . . ." Her hand moved toward the Kabadhai. "What does this mean?"

Hassan took a step toward her. "Holly . . ." He could say no more.

"You will be married to Wahid. Here and now," snapped her father. "No words can speak of my shame. No words can speak of my . . . heartache . . . that you, my Khalda, should be the cause of my pain."

She was moved by his pain, but marry Wahid here and now was something she would not do. She screamed and lunged for the kitchen counter, and when she turned to meet Hassan she had a long carving knife in her hand. *"Do not touch me!"*

"It was pointed not at him but to her own heart, and her eyes glared her determination.

Hassan felt his heart contract, and his eyes glazed as he met her glance. There was no doubt what she was thinking. Even so, he pursued, "Holly . . . try to understand. Think about what you have done. Even for an English daughter, is it right to go off without a word, is it right to leave your father to worry about you? Are you not ashamed?"

"I am ashamed that my father had to suffer, but he gave me no choice. Hassan . . . I am not an animal. I am a human being first, before anything else. I am a human being, I think, I feel . . . and you are asking me to submit like a slave. I won't, can't . . ."

"Holly . . . Holly . . . look . . . here is Wahid, who loves you still. He does us great honor by wanting you to marry him in the face of all this."

She raged up at him. Nothing she had said had made him see. If Hassan wouldn't see, how would her father? It was useless.

"I will not don the *aba*. I will not crumble before all of you and go humbly on Wahid's arm. How can you think that I would?"

"Enough!" It was an anguished cry from her father. He was angry, he was in pain, and he was moved to hiss, "Enough words, Hassan." He indicated with a quick movement of his head that he wished the Kabadhai to begin.

Sir Justin stepped out of his shower and was drying his bright-ginger hair vigorously with a towel when a sound in the front room stopped him. He could hear some altercation proceeding, and a frown descended over his handsome face. What was this? He slipped on a pair of clean jeans and with nothing else on moved toward the scene in his living room.

The Kabadhai heard him and leaned into the wall as Justin came forward. Justin was brought up short as he saw Mustafa and Wahid facing him and Hassan standing between himself and Holly. There wasn't any time for questions, for at that moment the Kabadhai came from behind.

Everything flashed before Holly's blurred vision in the streaking swiftness of a moment. Before she could think, before she could act or cry out, the Kabadhai was on Justin. Her hand flew to her mouth, her eyes opened wide with her terror, not for herself but for Justin. Horror engulfed her. What had she done? What was going to come out of this? It was her fault that Justin was now in this danger. She knew what Moslem beliefs were. She knew the many stories of what happened to lovers of Moslem daughters . . . she knew!

Justin felt someone at his back and acted instinctively in the mode he had been taught many years ago. He had been skillfully trained in the martial arts and held a first-degree black belt. He knew well enough how to protect himself and had on more than one occasion been called upon to do so. His body moved with agility and speed. His elbow went back sharply and caught the Kabadhai in the ribs; his doubled fists swung together as one block and landed heavily on the Kabadhai's head. Justin stepped back easily into a cat stance, his fists poised in perfect harmony with his own body and ready to take on his winded opponent.

The Kabadhai immediately recognized his adversary as one to be respected. No easy target here. Out came his knife, a long, curved, and deadly-looking blade. He whipped it through the air and smiled as he regained his breath. He said nothing as he moved, whipping the blade and smiling.

Justin took the offense by suddenly jabbing with his

fist, checking as the Kabadhai lunged forward and faking him out by then bringing up the unexpected round kick. It threw the man off balance, and while he was in that position Justin came up quickly with yet another kick to the man's chest. The Kabadhai bent in half, and Justin was on him, chopping at the man's wrist. The knife went thumping to the carpet floor, but before Justin could take it up Hassan had it in hand.

Holly went to her brother at once and held his arm. "Hassan, if you love me . . . only you can stop this: Hassan . . . it is wrong. So wrong. It is not his fault . . . I ran away on my own . . . he had nothing to do with it. Stop this, Hassan . . . don't let them ruin my life . . ."

She was breaking his heart. Hassan felt a wealth of emotion tear at his guts as he watched the Englishman and the Moslem strongman still in battle. He looked toward his father, who stood wavering. Mustafa no longer looked so determined. He was caught in a bind. He came from an age that demanded this, but somewhere there was Delia chiding, Delia crying. Tears welled over in Mustafa's eyes, because he heard Delia in Holly's voice.

Wahid knew only that this big strapping English stud had to be put into the ground. The Englishman had debased his intended bride. He wanted this woman with her gold hair and her aqua eyes. Her beauty had always haunted him, but first he needed his ounce of blood. . . .

The Kabadhai was not faring well. Sir Justin's training in the martial arts was quickly bringing the large Moslem down. Wahid saw this, and with a shout of rage he brought out a gun and swung it into play.

Holly screamed and ran toward Wahid. Hassan cursed silently and put away the knife to take chase. Simultaneously Sir Justin went to push Holly out of harm's way. It served to bring him closer to the gun and closer to Wahid. Again the use of that leg and the skilled foot. It came up and out with a sharp deft movement, and the gun went flying toward Hassan.

Wahid dove at Sir Justin and found himself no

match. Even in his fury, he was quickly, easily sent to the ground, where he remained for the moment, winded. Sir Justin spun around, waiting for more.

Hassan brought up the gun and looked at it and then at Justin, keeping himself a safe distance back. "That is, I think, quite enough." His voice was low, dangerously low.

The Kabadhai was getting to his knees, shaking his head, attempting to bring things into proper focus. Hassan addressed him.

"You . . . go into the bedroom . . . bring a shirt for this devil. Holly . . . you will get dressed and reappear here immediately . . . if you care about your Englishman's life."

He waited for his orders to be obeyed before he looked at Sir Justin full and answered Sir Justin's question.

"Why? You ask why?" He shook his head. "Holly was to marry the man you have rendered unconscious." He could see Wahid moving with a groan and sighed some relief. "She is daughter to Mustafa el Zahour, she is my half sister. Does that answer your question?"

Sir Justin's jaw dropped. Of course . . . this answered many of his questions. Zahour? He looked at Mustafa. Was he not on a committee that dealt with the oil prices? Was he not a part of that organization? Not now, couldn't think of that now. "Well, then . . . what do you plan now?"

Holly had reappeared in the blue blouse and blue print skirt she had worn the night before. She was slipping into her sandals. Her aqua eyes were wide with apprehension. Her movements were wary.

"He plans to marry me to Wahid," she snapped. "Against my will."

Wahid had risen. "No . . . your will is no longer the issue, my beautiful Khalda. Now, *I* must be begged for the honor." He was in a mad rage.

Mustafa closed his eyes. He had been afraid of this. Wahid's pride had been offended more than he could bear. He was not surprised.

163

"Holly, you will beg Wahid's forgiveness!"

"No. I will not." Her voice was quiet.

Dangerous! thought Hassan. Holly did not realize what she was doing. She did not realize she was pushing their father over the edge. She could not see that she was calling for the ultimate punishment to herself. That she was putting their family name on the line, and that in the end a cleansing of that name would mean her death as well as that of her lover! Hassan stood back in some horror, for he saw all this. He saw the thought of that ultimate punishment flicker across his father's face. He saw the anguish of the sudden dawning hit Mustafa fully, and it rocked him into action.

"No, Father . . . pride and honor are intangible things. This is the daughter of your Delia . . . she is your flesh, your blood, but she is also Delia's. You have no right to what you are thinking."

"She gives me no choice," raged Mustafa.

Hassan turned to her. "She refuses to beg Wahid's pardon. She refuses to marry him." He shook his head. "But she will not refuse to beg his pardon if her Englishman's life is forfeit for her refusal."

"Enough!" This from Wahid. "No woman must be threatened in such a manner to marry me. I have seen enough . . . I have heard enough." He gave them his back and moved to the window. "Mustafa . . . honor calls for her death as well as his."

There, the words had been spoken! Hassan felt his heart wrenched from his body. No more. He was taking matters in his own hands! He looked Sir Justin over. The Kabadhai had flung Sir Justin's shirt at him, and the Englishman had carefully put it on. He met Hassan's dark eyes and felt a flash of fear for Holly. He called to her softly.

"Come here, Holly . . ."

Sir Justin's voice was an anchor in treacherous waters. There was her father, a stranger, a man who would have her dead rather than happy. There was Hassan. What did he intend for her? The same? She ran into Sir Justin's arms.

Her father's fist came down on the table beside him. "Look how she flaunts her behavior. What . . . is this *my daughter?*"

Hassan spoke quietly, and it was a threatening sound. "All will be righted soon." He turned to Sir Justin. "You will save not only your own life but that of my sister by agreeing to give her your name and therefore your protection."

"No." It was Holly. "You can't do that . . . he is a British subject."

"He is that. He could also be a dead British subject," said her brother drily.

"Hassan . . . I don't want to marry him . . . I have only just begun to live . . ."

"Enough, Holly! You will marry him," said Hassan.

Sir Justin scoffed, "It takes more than a pistol to perform a wedding."

"The minister we have obtained has been paid well . . . he awaits our pleasure outside in our limo," said Hassan.

"And he will perform no wedding against our will!" snapped Sir Justin. Last night with Holly had been a paradise of sensation, but he didn't mean to get trapped in this manner. It was ludicrous. This whole scene had taken on the aspect of a French farce.

Holly went thoughtful. Here was a way out. She could marry Sir Justin and be free of her Moslem world. Quietly they could divorce . . . ? Oddly enough this brought a sadness to her eyes, to her soul. She wanted her freedom. She couldn't bear to be tied to a man after all this . . . but marriage was a thing she had dreamed of doing only once.

"Make no mistake, Laeland. He will do as I want," growled Hassan between gritted teeth. He was going against his father's will. Mustafa had retired to a chair. He was sitting stiffly, and his thoughts were unreadable. "Have you no idea that I am now a desperate man? I am flaunting my father's orders . . . I am losing a lifelong friend in Wahid . . ." He shook his head. "You will do as I say. If you do not, you bring

165

about not only your own death, but that of my sister, and as the minister will be a witness, he too will be eliminated. You have no choice."

Sir Justin's face was grim. He was in a bind. There were reasons why he would not be able to immediately have the marriage annulled, but it was a possibility for the future . . . if they lived apart. This is what first came to mind, and then he saw Holly's face, and he was shaken with conflicting emotions. "As you say : . . it would appear that I have no choice."

Part Three

Chapter One

It was over. Had it really all happened? Was the grave-faced man standing apart from her actually her husband? Was her father really gone? Hassan. Would she ever forget the awful, the haggard look in Hassan's black eyes? They were gone. Mustafa, her father, Hassan, her brother, were gone. They had left without a backward glance, without a word. . . .

Her heart ached and her mind rebelled in pain. What now? She discovered Justin's gray eyes, and gone was the twinkle that had stroked her last night and then again in their early waking hours. He was filled with irritation. She started to speak to him, but he stopped her with a hand movement and quick, clipped, sarcasm.

"So the little story you told me was only half a lie? You weren't running from your Moslem lover . . . but from your family. It explains some things. . . ."

"And if I had told you the truth? Would you have believed?" she bit back at him.

"That is not the point, is it? You lied to me . . . all this time you have been lying to me. I introduced you to my aunt as Holly Winslow . . . you allowed it. You never thought to warn me that I might be putting myself, my family, in some danger!" He was at the moment without compassion for her predicament.

Her lashes dropped to her cheeks and her voice was scarcely audible. "I . . . I did not think . . ."

"No, you did not indeed!" He paced in some agitation, and then he rounded on her. "Or did you, Holly . . . last

167

night . . . when you came to me . . . did you have this end in mind?" His dealings with the fair sex had aroused his suspicions again.

She bristled at once. "Damm it, Justin Laeland! Haven't I had enough for one morning? Look here . . . I didn't marry you because I wanted to. Marriage is not something I want just now. I was subject to my father's will this morning . . . as you were." She turned away from his dark-gray eyes and looked outside. Everything looked dismal, and her voice dropped again. She felt like a beaten child. "I don't mean to hold you to this marriage . . . nor do I expect you to hold me to it. I shall file for divorce."

He moved to her and took her shoulders in his hands, but pushed her away almost immediately. Why he couldn't say. His hand ran through his bright-ginger hair. "Damm it, Holly . . . I wish you could, but the sorry truth is that you can't . . . not just now."

His reaction pinched her more than she thought possible, but her chin was up. "Why not?"

"Because I am secluded here in the country with . . . with good reason. I need my privacy just now. If you go filing for divorce you will bring down the media around our necks, and I can't have that just now."

She sank into herself. The media? She couldn't have that either. What would her father do? Would he come after her again? No, she couldn't take that chance. Somehow she would have to arrange a divorce in secret. "What, then?" her voice dropped with her spirit.

He frowned. "You will go on at Sophie's just as you have done. There will be no mention of our . . . er . . . marriage. In a few months' time we will have the marriage annulled. We both have ample cause."

She thought this over and looked full at his rugged handsome face. He had handled himself well this morning. He had fought the Kabadhai, he had fought Wahid . . .

"And how shall we go on? How do we behave?"

"As we have done." His voice had softened. What was she asking?

"Then we are free to see other people . . . do as we wish?" she pursued.

He was caught off-guard. He had not expected this. Was she asking for herself? Was she curious about his seeing other women? Was there another man she was interested in? The memory of Holly in his arms teased him. He didn't want to think of her with anyone else. She had been a virgin . . . his pretty little virgin . . . but hell, he wasn't tying himself to a woman in this jest of a marriage!

"Of course," he answered curtly.

"Right, then," she answered and started for the front door.

"Where in hell are you going?" he thundered after her. He wasn't done yet . . . was he?

"Home," she answered. It occurred to her that the lovely plans they had made for the day were now smashed to smithereens.

He wanted to stop her. A rush of absurdly illogical feelings had shaken him. He curbed them. He looked out the window to note with a frown that it was still raining.

"You are not going to walk through the woods in the rain. You'll get soaked through." His tone was full of harsh reproof.

"I want to." She was already at the door.

He was on her immediately. Her arm, slender and limp, was in his bold hand, and the touch sent a shiver of anticipation through him. Her body, soft and pliable, braced against him, and he felt a sudden deluge of irrational hunger sweep through him. He curtailed this and spoke crisply.

"Then soak yourself in your bath. I am driving you . . . home."

Chrissy had not gone to classes. Her mother was off for a day of social functions and wouldn't notice. Her father was away on business. She decided after some deliberation to make it over to Laeland Grange. The rain was subsiding into a drizzle when she arrived, but

169

she ducked into the main barn in hopes of seeing Greg. He wasn't about.

Joy was tacking up Drifter, the gelding she normally hacked out, and saw Chrissy's entrance. They had often taken hacks out together on the New Forest trails, and she waved a greeting.

Chrissy went to her at once. She liked Joy. The older girl was sophisticated fun. Yes, if anyone could help her with her problems, it would be Joy. She so needed someone to talk to, for her plans for Greg were beginning to frighten her.

"Joy . . . oh, I am so glad you are here today."

Joy looked up. "What are you doing out of school, Chrissy?" she was teasing amicably.

"Never mind that. Joy . . . I need to talk to you . . . but will you promise to keep what I tell you a secret?"

Joy considered the teenager a moment. Chrissy was a Penbroke. She had tolerated the girl's confidences before because there was always the chance something might prove to be useful. She was fully aware that Greg and Chrissy had been messing around. She also knew that Chrissy had a taste for variety in her quickly growing list of male friends. What could the girl want to tell her that she didn't already know?

She answered sweetly, "Of course, love," and touched the girl's cheek gently.

"Right, then. . . . Will you bank me today, Joy? I haven't any cash on me."

"No sweat, little girl. Go tack up a horse. I think the rain has pretty well subsided for the day. I'll go pay your way," said Joy, looking after her thoughtfully.

Armed with an umbrella and newly outfitted in jeans and a bright-yellow rain slicker, Holly trudged through the woods to the main country road toward Brockenhurst. She had a few things she needed to buy in the way of groceries, and besides, she told herself, she needed to get out and think clearly.

Everything at the Grange seemed to be running fairly smoothly. She had seen Chrissy Penbroke riding

170

off with the same oriental girl she had seen in Justin's arms last night. Odd, that. She had never asked him to explain . . . why should he? He was free and so was she. Even now. They were married, but not really. They had been forced to it.

The sweet thought of his hands on her body intruded at this point. Brutally she whipped the memory away. Wondrously did his voice in her ears come to mind. Irritably she brushed it aside. Over. That was something that was gone. It was relegated to the past. She had only the future to move into. . . .

Greg recalled his mother's stern lecture that morning. She meant to sign over a total of fifty percent to Thomas Martin if he did not prove his worth to her. He drained off his ale and called for another.

"Sorry, lad . . . it's close onto two o'clock, and you know I can't be serving then."

But Greg was in no mood to contend with the law. "Have to serve me . . . I'm a customer," he said.

"Off wit' ye, Greg . . . don't be giving me no trouble, now," said the proprietor with a shake of his head. Poor lad. His mother held the strings too tightly, he thought. It would be the lad's ruin in the end.

"Nowhere to go, Ed," begged Greg pitifully. "It's raining . . . no lessons today . . ."

"Then see to the barn. There is bound to be something they'll be wanting ye to do up there by now. So off wit' ye."

"You're a cruel man, Ed," said Greg, getting uncertainly to his feet. He had downed more than a few ales. He blinked as he made for the front door of the pub, and as he fell out of the portal and landed in Holly's arms, he repeated, "A cruel man he is . . ." Then he smiled up at her startled face. "Holly . . . *you* won't feed me to the dogs, will you?"

She attempted to help him into steadiness. "No." She said soothingly, "now what kind of a question is that?" She looked around for his car and found it no great distance from where they stood. She took his arm and led him to it, opened the passenger's door and plopped him in.

She stood a moment and sighed over him. He was in no fit condition to drive. She had only a beginner's knowledge of it herself. Hassan had given her lessons until her father had put a stop to it. It was a manual stick shift.

She got into the driver's seat and appraised the instruments. At least they were all similar to what she had learned on. It was four speed, and she had learned on a five-speed . . . but never mind. She shifted into neutral, started up the engine, and caughed the car onto the country road.

"No . . ." Greg cried. "Not home . . . don't take me home."

"Where, then?" She shifted into second gear and then into third, ground the gears but finally found the correct groove.

"Anywhere . . . but not home. Must see that . . ."

She could see a drive into the forest itself. It would end in a square parking lot for tourists. She turned the car onto the gravel drive and eased it to a stop. The parking lot was empty. She sighed but felt a sense of accomplishment. She hadn't done the shopping she had come to town to do, but never mind; she had driven a car.

"Do you want to talk?" she asked gently.

He looked at her. His hand reached out and took hers, and suddenly he was putting it feverishly to his lips. "You are so beautiful, Holly . . ."

"Stop it, Greg. You are just drunk, you know."

He moved in closer, tried to take her in his arms. "Let me, Holly, let me . . ."

She pushed him away and started to get out of the car. "See you, Greg."

"No . . . I'm sorry . . . Holly . . . stay." He halted her with the plea in his eyes as well as his voice.

"Okay, we'll start again. Want to talk?"

"It's m'mother . . . she doesn't think I'm fit to run the Grange!" he blurted out.

She leveled a look at him. "You mean you want full control of the Grange now and she wants you to wait?"

He laughed bitterly. "I wouldn't mind that. . . . No, she wants to give that two-timing husband of hers equal shares with me!"

"But . . . but the Grange is your inheritance from your father, isn't it?"

"Not the academy . . . not the business . . . only the lands," he moaned.

"Well then, Greg . . . getting drunk on a rainy afternoon proves your worth, doesn't it? I mean, really, Greg, what better way to show your mother just what her decision should be?" Her tone drew him up.

He stared at her a moment, and then he dropped his head into his hands. "Oh, God, Holly, I've made a mess of it. . . ."

"Yes, you certainly have, but not so that it can't be righted. Shall I take your life in my hands and drive you over to Southampton?"

"Why?"

"My driving may help to clear your head, and if it doesn't, its a large enough town . . . we should be able to find a coffee shop where no one knows you." She was smiling brightly.

He eyed her for a long moment and felt tempted to tell her about Chrissy Penbroke. Holly was a good friend. She might know just what he should do. Then again, she might be disgusted with him, and right now he needed her ready sympathy.

"Right, then, girl . . . drive on."

Dusk had settled on the Grange. Jim Jakes had spent most of his afternoon there tubeworming some of the horses, floating the teeth of others, checking out some of the broodmares for infections. He sighed now and stretched his long arms into the air. He rubbed his full head of yellow hair and then rolled down the sleeves of his blue shirt and slipped a heavy dark-blue sweater over his head.

"Well, Sophie . . . I think you had better start teasing

173

both Stockings and Dolly . . . getting them ready for the mating," he said as he moved toward the parking lot.

"Yes, I'll have Thomas see to it tomorrow." She was following his gaze, watching him as he looked up toward Holly's flat. There was a light on, and they could just make out Holly's form as she moved across her room.

Jim Jakes's thoughts flickered in his eyes, and Sophie smiled benignly. "Why don't you ask her to dinner? I'm sure it must be lonely for her eating by herself up there."

He turned and looked Sophie full in the face. "Bless you, Sophie, that is a first-rate notion!"

Sir Justin pushed away his scribbling and slammed down the phone. His man at his plant in Liverpool had fed some figures into the computer for him, but they had not turned out as he expected them to. Nothing had gone right today!

He stood up and ran his hands through his thick waves of hair. Holly, Holly, Holly! Damm it to bloody hell, why couldn't he get her out of his head? Damn that blasted marriage ceremony . . . damn the guilt he felt for the way he had treated her . . .

What had she said? Oh yes, she didn't want to be tied down to a marriage. Swell, neither did he. She wanted to be free to see other people. Sure, so did he . . . but last night when he had held her in his arms, touched her body, caressed her soul? No . . . that was last night, and now . . . now she was at her own flat, doing her own thing.

He stomped off, taking the stairs to the garage above two at a time. His man Cal had been gone these last few days on a holiday, and he thought of his driver fleetingly as he glanced past his assortment of motor vehicles. And then he stopped. Maybe he would just drive over and take Holly out to dinner.

He pressed a button, and his garage door glided upward. He took up his dark-blue blazer and slipped it on over the ivory-colored turtle-necked sweater he was wearing. He got into his little red sports job and started the engine. What are you doing? he asked himself. Come on, this isn't like you . . . forget the bird. . . . Don't want to. Want to see her . . . want to talk to her . . . want to . . . That's trouble, Justin, nothing but A-1 trouble! . . . Is it? The bird is my wife. . . . Like hell she is! No contrived ceremony can make a married man out of me! . . . Right, then, so where are you going? Justin, what are you doing?

He backed his car out of his garage with a gust of speed and took the drive with purpose toward the Grange. The question would not die. What are you going to do, Justin? What? What? What?

Hell! I'm going to go play with a little fire . . . that's what!

Chapter Two

Jim Jakes's blue eyes had followed Holly's movements in the past weeks as often as they could. He was drawn to her. His conversations strengthened the growing conviction that here was a woman worthy of his pursuit. She was more than just beautiful, she was more than graceful and feminine. He sensed in her the touch of aristocracy, and this interested him.

He heard her light footsteps as she descended the stairs and opened her door wide. His blue eyes smiled at her. She was casually dressed in jeans and a soft white cotton knit top. Her fragrance was light, inviting. His voice responded to the vision of her by dropping to a warm, "Hello, Holly . . ."

"Why, Dr. Jakes . . ."

"Jim . . . please, after all, I feel no compunction about calling you by your given name."

She smiled. "Come in."

"No, you come out," he returned with a grin. "I am half starved, and they are serving up a sumptuous hot meat pie over at the King's Head tonight. Would you join me?"

Holly had only just left Greg moments ago. She never had gotten her groceries. She put her hands together gleefully. "My hero! You cannot imagine what I was just about to stuff my face with . . . crackers and cereal."

"Ugh . . . horror of horrors. Come along, then!" he said and laughed.

"I certainly will." She reached behind her to the wall rack where her denim jacket hung and allowed him to hold it for her while she slipped it on. A moment later they were moving toward his mustard-colored Sirocco, and it occurred to her fleetingly that this was a fairly expensive car for a young country vet to own. However, this was soon forgotten, as he began to entertain her with quick and flowing conversation.

Lynn Patterson came out of the boarders' barn with her bridle slung over her arm and watched a moment as Holly drove off with the good doctor. She smiled to herself. She was glad to see Holly finally going out with someone. She dropped her bridle onto the back seat of her cream-colored Jaguar. Her boots were covered with mud, and she pulled a towel out to wipe them down, remembered that she still had her saddle to get, sighed heavily, and returned to the barn. When next she appeared in the parking lot she opened her soft brown eyes wide to note that Sir Justin was there and making his way to Holly's door.

"Sir Justin," she called after him. They had met on several occasions both at dinner parties of Sophie's and then with her husband, who had done business with Sir Justin from time to time.

"Holly's gone out," she said on a lower note as he turned to smile at her.

Sir Justin liked Lynn Patterson. She fit his design of what a wife should be. Pretty, faithful, active, and kind. A good wife, a good mother. Yes, she was a rarity, and he liked her. "Here, Lynn, let me take that," he said, reaching for her saddle.

She tried to resist. "Don't be silly . . ." But he had it already out of her arms and was depositing it in the back seat of her Jaguar.

She sighed. "Thanks, Justin . . . I thought I had better take it home and oil it over. Nothing else to do with Tracy always off with her friends these days and Mark going up to Liverpool."

What was this? Was there a trace of frustration in Lynn's dark eyes? Were things going badly for her at home? He liked both Mark and Lynn and hoped not.

"Getting bored with the English countryside, Lynn?"

"Hmmm. Bored. I've been thinking about chucking it all after the show and hopping a plane to Paradise Island, but Mark says he can't get the time."

"Well, you just keep pressing him, maybe he'll find the time." Justin grinned. "Now, what were you telling me about Holly?"

"Holly? Oh yes . . . she isn't home." Lynn hesitated for a fraction of a moment. Was Justin interested in Holly? Was that a good thing? He had quite a reputation with women . . . and Holly was such an innocent. She decided to spill the beans. "I saw her go off with that nice Jim Jakes."

"Did you? Long ago?"

"No . . . only a few moments before you arrived." She sighed again and got into the driver's seat. "Well . . . gotta run. Mark will want me to help him with his packing."

He waved her off and stood a long moment afterward. Holly and Jakes? He had seen Jakes on several occasions and did not like the man. They were both about the same age, and ruefully he thought that Jakes was no doubt a charmer with that yellow hair and his quiet style. So Holly was already exercising her right to see other men?

What was happening to him? Damm it all to hell! Dammit it all to bloody hell! And then he was storming

177

to his car and taking it down the drive. What was good for his beauteous little goose was going to be just as good for the gander!

Jim Jakes took Holly's hand in both of his. Between them on the table was his tankard of dark warm ale, half finished, and her glass of gin and tonic, barely touched. He was contemplating her blue eyes, and she was beginning to blush. He released a sudden laugh and touched her cheek.

"Just how old are you, Holly Winslow?"

She winced. Winslow? Laeland, Zahour, just what was her name?

She answered quietly, "I shall turn twenty . . . soon. Why?"

"Because you blush like a babe. It is most becoming."

She liked him, but he was moving in on her too quickly, and she wasn't ready for that, not now, not with Justin's touch still burning through her memory.

"I thank you, sir, but now I really do think you had better see me home. I have an early lesson to give tomorrow morning, and before that I want to do some work with Ulysses and Tinker. You know, the show is so very near, and they both still need work."

She was holding him at bay. He could sense it. Very well, he wouldn't press her, not just now. He pulled out the round table so that she could slip out, and then he was helping her into her jacket. "Whatever the lady wishes . . ." His voice was low and full of promise as he spoke into her ear.

Justin had taken himself to Lyndhurst, parked his car in the public lot, walked through the narrow alleyway to the main street, rounded a corner, passed the closed teahouse, and entered the pub. There he managed to imbibe no less than six mugs of dark ale, beat nearly every chap in the place at darts, find a pretty girl and snuggle her on his lap while he exchanged wisecracks with his newfound friends. It didn't help.

His mind itched with nagging questions. Where was she now? What was she doing? What was Jim Jakes

178

doing with her? Would she have Jakes up to her flat? Would she? Would she?

All he knew was that he had to get back to the Grange and see for himself. What if Jakes was with her? What then? Damn, I'll break his neck!

He took the A337 south to Brockenhurst. It was a ride of no more than eight minutes, he made it in four flat out. There was no controlling the indefinable thing that moved him. He only knew he was going to find her . . . find her and get her to himself. Hell, this was their wedding night!

Jim Jakes waited at Holly's back as she unlocked her door. His arms went up to the building walls on either side of her so that she was fenced in. She turned to find him hovering over her, close, so close, and his blue eyes were ablaze with something she had not seen in him before. Suddenly she was again reminded of someone . . . but who? There was no time for reflection; his voice was soft, low, and urgent as he bent to kiss her lips.

"Holly . . . ?"

She lifted her face and allowed him his kiss. She felt his passion mount as he pressed himself against her. Fireworks? No. Bells? No. Was she warming as she had done last night? No. Well, maybe the mood was wrong . . . maybe she was tired. Or maybe you are thinking of Sir Justin, she chided herself.

Gently she pulled away. "Goodnight, Jim. I enjoyed the evening very much."

So, then, she was a lady. She wasn't giving more of herself tonight, eh? He took her dismissal in stride. "Goodnight, pretty girl. Shall I see you tomorrow?"

"Maybe. Call . . ." She was letting herself in, closing the door.

He stood a moment and collected his thoughts. All night he had plied her with questions about herself, but she had skimmed them somehow in her own inimitable way. In the end they had talked about his growing practice, about her work with her students, her work with the black gelding, Tinker. Right, then, it was just as well she had dismissed him, for he had an appointment at his cottage back at the edge of Brockenhurst, and it was an appointment he couldn't miss.

Justin saw the headlights coming on as he started to turn onto the Grange drive. He pulled over and shut down his own lights as he waited for the Sirocco to pass. His brow went up. Going so soon, Jakes? Maybe it wasn't so soon. Maybe they had spent all this time up in her flat.

He gunned the engine and power shifted into fourth gear, taking the long winding drive at a dangerous speed. Once close to the parking lot, he downshifted and eased up on the gas pedal to reduce the noise of his entrance. He held his liquor well, but even so he was not all that clearheaded as he went to her door and began pounding.

Holly had already changed into her white nightgown. It was both a comfortable garment and a sheer one. Quickly she picked up a white satin robe and shrugged herself into it as she took the steps to the door below and opened it to find Justin in outraged fury standing before her. Her aqua eyes opened wide at his expression and state of disarray.

He sneered. "Well, well . . . look at you, sunshine . . ." He moved in on her.

She stepped backward and found herself against the wall.

"Justin . . . what are you doing here?"

"Checking up on my bride. Where have you been, Holly . . . or have you been here all along?" He stroked her long glowing amber-shaded hair.

"I have been out with Jim Jakes and just came home a little while ago." She didn't have to answer to him. Why was she answering to him?

"Did he kiss you goodnight?" He was quick to see the blush, quick to see the confusion in her eyes, and his rage picked up momentum. "Oh ho! Didn't you tell him you are a married woman? Didn't you tell him you are another man's bride?" He took up her shoulders and

180

brought her to him savagely. "What, Holly, did you spend our wedding night in Jim Jakes's bed?" The thought frenzied him, and he shook her hard. "Did you?"

"Stop it, Justin!" She yanked out of his hold and started for the stairs.

She hadn't answered him. It was driving him mad with jealousy, and he found himself chasing after her to finally tackle her on the sofa-bed she had opened earlier for herself. She was struggling beneath him, and when she heard the sudden plea in his voice she stopped to look at him full.

"Answer me, Holly . . . what has my little virgin done?"

"Oh, Justin . . . you have no right. You gave it away this morning. You said we were both free . . . and see . . . I ask *you* no questions."

"Holly . . ." It was an anguished growl.

"He kissed me goodnight, Justin . . . nothing more. He kissed me goodnight." She sighed at her own weakness. She hadn't meant to tell him anything. "He took me to dinner . . . we were in Brockenhurst the whole evening."

His voice when it came was charged, low and full with intensity, as his lips brushed her ears.

"And was his kiss like mine, Holly? Did you want him as you wanted me last night? Did he make you feel, Holly?" His mouth sought and set hers to burning as he pressed her to his hard lean body.

Oh, God, why were her hands clinging to him so desperately? Why was she arching to his touch? Why was her blood on fire? What was it about him that moved her, melted her? But as these questions loomed in her mind, she felt his fingers manipulating her pleasure points, and she was surrendering. . . .

"Justin . . . this is no good . . ."

His deft bold hands pulled away her nightgown and exposed her exquisite breasts. He groaned with his feverish delight and teased her nipples into pertness.

"Ah, sunshine . . ."

"Stop, Justin . . . you must stop . . ."

"Why? Why must I stop?" His lips flowed tenderly, deliciously, over her neck.

She pulled sharply out of his sweet hold and began to crawl away on the bed. In a moment his hands had slid over her legs and he drew her back under him. He was kissing her neck, her shoulders, whispering enchantment; bringing her to overwhelming passion as his hand stroked her derrière with an expertise that drew a groan from her reluctant lips.

He smiled triumphantly. "You don't want me to stop, Holly . . . you want me to . . . oh, love . . ."

"No . . . this isn't enough . . ." Her mind fought her body. "Justin . . . you can't wipe away what happened this morning . . . with this . . ." Her breathing came in spurts, her words in hesitant gasps.

He stopped abruptly and looked down into her face. She was lovely, and there was such innocence in her wide aqua eyes. He released a heavy sigh. "Holly . . . if you weren't my wife . . ." He smiled ruefully. "If you were the girl I held in my arms last night . . . again at dawn this morning . . . wouldn't you be mine right now?"

"But I am your wife . . . not by your or my choice, and that *does* set us apart." She now pulled free of him and took the sheets around herself. "I have to make a life for myself, Justin, and I just don't want you popping in and out of it."

"So? You want me to leave on our wedding night?" He couldn't give in that easily, and hell, why was he continually referring to their state of matrimony? It was something he wanted to forget.

She smiled wanly. "You want our marriage annulled." She shook her head. "Therefore . . . we never can have a wedding night."

"Then forget the annulment. You can divorce me if you like, Holly. Sue me for alimony . . . but come to me now." Again he was reaching for her.

He was desirable in every way. His masculinity was a magnet that drew her. His boyishness was a thing

182

that charmed. His lips moved her to sensuous heights. But she set herself to resist him now,

"I don't want to sue you for alimony. I just want my freedom."

He got up with a groan, a sigh, and a backward look at her. He was nearly trembling with frustration. He wanted her more than he had thought it possible to want any one woman. She made him forget all resolves. She made him forget himself. What was this power she held over him? But short of rape he wasn't getting any of her this night.

"Well then, sunshine . . . sleep well." He moved toward the stairs.

"You too, Justin," she answered quietly.

He turned and pulled a face at her. "No chance. I'm going to lie in hell tonight, Holly . . ." And with this he left her alone.

She listened to his footsteps on the stairs and then to the closing door. She heard the engine of his car start up, and she heard him pull off down the long drive. Her lashes brushed her cheek as she lay back against her pillow. It occurred to her that she wasn't about to spend an easy night either.

Chapter Three

Chrissy Penbroke was dead! The cry was picked up and sent around with hushed speed and hard, meaningful stares. Chrissy Penbroke was dead. Someone had shot her with a .38 handgun. Someone had shot her and left her off the Beaulieu Road in the New Forest.

"That's not all," Lynn was saying on a whisper to Holly as they sat on a white-painted wooden bench outside the boarders' barn. "Holly . . . she was pregnant." Her eyes were wide with shock.

"But Lynn . . . she was a child . . ."

"Yeah, but old enough . . . the poor thing."

183

"Who do they think . . . ?"

"That's it . . . everyone is speculating, but when you come down to it . . . well . . . any nut roaming around at night could have picked her up and . . . well . . . it happens."

"Not here . . ."

Lynn shrugged. "Well, it did, though . . . didn't it?" She nudged her suddenly, for the inspector called in on the case was just coming out of the big house.

Holly watched the man as he approached them. He was short, round, and unobtrusive in his baggy suit. He nodded to them and produced a wallet with his photo and ID. "Inspector Higgens here . . ." He waited for their acknowledgment. "Well, now . . . I'd like to ask you ladies some questions, if I may."

"Sure, go ahead," answered Lynn. "Though I don't know what either one of us can tell you."

"I take it, then, that you have already heard about young Christina Penbroke?" he said ruefully. "Good . . . that over, we can get down to the heart of it. What did you know about the girl? Her friends . . . her activities?"

Holly shook her head, "I didn't really know her at all, inspector."

"Oh? Aren't you the riding instructor around here?" His bushy brow was up.

"Yup, that is what she is . . . but she only started here a few weeks ago," answered Lynn. "You want to know anything, you should ask Greg Laeland. He was Chrissy's group instructor."

"Was he, now?" The inspector frowned. "Mrs. Martin didn't mention that." His eyes receded into their darkness with his thoughts.

"Inspector?" said Holly hesitatingly. "There was a young woman that Chrissy rode out with yesterday . . . I saw them heading for the New Forest trails together . . ."

"Hmm. That's right," put in Lynn. "Joy Chen . . . she's a regular around here."

"A regular?" the inspector invited.

"You know . . . she hacks out once or twice a week . . . sometimes Chrissy goes out with her." Lynn sighed. "Chrissy didn't get along well with her school friends and girls her own age."

"Would that have anything to do with the rumors regarding Miss Penbroke's preoccupation with . . . er . . . older men?" he asked slowly.

"Older men?" asked Holly on a note of surprise. Of course she had not been deaf, and word had it around the barn that Greg and Chrissy had been messing around for some months.

"Rumors," added Lynn cautiously, "are too often only bad exaggerations of half-truths and conjectures. They rarely hold water."

"Ladies . . . we are not dealing merely with rumors. Young Miss Penbroke was carrying someone's baby." The inspector's voice was dry. "Ah, now you understand . . . fine. Perhaps we can begin once again."

"I . . . I don't know how we can help you," said Holly.

"Don't you? A pity."

"Look, inspector . . . we kinda thought some nut case was responsible. You know . . . I mean . . . who else would shoot a fourteen-year-old girl?"

"Who else indeed? I thought you might wish to speculate on the matter."

"How could we do that?" asked Holly sharply.

"You, Mrs. Patterson, have a horse boarded here. You spend a great deal of time here. Your daughter takes lessons here. You, Miss Winslow, work here. I thought you might wish to help by telling me whom Miss Penbroke spent her time with. I thought you might certainly know." He sighed. "You see, I have a feeling that she knew her murderer, and for the time being I am going to pursue that feeling." With this he moved off toward his dark-blue police car.

"Lynn . . . this is awful," said Holly on a hushed note.

"No kidding," said Lynn with a shake of her head. "That's putting it mildly. And I tell you what. I feel for poor Sophie."

"Why . . . what do you mean?"

185

"Look, you innocent . . . you and I both know that there was more to the rumors about Chrissy Penbroke than just talk."

"Yes, Lynn . . . but . . ."

"But nothing . . . this could mean real trouble. I happen to know that one of those rumors was absolutely true. Greg Laeland and Chrissy were definitely fooling around together . . . until you came to the Grange. Then it seems to have cooled . . . but Holly, think about it. She was pregnant, and it could have been Greg that was the father."

"You know for a fact that they actually . . . ?"

"No. I wasn't there to actually witness them going that far, but I did see them very late at night together driving down the Beaulieu Road . . . and before you came to the Grange, I saw them one at a time coming out of what is now *your* flat."

Holly thought about the rearranged furniture, the key on the floor, the looks Chrissy had given Greg more often than not, her own hunch about the two. "Oh, Lynn . . . he couldn't have killed her."

"No . . . I never thought Greg was more than just wild." She shook her head. "But we can't tell what a wild boy will do when he's pushed, and maybe Chrissy pushed him too far."

"No. It couldn't be Greg . . . there must have been another man in Chrissy's life."

"That's where I am out of my facts and into rumors. They say she ran around with some of the bloods in town. Some of the really weird kind . . . but why would one of them kill her just because she threatened to tell? *They* had nothing to lose. Greg did, you see."

"No, Lynn . . . no . . ."

Lynn Patterson studied her. "Thing is . . . whether or not he killed her . . . in the end he just might come up with the blame."

Holly shook her head. "Then you are right and Sophie does stand to really be in for a time of it."

Lynn bit her lower lip. "The poor woman . . . what with Thomas for a husband and Greg for a son . . ."

"What do you mean by that?"

"Oh, no." Lynn shook her head. "I'm not going to bring the world crashing around your ears in one day."

"Lynn . . . tell me," she insisted. "I work here . . . and I should be aware of what we are going to be up against. Are you telling me that Thomas Martin was interested in Chrissy?" Shock was written over her face.

Lynn was taken aback. "No . . . not that I know of. Thomas never went that young."

"You are saying that he is unfaithful to Sophie?" It was what Greg had said, wasn't it? Greg had called Thomas a "two-timer" . . . and here was Lynn confirming it. What kind of a world had she entered?

"Look, Holly . . . there is bound to be a miserable amount of mud raked up over this thing. No doubt many things will surface that ordinarily would have gone on without anyone the wiser. You're a baby . . . I don't know how that is with your face and body . . . but there it is."

"What mud, Lynn? Tell me."

"No. I don't want to go into the gossip around here. It's ugly. But I will tell you something . . ."

"What?"

"Don't go out with Judy and Thomas."

"Judy . . . you mean Judy Baines? Why . . . what's the matter with riding out with them?" She had for her own reasons been avoiding Judy, but that had to do with Judy's behavior toward her husband, John.

"Just don't . . . not now with all this going on."

Holly frowned. Just what was going on? What did it all mean? She thought of Joy Chen suddenly. She had seen Joy in Justin's arms. Then Joy was going out riding with young Chrissy. Here was Lynn warning her off Judy and Thomas. What was she suggesting? She thought of Judy's own confessions about another man. Her hand flew to her cherry lips.

"Oh, my God!" She knew in a flash. Judy Baines and Thomas Martin. It was obvious now. All those little things she had seen pass between them. Looks, jokes

187

slyly passed, touching ... Judy and Thomas. "But Lynn ... Judy is so young ... lovely ... and Thomas is old, next to Judy, he ... he is nothing but a gnome. It doesn't make sense."

"No. There is too much that doesn't make sense. Whoops, here comes Greg." Her chin went toward the sports car Greg was parking in the lot.

Sir Justin grimaced and released a long heavy sigh. He looked around in some frustration. He'd been at it for hours but he hadn't progressed even a fraction. He was getting nowhere. Every direction had come to a dead end. There was a gene in the *Euphorbia* that he had to isolate somehow and then insert into a prepared fungus.

Damn! It was her fault. Holly's fault. Her face followed him into his dreams, woke him in a fever, followed him in a frenzy. His night had been hell, and now his day was proving to be much the same! Had she planned for her father to find them together, force the marriage on them? Why not? She had everything to gain. Her freedom from her Moslem connections ... alimony when they parted ... the Laeland name. Damn.

The phone rang, and he reached for it in some irritability.

"Yes?" His tone was curt.

"Justin ..." His aunt, hesitant, almost hushed. "I am so sorry to bother you when you are working ... but something ... something dreadful has happened, and ... and I need to see you immediately."

"What is the matter, Sophie? You sound as though the world were about to cave in around your ears ... and you know that it can't." He was trying to bolster her, sure that she was being overly dramatic. She had that tendency.

"It is ... Greg, Justin. Please come."

"Sophie?" He was worried now. "What is it?"

"One of our students has been murdered ... she was discovered off the Beaulieu Road near Grange land. ... Justin, it was Chrissy Penbroke."

188

There it was. Not spoken but understood. The Grange riding trails were all off the Beaulieu Road, and Chrissy Penbroke had been Greg's student. "Right. I'll be over in ten minutes, Sophie."

Sophie put down the phone and discovered her son standing in the doorway of her antechamber, and his blue eyes were hard as he studied her.

"There is always someone stronger, wiser, more capable of handling matters than your own son." He was in a low sweltering rage. "The Grange might fall into scandal, so whom shall we call to discuss the matter with? Not your son, no, that wouldn't do. Justin? Yes, of course, even better than your husband, call in Justin to the rescue!"

"Greg . . . you love Justin . . ."

"Yes, yes I do. I also love the Grange. It is mine."

"No, not yet it isn't . . . and this latest matter . . . makes it less so," she said quietly.

He stood for a moment stunned. "You don't know what you are saying," he answered her quietly as he attempted to retain some composure, as he attempted to keep from throwing Thomas's unfaithfulness up at her.

"Just answer me, Greg . . . is it true?" Her hands had clenched one another at her waist. He could see her knuckles go white with the strain.

He turned away from her and took to pacing the width of the small room. Outside he could see one of the stablehands tooling a wheelbarrow away from the sawdust pit. So much had happened. How to right himself? Briefly he glanced at his mother's face. She was looking fagged to death. He didn't wish to add to her heartache. He knew things were not going well with her and Thomas.

"Greg!" her voice was nearly a shriek. "I asked if it is true!"

"Is what true?" He had put on a cool facade.

"Don't play games with me! Were you involved with that child?"

189

"She was no child, and yes, dammit, I was!" There, it was out.

Before she realized what she was about she had taken a step forward and landed him a blow, his very first from her. It left a red mark across his cheek. She choked back a sob.

"How . . . how could you have done . . ."

He stood, hurt, angry, ashamed, defensive, and a look of disgust flashed across his face. "How could I? Why not, Mother? It fits with everything you have ever thought of me."

She gasped. "Just what do you mean by that?"

"Never mind. Oh, look . . . I can't defend myself on this score. She was there . . . she was experienced . . . long before me, and she seduced me . . . not the other way around. That doesn't excuse me, I know . . . but . . ."

"But? There is no but in the matter. Greg . . . Greg, was the baby yours?"

"How in hell should I know? Chrissy Penbroke wasn't my private property . . . it wasn't that kind of thing."

"You make me sick!" snapped his mother. "Get out of here . . . out of my sight." Heartache swept through her. Here was her son, and he seemed a stranger.

Greg Laeland's pride came up furiously. "Gladly!" He slammed out of his mother's inner sanctum and stomped across the highly polished wood floors to the main door and left the house.

"Good girl!" It was Andrew Benton's voice over the receiver. "I knew you could do it, Joy! Now all you have to do is wait for the right opportunity to get into his lab alone and make copies of all his notes—"

"Hey, now just a moment, Andrew." She cut in sharply. "We agreed that I would get paid as soon as—"

"As soon as you came across! You haven't done that yet, have you? I mean, really, Joy, what is a key? I can't go to my people and give them a key. We know that he is close to a conclusion . . . all we are asking you to do is make copies of whatever you find in his lab. Our people will unravel it."

190

"Damn you, Andrew. I don't like this. I am the only one taking all the risks."

"What risk, Joy?"

"Well, his lab is not exactly near his bedroom, honey!" she snapped. "He'll know what I'm up to if he finds me there."

"Don't let him find you. Make sure he is out . . . and be quick about your business. It should be fairly simple."

"You frigging creep. Sure, simple for you . . ." She looked toward her front door. "Someone is at my door. I'll ring you later."

Thomas let himself in as Joy slipped off her sofa and moved across the room. She exclaimed happily at the unexpected pleasure, and he could see the sincerity in her dark oriental eyes. He opened his arms to receive her.

"Thomas . . . darling . . ." Their kiss was affectionate more than passionate. He gave her a warm, gentle squeeze, and she sensed his mood at once. She stood apart, still touching, so she could see his face.

"What is it? What's wrong?"

He sighed and for a moment felt very old. "Joy . . . something has happened."

"Ah, yes, I know." Her oriental eyes moved, and he was reminded of a cat, graceful and sly, so very sly.

"You know?" His brow went up.

"Hmm. An Inspector Higgens was up here a short while ago. He wanted to know about my friendship with Chrissy Penbroke."

"And what did you tell him?"

"Ah, now what should I tell him? Chrissy and I rode together from time to time. She was too young to trust me with confidences." Again the look. "Wasn't she?"

"And he was satisfied?"

"I don't know. He is a man who plays by instinct. But never mind that. Sophie no doubt has made up her mind now to give you fifty percent of the business?" She giggled.

He took her shoulders in a sudden desperate move. "Joy . . . Joy . . ."

"What, my Thomas?" Her voice was soft, soothing. "Why so worried?"

How much would Joy Chen do for him? How often had she told him she would do anything . . . *anything?* What was gnawing at him?

"Worried? This will not do the Grange any good, you know."

"It will pass." She was already unzipping his pants. "People tend to forget . . ."

"It's not so simple, and the Grange is my bread and butter."

"And with Greg . . . out of it . . . as he might be one day . . . you will do fine. . . ." She was nibbling at his mouth. "How much time do we have, Thomas?"

He gave in to her caressing with a groan, and his hand moved under her red silk top. "Enough, little bitch, enough."

Holly had been training Tinker for some weeks now. He didn't have the power or the judgment to take on the jumps without his rider working him over them. Holly would be entering the bay gelding in the Hunter Hack class, which would mean he would be required to take two jumps in addition to being shown in his gaits. It was important to the Grange that they do well, since much of their business depended on the sale of their horses.

Holly took him around and headed him toward the series of three crossbars she had set up. His ears flicked. He had done this before, but the bars now seemed higher. His eyeballs rolled nervously, but Holly kept him in rein, timing it just so, and at the proper moment she released the reins and urged him over the jump with a clicking sound. He flowed over gracefully, taking the canter and the remaining two jumps with effortless grace. She stopped him in a straight line and rewarded him with a pat to his lovely neck and high praise.

"Now, Tinker . . . now, beauty . . . the water . . ." She put him in stride. She could see he was already preparing himself for this. He didn't like water. She had been attempting to cure him of this phobia by repeatedly taking him over streams on the trail, hoping the natural wetting of the water would ease him over this particular jump. Now was the test.

Again the gelding's eyeballs glinted white as he approached the jump. It was different. Familiar in some obscure way, but frightening all the same. He heard his rider assuage him with gentle words, pushing him on with her clicking, tooling him with her leg. There was alarm in his manner as he brought himself to the jump, but he could feel her leg urging, demanding. He took the jump with determination, raising his quarters upward, his rear legs tucked beautifully as he rocketed over the water.

"Well done!" It was Jim Jakes at the fence.

Holly was grinning with pleasure as she brought him around and stopped before the young veterinarian. "Hello . . . I'll say thank you the day of the show."

"Oh, he'll do. He is looking fit. You've done quite a job with him in these weeks." He shook his head. "I thought that Tinker here had a thing about water? Heard Greg mention it once or twice."

"He does . . . but I've been pushing him at waterjumps from day one." She dismounted and breathed a satisfied sigh.

He looked around. "Quiet today . . . no lessons?"

She frowned. "Maureen tells us that nearly everyone has called to cancel."

"Oh?" It was a question.

"I suppose it has something to do with the poor Penbroke girl . . . what with that Inspector Higgens asking questions all over town. People do react," she answered thoughtfully.

Greg was coming out of the barn, coming to them. "Hey . . . Jim . . . want to help me mate Timmy with Stockings?"

"Where's Thomas?" asked the vet on a note of surprise.

"I told him that you might need help with this particular breeding."

"Well, he's not around, and I don't want to wait any longer. Stockings is ready, and Timmy is going crazy out in the stud paddock. I'd swear he can smell her scent all the way out there."

Jim smiled. "Right, then . . . go and get the mare. I'll go lip-chain him." He turned to Holly. "Want to watch?"

"How ashamed I am that I do," she said on a smile

"Why ashamed?" He laughed.

"I don't know. I feel like a voyeur."

"Well, that's what we are," shouted Greg as he moved off. "Every last one of us."

Jim Jakes frowned but then turned a smile to Holly "Go on . . . give Tinker over to be walked down and join us in the breeding paddock."

A few moments later Holly was bracing herself against the gray wooden railing and watching Jim Jakes handle Timmy. The stud was in a frenzy. His neck was arched his body tense; he could see Greg leading the pretty black mare with the white stockings toward him, an he began to prance and snort wildly. The stud's penis dropped from its sheath, and he attempted to rear. Jim Jakes twitched the metal chain in the stud's mouth bringing the horse down, but he continued to blow grunt, and deliver a resonant display of his eagerness The mare came along with Greg quietly, although her ears and attention were up.

Holly watched in fascination as Greg allowed the mare and stud to touch noses. Timmy blew into the mare's nostrils, assuring her of his friendliness. She accepted this show of affection. He proceeded to nibble at her face. She allowed it. Thus encouraged, the stallion sniffed beneath her long black tail, and so exquisite was the scent of her heat that he raised his head straight up and out and curled up his lip with ecstasy

Holly giggled. At her ear a familiar, strangely stimulating male voice said softly, "But it's not funny you know . . ."

She spun around to find Justin towering above her

In his denim waisted jacket and blue knit shirt he looked boldly appealing. She attempted to recover.

"Of course it isn't . . . but just look at Timmy . . . *he* looks as if he's laughing," she answered on a hushed light note.

The mare lifted her tail and spread her rear legs. The stud went into a frenzy. Jim cropped the stud. "Up . . . up!" he commanded as the stud lifted himself onto the mare's back and entered her.

"Why does he have to crop the stallion's legs?" asked Holly on a whisper.

"In the wilds the mare would kick the stud to get him up high enough to penetrate her properly. In a controlled situation like this, she will too often take the thing passively, and his penetration will not be deep enough to impregnate her." He was frowning. "Like now. . . . *Greg* . . . Timmy is not well enough into her!"

Greg still held the lead rope to the mare. He backed her as Jim cropped the stud up farther. The stud lay on his mare, his front hooves dangling on either side of her body, and his tenderness with his mare was remarkable as he nibbled blissfully at her neck and kept his hooves from scraping her. A moment later he was done and retreating from her.

Holly was bolted in place, unable to tear herself away. "Look at Stockings . . . she isn't moving. Is she asking for more?"

"Indeed, the mare was again lifting her tail. "Dammit, Greg, walk her!" shouted Justin. "Before she drops her scent and loses it!"

Greg began walking the mare around, anxiously watching her hinds. If she dropped her scent now, they would have go through the entire thing again. Jim had his hands full with Timmy, who appeared in a mood to boast as he pranced and jumped on his fores. He took him in toe and walked him back to his paddock.

Holly sighed. "My goodness. It all seems so contrived. I mean, how do they ever manage on their own in the wild?" she teased.

"A great deal better." He was smiling at her. He

looked around, puzzled, for it was quite early in the day and the place looked abnormally quiet. "What's the matter?"

"I don't know what you mean," she said quietly, evading his inquiring eye.

"Oh?" His brow rose, for it was apparent to him that she did. "No lessons . . . or did the good doctor have a reason for inviting you to watch this breeding session?" There was the sneer to his lip.

"You are disgusting, despicable, and horrid!" she snapped and moved off.

He thought to follow and continue this, but he was here to see Sophie, and so he allowed it to pass and continued toward the house.

Chapter Four

"Where the bloody hell were you, Thomas?" demanded Greg as he stamped across the gravel parking lot and faced his stepfather.

"Why?" Thomas was never flustered by Greg's open antagonism. He even found it understandable. But the lad was a nuisance.

"Because you might recall that you were supposed to be on hand to help with Stockings!"

"Oh, damn . . . that's right. She was ready to be bred today. Well, we can take care of it now."

"Never mind. Jim was here and helped me with the thing."

"And how did our young mare take her first stud?" There was the hint of amusement in his voice. The test at banter. There had been a time during Greg's father's life when he and Greg had been friends.

That time was gone, never to be recalled. Greg did not pick up on it. "Well enough," he grumbled, "but I think you should have advised one of us where you were off to."

Another car was coming up the long drive. He looked up and recognized Joy Chen's blue Datsun. Greg's features hardened. He had had quite a day. Inspector Higgens had returned to ask him about Chrissy's pregnancy. It seemed during his interview with Joy Chen he had understood that Chrissy had confessed to Joy about her relationship with Greg. Without another word, he turned and stalked off. Thomas looked after him and waited till Joy had parked her car.

"You didn't say you were going to ride, Joy," he asked in some surprise as he helped her out of her car.

"I'm not . . . I left my slicker here the other day . . . I just thought I would pick it up and then be off," she said, moving away from him to the main barn. She noted that Sir Justin's car was parked there, and as she walked past the little red sports car, she casually touched its hood. The engine was still warm. Good, then . . . he had only just arrived. Perhaps now was the time to run over and do what she had to do. Or maybe she would just wait and see where he went from here.

Thomas watched his little oriental love, and he could see she was deep in thought. What was she up to? Joy was forever plotting some deviltry. It was part of her nature. No matter, whatever it was she would never hurt him. He never had to worry about Joy. Judy Baines, on the other hand, might be trouble. Maybe he would cool it with Judy for the time being . . . until the heat from this thing with Chrissy dissipated.

The Grange had a large garage. Within its spacious walls reposed one grand old car. It had been Sophie's first husband's joy. A large, roomy, silver Laeland Cloud. It was a classic, but a gas-eater, and as such used infrequently and only by Sophie. This suited her, as she didn't leave the Grange much these days, but when she did, it was always in her silver Cloud.

A door to the dark garage creaked as it opened, allowed a shaft of dulling sunlight to enter, and then shut it out again. The stale air shifted as someone moved around the large car, flicked a flashlight on, and pulled out a pair of sturdy wire cutters. The brake line was discovered easily, for even a layman once shown this will recall its location and appearance without effort. Severing it took even less skill.

Tools were put away and, no one the wiser, the garage was left behind. It was Sophie's club night. She always drove her car to her club meetings, and she always took the Round Hill Road south, a winding country road with treacherous curves.

Holly had stalked off angrily from Justin. She went to her flat, undressed, and, still much in a huff, took a quick shower. Some twenty minutes later, she was dressed in a tight-fitting knit green shirt and pale-blue Britannia jeans. She grimaced at herself in the mirror. Gone were the Diors, the jewels, the constant attention to her hair, her complexion, her nails. Was she happy?

She could be. She liked working with the horses, she enjoyed giving lessons. She was becoming involved with the friends she had made at the Grange. But . . . but what? This ridiculous marriage to Justin has ruined everything!

In something of a strange mood, she started downstairs, opened the door, and found Jim there, his hand poised and ready to knock.

"Hello!" he said with his open smile.

Again she was reminded of someone. Who? She couldn't pinpoint it to a name. It was just something about his face. Never mind.

"All done?" She returned his smile and stepped outside. Her eyes went to the parking lot and noted that Justin's car was still there.

"Yes. You must know I've been thinking all day about seeing you . . . asking you to join me for dinner and a movie tonight." He was taking up her hand, wielding her steps away from the open stretch of lawns and riding rings.

She stopped and frowned. "You are very sweet to think of me, Jim, but I can't tonight."

He looked disappointed. "Oh? Another engagement?"

She nodded, and he looked so taken aback that she laughed.

"It's not what you think."

"Then break it," he said at once.

"I can't. I don't do that to friends, and Greg is a friend. It's his mother's night to have dinner with her club. With this mess over the Penbroke girl I told him I would keep him company. I don't think he should be alone."

He eyed her for a long moment. "No chance I could change your mind?"

"Why?" She laughed good-naturedly. "Do I look the fickle sort?"

He squeezed the hand he held. "No, no, in spite of your devastating beauty, your eyes tell me you are sure and steady."

Justin was shaking his head, and his ginger locks strayed over and across his forehead. "Look, Sophie . . . I think you're wrong. I have just got to say to you that you are not behaving fairly to Greg. The Grange would have come totally into his hands if he were twenty-five."

"Not if I had deemed it otherwise. That is precisely why I am doing this now . . . before he gets full control," she answered quietly.

"You are being very hard on him," said Justin just as quietly.

"She was only . . . a child . . . and his student. He should have used more self-control . . . better judgment. How can I possibly allow him to take charge of the business his father adored? He will ruin it . . . if he hasn't already!"

"Look, Sophie, I am not going to argue with you over Greg's indiscretion . . . but Thomas should not be the one to gain by it!"

She put up her chin. "Now . . . I know you have never approved of Thomas . . ."

"Precisely!"

She cut in again, "Don't let's argue, Justin. I am

199

having my solicitor draw up the papers, and fifty percent of this business will be put into Thomas's hands . . . to revert to the family again in the event of his death."

He touched her cheek. "Won't you hold off, Sophie? Give it more thought, more time?"

"No, I have made up my mind."

"It won't look good for Greg just now . . . with this hanging over the Grange."

"It will not be generally known." There were times when she could be stubborn in her way. She was now.

He sighed. "Right, then . . . as far as the talk that will hover around Greg's head, we are agreed that the best course of action for now would be to ignore it." He was doubtful that this would serve, but there did not appear to be a ready answer.

Sophie colored up but proceeded, "Justin, Greg said to me that he wasn't Chrissy's only . . . male interest. He indicated that she saw other men . . . intimately . . . that the police would discover this."

"Oh? Well, if that is true, Sophie . . . her parents are influential enough to keep it hushed."

"Yes, I know . . . but will it . . . will people still look askance at Greg, at our school, when they enlist their daughters for lessons?"

He eyed her a long moment. "Sophie . . . in the end, it will be all right. Her death is the issue here . . . not her social activities."

"Then why do I have this dreadful sinking feeling that it's not over."

Greg didn't want to go into the house. Justin was there, closeted with his mother, and at the moment his resentment toward both was overwhelming. He took up the hose and ran it over his face and hands, took up the paper towels Holly shoved at him, and grinned through it all as she hurled friendly abuse at him.

"Clumsy oaf . . . you have sprayed me all over . . . stop shaking your head, fool!" She laughed as she stood apart from him and watched him comb his long damp

200

hair of fair waves. "Just look at you!" she ordered mercilessly. "You are water-spotted all over! Do you mean to say that you are taking me to dinner looking like that? No self-respecting English country gentleman would be seen in your clothes clean, let alone in their present state!"

"Take a damper, you silly bird! I am doing you an incredible honor by taking you along with me." He was grinning wide. Holly was restoring his good humor.

"Oh ho! Listen to the fop! What you need, Greg Laeland, is a good thrashing!" she flung at him.

He reached for and caught a quantity of her long amber hair.

"Come on, then . . . see if you can train me!"

"You know, of course, that this means war!" she threatened as she undid his hold and swung around to give him a friendly kick across his shin.

"Ouuh!" he cried and started after her.

Justin stepped outside in time to see some part of this exchange. There was his cousin chasing his wife around his car! Holly was screeching in happy glee as she avoided Greg's attack, but he could see that his cousin was closing in.

He moved toward them and called them to order curtly. "I don't think your mother would appreciate this behavior, Greg . . . in view of your present differences." He sounded even to himself ill-natured and fusty.

Greg's color drained immediately from his face, and he stood in mute, abject misery, unable to defend himself. Holly's temper flew to the fore.

"You sound like a sour old man, Justin Laeland!" she lashed at him. She turned to Greg. "Come on . . . I'm starving, and you promised me dinner." It occurred to her that it would be nice if Greg invited Justin to join them. He didn't, and she felt a sense of loss.

A few moments later they were driving off, and Holly couldn't stop herself from turning back for another look at Sir Justin. She sucked in her breath, for he was still in the lot, standing, watching their retreating car. What did she feel? Ludicrous. But what was it about him that moved her to this physical state? What physical state? Heart pumping furiously. Flesh trembling. Legs wobbly. Head booming. He made her absolutely miserable.

Sophie pushed the button and stood back as the garage's door slowly eased upward. She went inside, opened her car door, dropped her blue leather bag inside, and held the blue silk of her dress as she slipped into the driver's seat. Such a luxury, this car. An automatic.

She sighed. Her makeup was fresh, her hair stylishly in place, her perfume just enough, but she felt old and tired. Her interview with Justin had made her uneasy. Was she wrong? She put the key into the ignition and started the car engine.

Some moments later she was steering down the long drive of the Grange, slowing over the cattle grid, stopping at the intersection where their drive met the road, and turning the car south toward Round Hill Road. Greg was off with Holly. Thomas had made a point of mentioning it. Not a good thing, he had said. It would cause talk. Would it? That was ridiculous . . . but with this Penbroke thing hanging over their heads?

And Thomas . . . tonight he had said he would stay at home to await her return. He had been so warm and affectionate. Gentle and understanding, the way he had treated her when they were first married. Why had things changed? Did he sense her growing convictions were pointed toward a divorce?

Divorce? She had never thought she would ever contemplate the word and what it meant, but she had put up with too much from Thomas. She knew that he was a womanizer. She knew he had Joy Chen as a lover. At one time she had thought he had given all that up, but not now. Now she knew he never would. He was a gambler. He was a selfish, cruel man. But what was worse, what was far worse, was the sure knowledge that he didn't love her, he had never loved her.

She touched the brakes. What was this? The car was not slowing. She had first noticed it when she had stopped the car at the intersection. The brakes had seemed low ... too low ... and now? She put the automatic shift into low gear, for she was coming to a narrow bend in the road and the car was picking up speed. Her foot pressed the brake pedal down to the floor. Nothing!

"Oh, my God!" she breathed out loud as the car screeched around the corner. What to do? Emergency brake? Yes, yes ... she yanked hard. Nothing. No brakes, and the car was picking up speed. Frightened now, she began to take the car near the side embankments in order to slow it down and then she noticed the headlights of an oncoming car!

She swerved out of its path, jumped the high ridge of earth and grass, took down the bushes in her way, and careened through the woods. She screamed then, for there were trees ahead. A clump of trees too wide to avoid, and she ended by hitting them full force!

Sophie went forward sharply, hit her head, and fell back unconscious!

As Justin watched Greg drive off with Holly, he realized just how very little control he wielded over his new bride. He had never meant to get married, he had never meant to be divorced.

Dammit all! He got into his car and drove back to his cottage. He slammed the car door shut, looked toward the garage. He should work in his lab ... put her out of his mind. Hell! Not now. He stomped off, made his way to his kitchen, and in a fit of temper heated a can of chili without removing it from its tin.

This done, he sat in front of the tube to watch the evening news, drink his dark ale, and eat his chili. Holly, ah, Holly ...

He had had enough. Dammit all to bloody hell! What was wrong with him? What was he doing? He could

have any beautiful woman he wanted. He had the
wealth and the title to obtain them. But you can't have
Holly, he thought. . . . What the deuce do you mean?
had her. . . . So you did, but you want her now, don't
you, and she won't have any of you!

He felt like a little boy deprived of a sweet. He
wanted her. At that moment in time he would have
paid any price to have her.

The phone rang, and with a frown he took up the
receiver not far from his elbow. "Yes?" His voice was
curt and unfriendly, although only close associates and
intimates had the use of his unlisted number.

"Justin?" It was Holly's voice, upset, unsure. "Justin
. . . something terrible has happened. Oh, Justin . . ."
She felt near to tears.

He heard it in her voice, and it shook him, but his
own voice came as a clipped command.

"Easy, sunshine. Take your time and tell me what
has happened."

She said his name again. "Justin . . . oh, Justin . . ."
She took in and let out air. "Thomas came for us, we
were at the King's Head . . . they called him, you see
and he knew where we were—"

"Why would Thomas come for you and Greg?" he cut
in, attempting to get at the meat of the matter.

"It's Sophie . . ." She felt the sob well up in her
throat. She was genuinely fond of the flighty, affectionate woman, and she knew that Justin was as well.

"Sophie? What's wrong with Sophie?" A flash of fear
put emotion into his voice.

"I don't have the details . . . but what I understood is
that she lost control of that big car of hers and went off
the road to hit a tree."

"My God . . ." he breathed. "Holly . . . how is she?"

"We don't know exactly . . . she was unconscious . .
but when she came to, the doctor says she asked for
you. Greg gave me your number."

"She asked for me? Why would she do that?" he
allowed his thoughts to form the words. There was
Thomas, Greg . . . why would she ask immediately for

him? "Never mind that now . . . which hospital are you at?"

"The Knowles . . . Justin . . ." But she didn't know what she wanted to say. It was absurd. She was calling to him like a child. She had to stop this, get hold of herself.

He was not immune to her, and his voice came like a caress.

"I'll be there shortly, sunshine. In the meantime I trust you to keep things together for me."

"Right," she said softly and put away the receiver. When she turned it was to find Thomas and Greg once again at one another's throats.

"Stop it! Both of you. This is not the time nor the place for this stupid bickering."

Greg glanced at her sharply, but gave in to her good sense. He chose to saunter down the brightly lit hall to a vending machine. Thomas appraised her thoughtfully and said on a quiet note, "I would be wary of Greg if I were you."

She raised an eyebrow. "I am not going to pick up on that very provocative statement, Mr. Martin." With that she turned away and went to a nurse to once again inquire after Sophie Martin. No word yet. No one seemed to have word on Sophie. At this moment she could be dead . . . or near to it. Oh, God, she wished Justin were there already!

Chapter Five

Joy Chen blew the smoke from her cigarette out her window and watched as it waved and convoluted through the trees. Her small Datsun was well hidden in the woods that lined the Grange drive. Maybe she was wrong. Maybe Justin would not be notified about Sophie until the morning. Drat! He was her favorite nephew, and more . . . Sophie so often relied on Justin's judgment.

How often had she heard Sophie say that Justin was much like her first husband, William Laeland?

Payoff! Headlights turning off the cottage road onto the Grange drive. She ducked low, but her eyes watched as Justin wielded his sports car speedily down the drive and onto the country road. So, she had been right after all. She smiled to herself. It was a lucky thing that she had called and found Thomas as he was about to leave for the hospital . . . a lucky thing indeed!

She started her engine and slowly eased it over the rough forest ground to the Grange drive. Imagine Sophie's hitting a tree with that big car of hers? She smiled to herself. Thomas a widower? The thought gurgled inside her throat, and as she parked her car outside Justin's garage she gave a whoop of laughter.

Some fifteen minutes later she was driving at some speed to be off the grounds unseen. Most of Justin's notes were on film safely within her purse. Well, well, Joy Chen, you seem to be capable at all things you undertake . . . at all things!

Holly stood and watched the doors anxiously. Greg glanced at her moodily from time to time. He resented the fact that his mother had called for Justin. He resented the fact that the doctors would tell him only to be patient. He resented most of all Thomas, Thomas standing to one side continually studying him. It galled, everything galled!

Holly's aqua eyes flickered as Justin came through the swinging doors toward them. Tall, authoritive, and brisk, he smiled to find her meeting him halfway.

"Justin . . . they won't tell us anything . . ."

"It's all right. Her doctor spoke to me downstairs. She is out of danger, but extremely fatigued."

Greg picked up on this immediately. "What right has he to speak to you first? I am her son, dammit!"

Justin's brow went up. "But I understood from the doctor that he had already come to you and Thomas with the information that Sophie had suffered a concussion and would be spending the night."

206

"That's right," put in Thomas, "but we asked for something a little more concrete, Justin."

Justin frowned. "Look . . . I am certain there is nothing to worry about." He was moving away from them toward Sophie's private room.

"Why do you get to see m'mother?" Greg spat angrily.

"I don't know, Greg. I am sure there is a good reason," said Justin, disappearing on the other side of the double white doors and down the hall that housed the private rooms. He could see from the corner of his eye that Holly's assuaging hand went to Greg's arm. He could just catch her saying something soothing. It pleased and annoyed him all at once.

"Now, Sophie, love, what have you gone and done to yourself?" The affectionate smile was wide across his lean face as he stepped inside Sophie's hospital room. Instant relief. She looked a great deal better than he had imagined she would. After all, she had refused to see her son and husband.

She smiled wanly, and he could see her trouble was far worse than a few bruises to her body. "You should know what a hard head I have, Justin."

He came right to the point. "Greg is rather upset that you have asked for me." He didn't have to say more.

"Yes, I imagine he would be. . . . and Thomas?"

"Not angry . . . maybe surprised, but no, not angry."

She sighed. "I am not ready to face Greg . . . I don't feel well enough emotionally, and if I allowed Thomas in it would only serve to further antagonize Greg."

"Why, Sophie? What is all this?"

"There is something I want you to do for me . . . discreetly."

He had her hand and put it to his lips. "Right, then, haven't I ever been a paragon of discretion?" There was the tease in his eyes.

She laughed, but it was gone almost immediately as she returned to the matter at hand. "Justin . . . tonight I went off the road . . . hit a tree . . . because I had no

207

brakes. The pedal was down to the floor . . . and I had nothing."

"Emergency brake?"

"None."

He frowned. "When was the last time you put brake fluid into your machine?"

"Justin . . . I want you to look at the brake line," she said gravely, ignoring his question.

He felt a chill tingle his intellect. "What are you saying, Sophie?"

"Only that I had no brakes, and I want you to look into the matter for me . . . quietly." She sighed. "There are reasons why I can't ask either Thomas or Greg." Certainly there were reasons . . . such desperate reasons . . . but she wouldn't think about that now.

A few moments later, Justin was explaining to his younger cousin as reasonably as he could, "Sophie seems well enough, Greg, but she is tired and sedated. Your mother would just rather not be seen until the morning."

"No doubt she has her reasons for choosing to see you tonight?" put in Thomas purposely.

Justin glanced his way, but there was a friendly smile across his face. "It was a matter of her car." He looked at Greg. "You know how your father felt about that car . . . well, Sophie was nearly comical in her concern over it. Wants it restored to its former beauty . . . wants my company to do it." He gave a short laugh. "Which shows just how fit your mother really is, so there is no cause for alarm."

This seemed to satisfy Greg, and he breathed a long sigh. "Oh . . . so that was it?"

Thomas shrugged. "Well, since there is nothing else that can be done, I think I shall call it a night." He turned and left them.

Greg smiled at Holly. "So, girl . . . it's off to Bournemouth for you and me. I have some friends I'd like you to meet."

"Oh, no . . . not tonight, Greg. I am a bit tired,"

answered Holly quickly. "Why don't you go on, though? It will do you some good."

"Well, if you are sure you don't want to, Holly I'll take you home first."

"No need for that, Greg," put in Justin quietly. "I am going straight home myself, and I can drop Holly off at her flat."

Greg considered his cousin for a moment. What did he feel about Holly? He glanced at her and saw her eyes sparkle with a glint of anger and something else.

"I don't mind seeing Holly home, Justin."

"I'm sure that you don't, but it is out of your way, so there is no need," said Justin with some determination.

Holly could see the two would come to battle over this. She touched Greg's arm. No time to consider her motives. "You go on, Greg . . . really, I'll see you tomorrow."

He sighed, touched her nose. "All right, girl . . ."

Justin and Holly watched him sidle off for a moment before turning to one another. "You two seem friendly enough," said Justin, starting to lead her off.

"And why shouldn't we be?" she challenged immediately.

"Don't misunderstand," he said blandly. "I don't mind . . . but I wonder that Jim Jakes doesn't object."

"And why should Jim Jakes object?" she demanded, her eyes flashing at him, her hand moving to swish her long amber hair behind her.

He wanted to sweep her into his arms. He wanted to touch her, hold her, kiss her. He answered her instead, "You should have the answer to that better than I."

"Now, just what is that supposed to mean? Jim Jakes can have no objection. For God's sake, you sound as though you think I am leading the man on." There was a troubled look about her eyes, and she was biting her lower lip.

"Aren't you?"

"No . . . no, of course not."

He started the engine and glanced sideways at her.

"Then you aren't becoming involved with the good doctor?"

This was ridiculous. She didn't have to answer his questions. What was she doing? Putting herself on a stand?

"Look, Justin, this is none of your business!"

"Yes it is. You *are* my wife."

"In name only," she countered angrily.

He remembered the events leading up to the morning that had joined them. "Not quite in name only."

She looked stunned. "That was before . . ."

"Wasn't it, though," he said softly.

The remainder of the ride was managed in silence. It wasn't uncomfortable silence, for they had their thoughts to sort out, and it was with some surprise that Holly looked about to find they had already turned into the Grange's private drive. She was touched with a sense of disappointment as well until he made the sharp turnoff to his cottage road.

"Just where are you going?" she demanded.

He had decided to try something new. "Holly . . . would you mind keeping me company for a bit? This has been a bad day for me."

She eyed him warily. "I am certain, Justin, that you don't need my company to stave off your blues."

"Right, then, I won't ask for it," he said on a hurt note and put his gearshift into reverse.

Immediately she relented and put her hand over his before he could move the car. "All right . . . but just for a little while."

They were inside, only one mood light was on, and he was pouring two snifters of V.S.O.P. brandy, handing her one, sitting back with a long weary sigh, and taking a sip of his. He didn't say anything.

She sipped her brandy and watched him. He wasn't making any move to come near her, and he wasn't talking. This was unexpected.

"Justin," she said curiously, "just what do you do here all day?"

"Research," he answered laconically.

210

"Research? Just what sort of research?" Her tone was nearly a chuckle.

"I'll have you know, my girl, that I am a scientist of sorts!" He was smiling now.

"Really? How very interesting. . . . But I thought you were president of your car thing."

" 'Car thing' indeed!" he bantered. "I'll have to teach you to have proper respect. I am president, but only because my father died. Have I told you about my father? Disappointed in me, he was." He was musing now, genuine in his approach, sincere in his desire to confide in her. "Wanted me to be more of a business-man . . . but I never enjoyed it. Went in for genetic engineering instead. He hated that. Wanted me wheeling and dealing with him." He shook his head. "Had to die to get me to run his firm"—a short snort of a laugh—"and in the end, ironically, it's my field that will be the making of his firm."

"What do you mean?"

He glanced at her. To trust her or not? Halfway measure? "You see, Lady Laeland, I am working on a method of producing oil at a relatively low cost."

"Are you?" She was surprised. Proud? Was she proud? Nonsense.

"Hmm. So now you know what I am doing here . . . in secret . . . and why we cannot mention our marriage. It would bring too many reporters around our heads."

"Why would it be dangerous for anyone to know what you are doing?"

"Because, my dear, I should like to get my formula completed and a patent pending before some ambitious soul decides to kill me and steal it or before the Middle East powers decide they had better kill me to bury it."

She went closer to him without realizing it. She had been standing; now she sat beside him on the sofa. "Oh, Justin . . . are you saying you could be in danger?"

He shrugged. "Perhaps."

"Justin . . . shouldn't you have bodyguards?"

He laughed. "It isn't necessary yet." His arm went

211

around her shoulders, his face went suddenly serious. "Do you know . . . I can't remember ever having talked like this with a woman. . . ."

She scoffed, "Oh, stop . . . you mean you were never serious with a woman before?"

His face, his gray eyes, hardened. "I was once."

She cocked her head and tried to ignore the twist of jealousy she suddenly felt. "And . . . ?"

He gave a short laugh, but there was a taste of bitterness in it. "I poured my foolish young heart into the woman's experienced hands. I rather thought at the time we exchanged . . . vows. I woke up to find that she had decided to become my stepmother instead of my wife."

Holly leaned back to better view his face. "Oh, Justin . . . how very dreadful for you. . . ." She tried to imagine the hurt he must have experienced, the disillusionment. "How did you cope?"

"Not very well. It was not a pleasant time in my life . . . it was not a good year."

"What do you mean? You got over it in a year?"

He pulled a face. "Not exactly. You see, a year after the wedding, fate sent her flying to Paris in a plane that never made it. She was one of eighty odd people that were killed."

Holly's arms went around Justin at once. Softhearted, she had never been able to hold herself aloof to another's pain. "Oh, my poor Justin . . ."

He received her thankfully. He held her tightly, tenderly, and felt a swelling of joy he could not understand. It gave over after a moment to something else, more urgent, and he pulled away to look at her face, into her eyes. Suddenly his hold had altered, his position had shifted, and his mouth had taken hers. His kiss was sweet, but it heightened into passion as she pressed herself against his hard, masculine body. His touch was gentle, but it moved deftly with command. His whisper was a caress, but it charged her with desire, and she found herself responding to his every brush of hand with a fever that stirred him to mindless

212

ardor. Willingly she took his kisses and returned her own. Pleasurably she listened to the sound of his hunger and nearly cried with her own. Fitfully she attempted restraint.

"Justin . . . no . . . Justin . . ."

"Don't leave me now, Holly . . . not now . . ."

She was not proof against the boy in his voice. She was not proof against the man's hunger. "Oh, Justin . . ." Her mouth opened to receive and his tongue explored in wild sensation, and as the rockets bounded in bright confusion, she gave herself to his touch.

Chapter Six

Saeed stirred the strong black coffee and then stared hard into Andrew Benton's eyes. Joy moved uncomfortably beside Andrew. Why did she have to be here? All she wanted was her money. Why had Andrew dragged her to this meeting?

Saeed didn't allow his eyes to move from Andrew's face as he carefully chose his words. "There is a saying . . . now what is it? Ah yes, something to do with working two sides of the fence. My employers would not be pleased to discover that you might be . . . er . . . contemplating such a move."

"What ever gave you such an idea?" started Andrew. Nervous perspiration began to break out behind his ears, under his arms. He moved uncomfortably. It had been precisely what he had been thinking since Joy had arrived the night before with the film of Justin's papers. They had developed it and delivered the prints to Saeed. There should be nothing left but for Saeed to hand over the money that had been promised.

"There is something in your character that suggests you may have had such thoughts. But never mind, we realize you value your life too much to entertain them for long."

"I wouldn't dream of doing such a thing."

"No, you wouldn't, because there would be no sense in our paying for something that would end in Laeland's competitor's hands. Then we would have too many to deal with, and my employers would be most displeased, and when they are displeased ... it angers me ... greatly."

"I understand," said Andrew, nervously pulling at his tie. "But I have given you what you want ..."

"You have given us copies of Sir Justin's present work, work which is very much against our interests. It seems Sir Justin is very near a great discovery." He shrugged. "It was inevitable. Our people knew this, of course. However, we do not want him to complete his work before the end of this quarter. You see, we plan to raise our oil prices by a great margin. ..."

"How can you stop him?"

"Sir Justin will have to postpone his work until after the quarter." He spread his hands open. "Even if he were to come up with his synthetic ... even then it would take months ... perhaps more than eighteen ... to get it into production. If we have raised our prices it will enable us to weather the many years ahead when we will no longer be the oil kings of the world."

"Yes, but Sir Justin won't sell out," said Andrew incredulously.

"Everyone, it has been said, has his or her price. His may not be money. We shall, however, discover what it is and use it."

Joy sucked in breath. The Arab was getting to his feet. The meeting was at an end; an envelope was being passed toward Andrew. She waited. She needed cash. She had stayed with Andrew all night, helped him develop the film, went with him to deliver it, came to this meeting, all because she needed the cash. The Arab was gone, and she turned to Andrew, pushing her coffee cup away from her. "Well, hand it over and let me go. I'm tired."

He took out two fifty-pound notes and slid them to her. She gasped. "Are you joking? You promised me

214

three hundred, not a hundred! Andrew, I am warning you!"

"I promised you three hundred when I thought I was going to have a double sale. But you heard Saeed . . . there is no way I can sell those papers elsewhere. A hundred is what you get!" He got to his feet and left her seething at his back.

What was she going to do? She needed cash. How was she going to get it? Jim Jakes? She could give it a try . . . but it could backfire on her. Thomas? Thomas wouldn't be able to support her habit for more than a week . . . he would soon be in trouble over the notes he forged at Sophie's bank. What next?

Sir Justin unbent as he got to his feet and brushed away the dirt from his jeans. A troubled glint lit his gray eyes as he turned to gaze thoughtfully at his Aunt's bent-out-of-shape old Laeland car.

Damn, there was not a doubt about it. The brake line had been deliberately and maliciously severed. What was more to the point was the sure knowledge that this had been done with Sophie's end in mind! But who?

Not Greg. No, not Greg, not for all the shares in the world. He loved his mother, and even if he didn't, Greg wasn't capable of such a thing . . . was he? Thomas? What motive? No, Sophie hadn't signed over the shares to him yet. Then who?

Damnation and hell! What should he do? Notify the police, of course, but Sophie would not like this. More scandal just now would be damaging to the school. But someone had tried to kill Sophie! This was no prank. No game here. The brake line had been cut, and what was he going to say when the mechanic got around to finding this out? The car was not a total wreck, it was in the shop for repairs. The brake line would be seen and reported to the police.

He sighed to himself and moved off to his own car. Sophie would be home from the hospital by now. He would have to speak with her in private before a decision could be made. He got into his own car and started off. This was turning out to be quite a morning!

He had come awake startled to find the warm being he had made love to during most of the night was no longer in his bed. Holly had gone. She had chosen to dress herself and walk back to her own flat in the middle of the early-morning hours. Why? The question irritated him. Her absence agitated him, and he hadn't been able to sleep again. Instead he had gone to his lab, and his work had proved fruitful, but damn if Holly wasn't messing up his mind!

Their lovemaking had been beautiful, better than he thought possible, better than with any other woman he had ever had, better . . . but stop it, you're acting the schoolboy, he chided himself.

She left you in the middle of the night for her own bed. She makes you no promises. She asks for none. Isn't that what you want? . . . Yes, dammit, that is exactly what I want. . . . Right, then, so that's what you've got.

Someone was trying to kill Sophie! The thought suddenly exploded all others. What was he doing dwelling on Holly? Someone had cut Sophie's brake line. Who? Why? And just what was he going to do about it?

Holly dismissed her class and took a long sip of the iced tea Jim Jakes had put into her hand. He was smiling warmly at her.

"A good class?" he inquired with a laugh, for he had seen much of their antics.

"Oh, Jim . . . do any of them want to learn how to ride? I have been trying to teach them to rise to the trot for some three weeks now, and with the exception of Suzie, the youngest one, none of them seems to be able to catch on."

He chuckled. "They will. At their age they learn quickly enough."

"Do they?" she said with a mocking grin. "I do wish you would tell them that. No, for this group it's just

216

some time away from Clare's boarding school and credits." She sighed. "But now, tell me."

"Tell you what?"

"You've been up to see Sophie . . . how is she feeling now?"

"You saw her this morning, didn't you?" he asked with some surprise.

"Yes, yes I did. We had tea together in her morning room, and Jim, I am worried about her."

"Are you? Why?"

"Didn't you notice how despondent she is?"

"Nooo . . . preoccupied . . . but good Lord, Holly, she has had a nasty accident and a very severe head injury."

"Yes, poor thing . . . but what worries me is her mood. Jim . . . she seems so down, depressed, totally unlike herself."

"Really?" He thought this over a moment. "You know, a concussion can leave one extremely fatigued."

"Yes, of course, but it wasn't physical . . . it was something . . . a feeling in her eyes . . . a sadness, I think."

He laughed. "Holly . . . have you been at the novels lately? No doubt she is worrying about the upcoming show. You know she is entered into the jumping class event and is probably worried about getting enough work in before D-day!"

Holly smiled. "Of course, that must be it. But Sophie is a pro. She needn't worry about getting practice in, and I'll work her horse for her."

He touched her pert nose, allowed a finger to push away a wayward flick of hair. "In the showing business one always has to be on one's toes or one is o-u-t, and Sophie knows that better than most." His smile was a caress. "Don't let it trouble you."

Sir Justin's dark ginger brows drew together as he approached them. What was this? He was going to plant Dr. Jim Jakes in the mud, that was what!

"Good morning," he managed to say brightly enough and was gratified to see Holly swing around and blush furiously. Was she avoiding his eyes, or was there really something on her jacket she was so carefully picking off?

"Morning, Justin . . ." It was Holly's voice, scarcely audible.

"Hello, Sir Justin. Up to see your aunt? You'll be pleased, she looks really well," said Jim.

"Thank you, I am certain she does. Sophie always manages." He nodded and continued toward the big house. He wanted to grab Holly's hand, drag her along and away from Jim Jakes, but with a great deal of self-control he left her behind without glancing back.

Holly was surprised and a little piqued. Nothing. He had tried absolutely nothing. He didn't try to speak with her, didn't try to catch her attention, didn't seem to want to get her alone. What was this? She recalled his lovemaking during the night and shivered.

"Cold? Want me to fetch your sweater from the barn?" said Jim, bringing her attention back to himself.

"What? Oh . . . no, no thanks." She smiled a dismissal. "I'll be working Tinker for the next hour, and let me assure you, working Tinker will keep me warm."

"So the lady bids me adieu," he said, bowing her off. "And I have my rounds to make." He reached out for her arm. "Holly . . . tonight? I promise you a fabulous dinner . . ."

She wanted to be with Justin tonight. She wanted to sort things out in her own head. What did she want? She would play it safe. "I don't think so, Jim. I think I'll just relax with the TV tonight and make it an early evening."

"Change your mind, Holly . . . I want to see you," he cajoled in a low soft voice.

"Not tonight, Jim." She smiled apologetically. "But thank you anyway." She was moving off.

He watched her go, and his gaze was so intent that he never heard Joy Chen come up behind him until she released a gurgle of amused laughter.

218

"She is after bigger fish, Jim . . . don't you know that?"

He spun around. "Joy? How are you? Hacking out today?" He was irritated with her. He didn't know the oriental girl very well, and until now she had never gotten in his way.

"Hmmm. Just came back from London, and I thought I'd loosen up with a ride. . . ." She hesitated. "Look, pretty Jim . . ." She moved closer toward him. "If it's company you want tonight . . . I'd be happy to give it to you."

He smiled. "You are far too . . . er . . . dangerous for me, Joy."

Her black eyes moved, and a light flickered deep in their dark recesses. She hadn't meant to play this card, but she was running low on cash, and her habit was growing more expensive every week. "Take me to dinner, pretty blond boy, and I promise it will be to your benefit."

He felt suddenly wary of her. "Ah, Joy . . . I don't think that would be a good idea."

"Don't you?" She was losing patience. "But Jim . . . I don't think it would be a good idea for you to pass up this opportunity. There is a matter we must discuss."

His fair brow went up. "Is there?" Sly thing, just what was she up to?

"Hmmm. I'll meet you at the King's Head . . . but I think we will take dinner somewhere more . . . exclusive."

"If you like," he conceded, but his blue eyes flashed with his anger. "I'll come by for you at seven." With this he moved off, leaving Joy to watch him as he got into his car.

Holly had stood with Tinker and watched some of this scene with interest. Was Joy throwing herself at Jim Jakes? How very odd. She had heard about the oriental girl, who was near to being the number-one topic of gossip at the stables. She had seen Joy ride out with Chrissy Penbroke on the day of Chrissy's death

219

. . . and now as she watched Joy approach she felt a shiver of fear tickle her spine. This is absurd, she told herself, and mounted her horse.

Sir Justin put his hands on the arms of Sophie's cushioned wing chair. "Right, Sophie, we know the line was deliberately cut. You must agree to call in the police."

She looked away from him. "I can't, Justin. Don't you see . . . only one person stands to gain by my death at this time. . . ."

"Sophie!" Justin's voice was reproachful.

"No, no, don't misunderstand. I don't suspect my son . . . but Justin, don't you realize what the police would think? What with this dreadful thing about Chrissy Penbroke . . . they still don't have any leads . . ." She shook her head. "I just can't bring them in. That would be pointing a finger at Greg! It would!"

"Hush, Sophie. Don't get yourself worked up."

"But I've made such a muddle of everything. Thomas expects me to sign over the shares to him . . . Greg dreads it . . . as he should . . . and now . . . someone wants me dead!"

"But it can't have been Thomas, because he would only stand to lose if you should be killed at this time. You haven't signed the papers . . . and I won't believe it is Greg. Therefore, there must be someone else here who would stand to gain."

"There is no one else."

Justin had his doubts about that. Perhaps one of Thomas's ladies had finally decided to make him more available? However, this was not something he was going to suggest just now. Sophie was distraught enough.

"If you won't call in the police, you will promise to let me handle this problem," said Justin gravely.

"What . . . what are you going to do?"

"Make it known that I discovered the cut brake line of course." He shrugged. "That could accomplish one of two things. Make our culprit give up his or her plans or make our culprit more careful."

"You say, his or . . . her?"

"That's right." His tone was brisk.

She said nothing more about this but took to gazing out the window on the riding ring. She smiled to see Holly taking Tinker through his paces. "Look at that girl!" she exclaimed suddenly. "She handles Tinker as no one else ever has . . . she'll take a cup with that gelding, depend upon it!"

Justin's gaze followed his aunt's. It was amazing how the woman could jump from her own attempted murder to Holly's riding skills, but that was Sophie all over.

"I think Laeland will clean up at this event!" There was a chuckle in his voice.

"Yes, won't we though," returned Sophie proudly. "William would have been so pleased. . . ."

He patted her hand. "I'm going to run, Sophie . . . but if you want me, I'll be in my lab."

"Yes, dear." She watched him go. Someone was trying to kill her. Who? Her son, because he wanted to stop her from signing over the shares to Thomas, or Thomas, because he had forged her signature at the bank? It was no paltry amount that had been withdrawn, and she had only found out about it by accident. Of course, Thomas didn't know that she had discovered what he had done . . . or did he? Had he overheard her talking to the bank yesterday? He had walked in shortly after she put the receiver down. He could have overheard the entire conversation. It was why she had put off signing the stock shares over to him. Was he worried that she would have him arrested? Was Thomas trying to kill her? Or was it Greg? Either way it was heartbreaking to think about it.

Tomorrow she would ride. Tomorrow when she felt more the thing mentally and physically. There was, of course, one other possibility. Justin had not said it, but she knew it had been on her nephew's mind. There was always the chance that one of Thomas's mistresses had decided to . . . but this was probably an absurd line of thought. There was no doubt a reasonable explanation for the brake line's condition. . . .

Jim Jakes slowed his Sirocco, waited for Joy to jump out of her own car and into his before shifting and taking off. He didn't say anything for a long moment and waited for her. She only smiled and took long drags on her cigarette.

"Well?" he started hopefully, allowing some of his impatience to appear purposely.

"I really don't know how to begin," she said coyly.

He glanced at her sharply, and then thought to try something else, something he hadn't yet thought of. "My place or yours?" He sweetened it with his smile.

She laughed, throwing her head back with the sound, and then took a long look at him. "Perhaps afterward . . ."

"Afterward?"

"Hmm. After our agreement."

"Joy . . . I just don't understand what you want."

"I want money. Oh, not anything you can't afford, pretty man."

"Money? What in hell are you talking about?"

"Not now, sweetheart," she said firmly. "I'll just wait till we get to the motorway . . . during dinner we can discuss it, not now."

"Joy . . ."

She shook her head. "Not now. Later."

Holly paced the floor of her flat. She couldn't sleep. It was no use trying. All she could think about was Justin. They had shared more than passion last night. He had allowed her to see him, really see him, and she thought . . . but never mind. Evidently she had been wrong. He hadn't even bothered to stop to talk to her this afternoon. She had been working Tinker when he came out of the big house. He had looked her way, he had winked, and he had proceeded to his car. Gone. He was gone, just like that, without a word or a backward glance.

Last night had meant nothing to him. She was simply just one of his many women. He was the playboy Laeland, and she had been for a time one of his toys. A horrendous thought at the best, but apparently it was a fact. Another fact of life she could put down in her book of learning.

She had thought she was being wise. She had thought when she dressed and left him sleeping to return to her own flat that she was doing the correct thing, that in so doing she would make him all the more aware of their growing relationship. Well, she had somehow miscalculated, and she was alone, unhappy, unsure, and needing, needing only him.

She sighed and brushed a stray tear away from her face. Her father and brother were gone from her. They would probably never see her again. . . . Stop it! You are feeling sorry for yourself. . . . No, I am missing my father and Hassan. . . . You are wondering if it was all worth it? . . . Yes, and I am certain that it was, it is. Freedom is always worth the cost. . . . Freedom is heartache! . . . And its absence is worse, its absence is heartbreak!

She switched on the TV, discovered the local gentry to be on their knees, cameras tuned in on a family of foxes inhabiting an abandoned building not so very far away from the Grange. Fox-watching, it was called, and with some amusement she was distracted enough to cease her woes for the moment and join the fox-watching.

Sir Justin's excitement was near fever pitch. There . . . it had been right there all along. Bless you, Melvin Calvin! He had found the gene, he had successfully inserted it into a fungus yeast, and was astounded, overjoyed, gratified to find that it reproduced the crude oil from its donor plant. This done, the facts assimilated and retested, he had phoned his solicitors in London.

"What? . . . yes, yes, a patent. . . . I'll bring by everything you need in the morning, but Hopkins, listen to me, we have to patent the living organisms as well. . . .

223

Yes, not only the procedure but the new living organism. . . ."

"Hmmm. A complicated job you have set for me, but you are right. You will need two patents. In the meantime, I don't have to caution you to keep this under lock and key, do I?"

Justin was bursting with jubilation. He felt light-headed and giddy. "No, no you don't."

"What time shall I expect you tomorrow morning?"

"Cal is out of town visiting his daughter, but I'll drive myself into London tomorrow early and avoid the traffic. I'll be at your office at eight A.M."

"Very well, Justin, I shall see you then. And Justin . . . you will be careful. . . ?" The man's voice had lowered with the intensity of his meaning.

Justin was too thrilled with his achievement, with its meaning, to be put down with farfetched notions of industrial espionage. No one knew he was working on this. No one had any idea how close he had been to this final answer. "Yes, yes, of course, Hopkins. I'll see you tomorrow." He put down the receiver.

Genetic manipulation! Famous! Mind-boggling that the answer had come purely by accident. He started putting away his papers in the vault. For months now he had been right there, right on top of it, and he had seen it only by chance! He had followed the DNA guidelines set up by his colleagues. He had taken his experiment step by step cautiously until he had eliminated all other possibilities, and there it was, the gene he needed. Everything from this point on would be relatively simple.

Holly. Somehow thoughts of her slipped into his head. He had been working since early afternoon, and his work had managed to keep her from intruding upon his thoughts. But now here she was again, and he suddenly needed to see her, share his joy with her. He wanted to tell her what he had discovered, he wanted to boast to her, see pride in him on her face, in her eyes. He wanted to hold her.

He had walked away from her that afternoon, avoid-

ng her purposely. He didn't even know if she was at
home now or out with that blasted Jim Jakes.

He paced. Damn, why shouldn't I just pop on over to
her place and tell her my news? . . . What, at this hour?
Fool, it's nearly midnight! You have to get an early
start to London tomorrow.

He closed his lab door and double-locked it with the
new lock he had installed that morning as an extra
precaution. He took the stairs, crossed the dark interior
of his garage, and stepped out into the cool night air.
His sports car was in front of him. His key was in his
pocket. Well?

Hell, I can go the distance! I managed without her
today . . . I can manage without her tonight! . . . Right
then, leave her to Jim Jakes. It's obvious he wants her!
His gray eyes sparkled with something new and he
moved to his sports car; out loud he answered his mind,
"The Hell I will!"

Some moments later he was banging on Holly's door,
and when she opened it wide he didn't hesitate to take
her up in his embrace and kiss her long and sweet.
"Ah, sunshine . . . I've needed you."

She was breathless, she was petulant over his incon-
siderate behavior toward her, she pulled away. "Have
you?"

He was inside, kicking the door shut behind him,
reaching for her. She slapped his hands away and took
to her stairs. He was after her, and suddenly they were
both laughing, collapsing onto her bed. "Ah, Holly . . .
Holly . . ."

His kiss was long, hard, and full with his growing
emotion. She filled a void in his life. She answered a
need in his heart. Her touch recruited feelings he
thought long burned out of his soul.

Her arms went around his lean muscular body. Here
she was taking on this man, this dominant creature
who would forever try to rule her. Isn't that what she
had run away from? What was she doing? But she
couldn't think just now, not with his kisses covering
her face, his hands deftly working her body into a

225

frenzy . . . and then it flooded into her head that she loved him. Oh, God, she loved him. She wanted to say it, to shout it, but instinct held it back in her throat. Instead she whispered happily, "Justin . . . oh, Justin, I want you . . ."

This excited him into deeper, sweeter realms, but was it what he wanted to hear? Yes, dammit, but he wanted more, much more from her than that. No time now to consider this as his hands covered her breasts, as his lips brushed against the nipples, as he moved himself into position to take her. God but she was good. He whispered his delight with her, he taught her to understand as he spread wide her thighs. Had he ever felt this way before?

She felt a burning surge of hot blood race through her as his fingers worked the pleasure points of her body. Suddenly she could feel his impatience to take her, and he was working his rod against the lips of her womb, pushing, caressing, teasing her into blind sensation. She took him wondrously, passionately. She said his name, moved to his thrusts, fevered to his words. She loved him . . . loved him . . .

Chapter Seven

Sophie patted the chestnut mare she held still with the lead chain. "Well, Jim . . . infection all over? Is she ready for breeding?"

He nodded. "Hmm . . . she'll do, and yes, she is certainly ready for breeding." He glanced over the plump woman in riding breeches, boots, and a hard hat. "I am rather surprised to see you up and dressed for riding. You know, Thomas or Greg could have helped me with the mare."

She released a short laugh. "Greg is with our supplier in Southampton this morning, and Thomas . . ." Just where was Thomas? "Thomas is taking care of some other business." She put up her hand to stay him. "And I am dressed in riding clothes because, *young Jim*"—she used the adjective to reduce his sense of importance—"I plan on taking my jumper through his paces."

"You can't mean it! Sophie . . . you have more sense than that!"

Why did he suddenly seem so oddly familiar? What was that flash in his blue eyes? Never mind. She put it aside and raised a finely arched brow. "It is because I *do* have good sense that I mean to work my animal. Jim . . . the show is five days off, and I intend to win a cup!"

"Sophie . . . give yourself at least another day," he urged, his brows drawn in a frown.

"I am sure you have your rounds to do, sir, and I urge you to them," she said lightly, putting an end to his lecture.

He sighed. "Hmm. So I do, but where is that pretty instructor of yours? I thought I'd have a go at her before I left the premises."

"I imagine she is still in bed. She doesn't have a lesson till nine, you know." She was smiling sweetly but her thoughts were flickering to last evening and to the car she had seen parked outside Holly's flat. Justin's car.

"Okay . . . I'm leaving, but do give Holly my regards. Perhaps I'll stop by later to see her."

Sophie would only smile benignly at this and wave him off. She needed to work her chestnut. She needed to ride and shake off her dismal feelings. Nothing could have surpassed Thomas's tender care and consideration yesterday. He had jumped to her every sigh. She had almost told him that she knew about the money he had withdrawn from her account, but something had stopped her. Greg, on the other hand, had been moody, ill-tempered and unavailable for any length of time. Just what was she supposed to think?

* * *

Holly moved pleasurably as the sun stroked and warmed her face. Her thick curly lashes fluttered, and as she opened her eyes she smiled, expecting to find Sir Justin nestled beneath her covers. Gone. He was gone. A wave of disappointment flooded through her. She had hoped to sit across a breakfast table with him and see his face in the morning light.

Of course he wouldn't stay to embarrass her and cause gossip. And, of course, Holly, he wouldn't stay because eventually he wants an annulment! Can't get one if the whole world could testify to his having spent the night in her flat. . . . Stop it! Things were changing between them, weren't they? Yes, yes! After they had made love, he had sat up and talked to her about his work, his achievement, his plans. He had confided in her. . . .

He had told her about Sophie, about the brake line being cut. He had taken her in his arms, and he had trusted her enough to ask her to watch over Sophie for him. . . .

That was a frightening thought. Sophie in danger? First someone murders Chrissy Penbroke, and now Sophie . . . in danger? She had asked Justin if he thought there was any connection, but he had only frowned and the question had gone unanswered. Just what was going on at Laeland Grange? And when . . . when would she see Justin again?

Joy looked up from her pillow. Had she heard someone coming into her flat? At this hour? Why . . . it wasn't even nine o'clock yet.

"Thomas," she said with some surprise as she saw the small man come toward her. What was the matter with him? Why did he look so angry? She needed her pills. . . . She reached over to her nightstand drawer but his hand closed round her wrist and stopped her. "Thomas?" she repeated, this time in puzzlement. "What is it? What's wrong?"

"Just tell me you wouldn't do it . . . not now, no

228

when I am so close to getting the company shares," he said in a tightly controlled voice.

"What?" She blinked. "Just what are you talking about?"

"Tell me!" he demanded.

She hadn't seen Thomas yesterday. He had been trying to get in touch with her for two days now, but she had been avoiding him. No doubt he was referring to Sophie's accident. "Thomas . . . you won't get those shares. I told Judy to tell you . . ."

"She told me, and then she said she was going away with her husband on a short holiday . . . that things were getting out of hand here. I didn't know what she meant then . . . now I think I do."

"Thomas, you don't understand . . ."

"Then try explaining to me, bitch!"

"Will you tell me what she is doing up there?" demanded Lynn Patterson of Holly as she came up to the riding ring's weathered fencing.

Holly glanced at Sophie cantering her horse around the ring and then at Lynn's face and sighed. *"You* tell *me."*

"Oh, great." She grimaced.

Holly laughed. "Lynn, you are priceless. You say more with one look than anybody could with a dozen words!"

"That still doesn't give us an answer, does it? I mean . . . Sophie did suffer a concussion, didn't she?"

Holly nodded and watched as Sophie and her gelding cleared a four-foot rail and moved flowingly, smoothly to the next. "That she did."

"Well then, she should know better! Will you look at her?" She nearly screamed as Sophie headed her gelding toward the water jump. "Prince always gives me a refusal on that one."

"Her chestnut will take it—and I've seen you take Prince over that jump," returned Holly on a wide smile.

"Yeah, when I beat him he takes it. . . . Look at he glide."

"It would appear that she knows what she is doing said Holly quietly.

Lynn frowned for a long moment. "It's weird, thoug . . . don't you think? I mean . . . I thought English polic were supposed to be such wizards! I hear they still don know a thing about Chrissy's murder . . . and no Sophie has had this accident. I mean, Holly, she is on of the most cautious drivers I know." She shook he head. "If I were a suspicious person, I would be ver suspicious about all this right now."

"Speak of the devil!" breathed Holly as the sound of car brought her head around. It was a dark-blue polic car, and inside was Inspector Higgens. "I wonder wh; he wants here."

A moment later they had an answer when he aske to see Greg Laeland.

"He isn't here, inspector," said Holly quietly.

"Can you tell me where he is?"

"In Southampton on Grange business," she answere "Why?"

"Why? Because I wish to speak with him."

"Why?" asked Sophie as she dismounted her geldin and joined them. "Just why do you wish to speak to m son?"

"I am sorry to advise you, Mrs. Martin, that your so was not quite candid with me when we spoke a few da; ago, and there are questions I feel I must put to him

"I see. If you like you can wait for him in the house She turned to Holly and gave over her reins. "Will yo see to Friar?"

"Yes, of course," said Holly, watching them go off.

It was at just about the same time that Inspect Higgens arrived at the Grange that Justin was leavin his solicitors' London office and bumped into Ma Patterson. The two men shook hands and smiled.

"Justin! How the hell are you?"

"Very well, and yourself?"

"Not bad," said the American with a shrug. Truth was he had quite a bit on his mind. There was Lynn back in the New Forest, unhappy, lonely, upset with him because of all the time he put into his work. There was his work, and it was getting to be too much, too often.

"Look . . . I missed breakfast this morning. Why don't we take a taxi around to Claridge's and have a healthy English breakfast together?" said Justin.

Mark groaned comically. "Man, are you kidding? One of your breakfasts would weight me down for the rest of the day. But I'll have some coffee with you, and maybe a Danish if Claridge's can find one."

Justin laughed and hailed a cab as a thought occurred to him.

"You still have that tract of industrial land up at Liverpool?"

"Don't remind me," said the American with a grimace.

"Right, then, we'll talk about it over breakfast," said Justin. He knew just what he could use it for at the right price. If his company was going to produce his new oil, they would have to construct large vats . . . they were going to need land. . . .

Mark buttered his roll and laid some black currant jam on it before he took his bite and sat back in his chair. He was thinking over Justin's offer. It was shrewd—he hadn't realized Justin could deal in such a manner—but in truth it might be years before someone else found a use for that land. It would get him off the hook.

"But let me understand, you'll be constructing vats—"

"Right," cut in Justin. "Approximately sixty by a hundred feet in size. Liverpool's harbor is a perfect location. We will be drawing in the salt water to float the oil."

"Never mind the technical data . . . what we have to find out is whether or not that piece of property is right

231

for you, and then we will have to talk more about th
price, Justin."

"Fair enough, but I think the price we have dis
cussed is a good one for us both."

Mark laughed. "You would! And you call yourself
friend!"

Justin grinned. "When can we take a trip up t
Liverpool and have a look at it?"

Mark bit his lip and considered this. "Hmm . . . ove
the weekend?"

That was five days away. Justin was excited. H
wanted to see it now, but he had pushed Mark enough
"It's a date, then . . . where shall we meet?"

"I've got some business to finish up here in town
Then I'd like to drive into the New Forest this afternoo
. . . have a look at my wife and kid . . . it's been a while
you know . . . then I'm off for two days to Cornwall t
finalize another land deal. Saturday, though . . . tha
should be just fine."

"Good. How are you getting to Brockenhurst today
Train?"

"Hmmm. Why?"

"I've got a meeting with some of my staff here i
London, then I'm driving over to my cottage at th
Grange. I could give you a lift and we could go into thi
further on the drive down."

"Great. Okay . . . I'll come by your office aroun
four."

"No, make it my flat." He took out a pen and wrot
down the address. Some minutes later he was on hi
way to Laeland's offices and a staff meeting he ha
called. Things were now moving steadily, properly, an
he was excited because of it, but underlining his gle
foaming around his sense of contentment, was hi
growing feeling about Holly. Holly. He had beame
beneath the look of approval she had given him la
night when he had told her about his work. He grew i
the power of her love. Did she love him? Was that th
look he had seen last night? Did he love her? Holly . .
Ah, Holly . . .

* * *

Judy Baines brushed her short wisps of blond hair away from her face and paused outside Joy Chen's door. She had returned from a two-day excursion with her husband newly resolved to end her relationship with Thomas and Joy both. She couldn't bear it any longer. Their *ménage à trois* was sick, sick. Why had she allowed it to go this far? She would just tell Joy she was out of it. Joy would threaten her again, threaten to expose her to her husband but she was prepared for that. . . .

Odd, why was the door slightly ajar? Oh well, no doubt Joy had forgotten to lock it, forgotten to push it hard. It had a habit of slipping open if it wasn't shoved hard enough. She walked into the flat and found the drapes still drawn against the late-morning sun. Odd again. Joy was a late sleeper, but it was nearly noon.

"Joy?" she called and stood a moment. "Joy?"

Perhaps she was out. Should she wait? She sighed and moved to the sofa, changed her mind, and called again, "Joy?" This time she walked down the hall toward the bedroom. "Come on, Joy, wake up." She could just see Joy's form slumped across the bed, out on her pills, no doubt. "Oh, Joy . . . when are you going to learn?" she started to say, and stopped. "Joy?" She flicked on the light switch, and the beam of illumination lit glaringly on the blood running out of Joy's body.

Judy screamed and kept on screaming until a neighbor came to her support. Someone had shot Joy. She lay in the bed, her black hair shining around her shoulders, her sensual body limp in a graceful pose, her eyes opened with surprise. Joy Chen was dead.

Chapter Eight

"Ah, there you are, Greg," said Sophie thankfully as her son entered the room to join Inspector Higgens and herself. She put down her cup of tea. "Whatever kept you?"

"Smitty wasn't at the feed mill, Mother, and we really do need to settle the business, so I went looking for him all over town."

"Did you ever find your Smitty?" said Inspector Higgens casually.

Greg frowned at him. "No . . . but I expect he will call." He turned to his mother. "I didn't have any lessons scheduled till this afternoon, Mother . . . was there a problem?"

"No, no, that's not it, but Inspector Higgens here would like to ask you a few questions, dear." She started to get up. They heard the phone ring, and she smiled. "That's probably Smitty now. Shall I handle him, Greg?"

Maureen appeared at the doorway. "Sorry . . . but it is for you, inspector."

Sophie took up the receiver and handed it to him. She turned to her secretary. "Thank you, dear." Then to Greg, she whispered, "Shall we give the inspector some privacy?" and started to lead him out of the room. However, the inspector stayed them. A moment later he was off the phone.

He glanced gravely at Sophie. "I am very sorry to have to tell you this, but we have another murder on our hands."

Sophie sank into a nearby Queen Anne chair and bit her bottom lip. Greg opened his eyes wide and demanded, "Who?"

"A Miss Joy Chen. I believe she was a student of yours?" This he gave to Greg, quietly, meaningfully.

234

Greg colored up. "Dammit, inspector! I don't like that question. She was never my student. A few years ago she was Thomas's private lesson."

"She was, I think, though, a regular around the Grange?" pursued Higgens, not at all perturbed by Greg's outburst.

"She hacked out of our stable," said Sophie softly. Her mind was a flutter of thoughts, trickling with quiet fears.

"She was also a friend of Christina Penbroke's." It was not a question. This time the inspector was stating a fact, waiting for a reaction.

Greg sat down heavily, and he and his mother exchanged glances.

"I shall return later today, Mr. Laeland," said Higgens on a parting note. "There is a great deal we must discuss."

Andrew Benton was a problem, thought Justin as he slipped his key into the lock of his penthouse flat and stepped into the sprawling white-carpeted room with its panoramic view of the city. Fleetingly, he wondered if Holly would want to redecorate.

A knock. He frowned. Who could that be? It was only three. Mark Patterson wouldn't be by till later.

He opened the door wide and found there a man of average height, dark hair, skin, and eyes, in a European-styled beige suit. His brow went up. An Arab? What was this? More of Holly's relatives?

Saeed bowed his head respectfully. "Sir Justin. May I come in?"

"Who the deuce are you?"

"I am Saeed," said the Arab, as though this would answer all. "I think we must talk."

"Really? Why?"

"If I may come in . . . ?"

Justin stood aside and allowed the man admittance. "Have a seat, won't you?" He was slightly amused.

"Ah, it is appreciated. Thank you, I will," said Saeed, plopping heavily on the white-and-brown print sofa.

235

He sighed long and hard. "I am here on behalf of some gentlemen quite well known to you. An organization formed with the oil interests of the world in mind."

"I see," said Justin, just beginning to realize. They had approached him in the past, or at least they had tried to. What was this now?

"Ah, this is a good beginning, is it not?" said Saeed.

"Is it?"

"It has come to their attention that your work on a fuel . . . a new method of deriving oil . . . is . . . shall we say, in its final stages."

How did they know that much? He smiled to himself. Wouldn't they be surprised to know it all? He said easily, "May I know how you come by this information?"

"You must realize that we protect our sources," said Saeed.

Justin smiled amicably. "Of course. So, then, how can I help you?"

"It is evident, is it not, that if you manage to actually produce this relatively cheap form of oil . . . we will find ourselves . . . uncomfortable."

"No, you will simply have to make do . . . like the rest of us."

"Ah, but we have grown accustomed to—"

"To losing millions at the gaming tables and taking it out of the West's hide," said Justin sweetly, cutting in.

Saeed ignored this. "We plan . . . you may realize . . . to increase the price of Middle Eastern oil at the end of this quarter. We would not like to be embarrassed with your product suddenly hitting the market."

"That is too bad," said Justin, shaking his head sadly. "You will be."

"Sir Justin, are you not surprised that I knew you would be here at your flat? That you were no longer at the Grange cottage?"

"No, I imagine you make my whereabouts your business," said Sir Justin blandly. "Do get to the point."

"The point is that we are capable of many things."

236

"No doubt, but if you are asking me to shelve my experiment, you are out."

"We don't ask that you forget it . . . we know that a man like you would never accept that. Also, we are not fools. If you are working toward such a goal, there must be others. Eventually this thing would happen to us. We ask only that you . . . put it off until after the quarter, until we have raised our oil prices, accumulated enough to tide us over through . . . what we envision the lean years."

"No," said Justin.

"You don't understand. We realize, of course, that money means nothing to you in this instance. We are therefore prepared to offer you something else."

"Really?"

"Yes, Shall we say . . . the life of someone dear to you?"

Justin had Saeed by the lapels. "Tread easy, mister!" His threat was a growl.

"Abusing me can do neither of us any good," screeched Saeed. He could feel the power behind the man looming above him.

Justin released him. "Perhaps not, but it could bring me some measure of satisfaction. I don't like to be threatened."

"Nor do I like to threaten such a man as yourself. However, we must make our position known to you."

Sir Justin released a short laugh. "Then it is time to advise you that your source was, shall we say, a bit late with his information. I have already completed my experiment and achieved my goal. The patents have been applied for, and my findings will be publicly announced in the various media."

Saeed stood up in some consternation. "This is bad . . very bad for us both."

"I think not. You will tell your people that I was a heartless man who would rather see my entire family destroyed before I would give in to their threats. They would gain nothing but evil notoriety by going after my people. On the other hand, I have both the money and the power to strike back against them and theirs. No, I don't think they will choose that road.

"In the meantime, there is no way my vats can be constructed to go into production before the end of the quarter. Let them raise their prices if they must. For the time being, they will get the increase . . . until I bring them down, and, Saeed, eventually I will."

Saeed moved toward the door. "I shall tell them, Sir Justin." He sighed and turned to give him a full look. "It is, as you said, that our source was a fool, his information came too late. I think we should no longer protect him."

"Him . . . ?" Justin urged.

"Your own man. Andrew Benton. The fellow is untrustworthy." With this Saeed was gone.

Maureen put Dr. Jakes on hold while she went to get Sophie. He held the receiver in his hand tightly and felt a nervous sweat prickle across his brow. This was turning out exactly as he wanted. Now if only she would meet him. She had to meet him. Sophie came to the receiver.

"Hello, Jim . . . what is it?"

"Sophie . . . look . . . is there anyone near you right now?"

"Why, no." Surprise in her voice.

"Sophie, we have to talk. Something has happened. You know Joy Chen . . . has been murdered?"

"Yes, I know. It is dreadful."

"Worse than that, and . . . I'm sorry, Sophie . . . but we are going to have to come to a decision, you and I."

"What are you talking about?"

"I can't go into it over the phone."

"Well, come over then . . . we can be private."

"No, I would rather not. Look . . . you know the old well on the Grange New Forest grounds? Can you take a walk over there later in the afternoon?"

"But . . ."

"Sophie . . . it involves Greg, and I really think he shouldn't see me talking to you."

She felt a trickle of fear touch her spine and bolt upward. Tension filled her and stiffened her muscles. "Right, then, Jim. What time would be convenient to you?"

"Five-thirty ... and Sophie ... not a word to anyone."

"If you think this cloak-and-dagger stuff is necessary, Jim ... though I can't understand why."

"Please believe me, Sophie, it's necessary." He put down the receiver and smiled to himself. Indeed, it was necessary all right.

Chapter Nine

Greg Laeland moved toward his car. His face was drawn in misery. Egad but his life had turned upside down suddenly. One day everything was running along smoothly, and then whop-bam the world hit him in the face. Just what was he going to do? The police were breathing down his neck. They were getting into his relationship with Chrissy. That blasted Inspector Higgens had been all too impertinent. . . .

Their investigation was getting more and more calculated. And now Joy ... murdered? Oh, God, what was he going to do? He had almost blurted out to Higgens that Thomas and Joy were lovers ... but then he thought of his mother, of the pain, the humiliation, she would have to endure, and he couldn't do it. Eventually she would find out, but he suddenly realized that his dislike for Thomas, his unhappiness with his mother's attitude, and even the prospect of losing half the company to Thomas couldn't shake his love and respect for Sophie. So, when the questions zeroed in on Joy, on what her relationship with him might be, he had simply clammed up and said nothing.

Just great. What was he going to do? Dammit, he

didn't know! Higgens wanted him to be more specific about his whereabouts this morning. Hell, this was a another problem. Most of the time he had been in his car, driving around looking for Smitty. Just how could he prove that? What if they pinpointed Joy Chen's death to be a time when he had been driving? Oh, God, he was in trouble. This was real trouble. And why? Just who would want Joy Chen dead? Thomas? Why?

Jim Jakes. That was another thing. Strange that Jim should take him aside, insist on meeting at the old well in secret. What was it all about? Jim had hinted at knowing something . . . not wanting anyone to see them together. Why? Maybe it was a trap? Absurd. Why would Jim Jakes wish to entrap him? He was only a country vet. . . .

He opened his car door.

Holly was looking fresh and beautiful in her spring dress of blue cotton. When she had bought it she had smiled at herself—no Dior or Laurent this, but well within her budget. It had been a good independent feeling. Now she surveyed herself, gave a brush to her long amber hair, and with lively movement took her stairs. She couldn't stand it any longer.

She wanted to see Justin. Had to see him, and see where they stood.

She opened the door and saw Greg going toward his car. He was looking troubled. She would ask him for a ride to Justin's cottage and talk to him on the way down. He looked as if he needed someone to talk to, and she knew that Inspector Higgens had given him a rough time that afternoon. It wasn't a good thing for the riding stable, and it was frightening to think about. Two girls killed within a week of one another. Just what was happening here?

"Greg?" she called.

He turned and smiled. Lovely. She was always bright and lovely, and what was more, he discerned real friendship from her, a rare commodity. He stopped at his open car door and waited.

"Hello, pretty girl," he said, smiling for the first time that afternoon.

"Will you drop me off at Justin's cottage?" she asked on a breathless note, going around to his passenger door.

He frowned. "I will take you anywhere you want to go ... but Holly ... Justin!"

"Careful, now," she warned, finding that while she gave herself the right to criticize Justin Laeland she didn't like it coming from anyone else.

He grinned. "Look, he is my cousin, and a very good fellow at bottom ... but he is a charming rogue with the birds, and I don't want you hurt." He sighed. "Or have you passed the line already?"

"Ask me no questions, sir, and I'll be happy to tell you no lies." She sat in his car. "Now ... are you going drive me, or shall I walk?"

He gave a short chuckle and got in the car. "I'll tell you what, puss. I think Justin has met his match in you."

Jim Jakes pressed a hand to his forehead as he parked his car off the road and secluded it between massive evergreens. It was already getting dark. Damn, but he was such a clever boy. He smiled as he thought of his brilliance. Everything he had done had brought him to this moment.

He could have worked as a top man in his chosen field, but no, he chose to come here to the New Forest and take over a country vet's practice. Why? His eyes glistened in answer to the silent question. Why indeed? What else could he do? It was his destiny. He had often thought Sophie might guess. She had a way of suddenly cocking her head and considering him. But no, not even Sophie had realized.

He got out of his car and started down the woodland path that would eventually take him to Grange grounds and the old well. No one would suspect him. A thought of Joy Chen flashed through his head. She had been stupid enough to think she could blackmail him! Damn

241

her soul! But that had been easy enough to deal with. Everyone had cooperated. He had seen Thomas leaving the flat. The door had remained slightly ajar. He hadn't even had to disturb her to get into the flat. So easy. He left her there, her black hair glistening, her dark eyes opened wide with her surprise. His eyelid twitched with the sudden memory. No one had seen him. And now she was dead.

He heard a crackle of leaves and twigs and saw Sophie pacing near the old stone well. She was playing thoughtfully with the weathered but ornamental bucket, and he smiled to himself as he approached her.

Sophie heard him and looked up. There was something in his expression that sent a shiver through her but this was nonsensical. She sighed and went forward hand outstretched to greet him. "Now, Jim . . . do explain, for you have me frightfully worried."

"Of course, Sophie . . ." He was very near to her, and he was reaching into his pocket.

She stiffened. She didn't know why, but she was afraid of him, and as he saw her reflex action he chuckled. "Whatever is the matter, Sophie? I only want to show you a picture." He brought it out and waved it in front of her, not letting her touch it.

She looked down on the image, faded and somewhat yellowed, of William Laeland. She frowned. "A newspaper photograph of William? But . . . I don't understand."

"Don't you? Look at him. He wasn't even twenty when this was taken. He was still in Cambridge then . . . but old enough to take on a mistress. Oh, don't look so distressed, Sophie. He didn't know you then . . . but he took on a mistress and gave her a son. . . ."

He saw her draw back, and her hand went to her face. "That's right," he said. "It all comes together for you now, doesn't it? You have always thought you saw something familiar in me . . . didn't you?"

"Jim . . . Jim . . . are you telling me . . . ?"

"I am telling you that William Laeland was my father, though he never owned it in any way that could

242

have made the difference. Oh, he was generous all right. He made certain that I was clothed, fed, and educated, but not once did he visit me." His face contorted into bitterness. "I was his firstborn son! If it hadn't been for you, he might have married my mother and given me a name . . . but you came along, and he was so damn afraid you wouldn't have him that he never . . ." He shook his head. "That doesn't matter now. I mean to set things right."

Sophie knew now why she was so afraid. "Set things right, Jim? Have you been working on that? Did Chrissy and Joy Chen have something to do with that?"

He laughed harshly. "I always thought you were shrewder than you let on." This time when his hand went into his pocket it was to return with a .38 gun. He handled it easily, lightly, and looked at her long. "Chrissy . . . yes, I think you should know about Chrissy. A mother should know about her son. Your Greg was fooling around with that little fourteen-year-old slut, though in fairness to him, it was easy to forget that bird's age. It was then I realized how I could use their little affair to advantage. I took her on myself, and we met in secret . . . but as it turns out, she did tell Joy I was the father of her baby."

Sophie felt the earth tremble beneath her feet. Here was Jim Jakes telling her he was a murderer, telling her that he had planned it all. "But . . . but why?"

He sneered. "Don't you know yet? Dammit . . . my mother died when I was eighteen. Do you think he came? No . . . but his checks did, they kept on coming. A lawyer came out and said that my father still wished me to continue my education . . . and I did, for him, hoping one day he would acknowledge me."

"I never knew . . . he didn't tell me . . ." Sophie whispered.

"It doesn't matter! I decided that he owed me. I am his firstborn. I am entitled to the Grange . . . to all of it!" He was nearly shouting now.

Demented. This poor man was demented, that was all Sophie could think. Time. She had to stall for time.

"But, Jim . . . I don't understand. If you kill me . . . the Grange will still go to Greg."

"You still don't see, do you? Who do you think tampered with your car? I wanted Greg suspected . . . for this moment."

Sophie closed her eyes. What could she do? What was she going to do? "Greg . . . are you telling me that . . . that Greg will be arrested for my murder?"

"A good notion, but not safe enough for me. No, Greg won't live long enough."

"That still won't get you the Grange," she tried desperately.

"Yes it will. There is a clause. It was explained to me when my father died. If I kept silent about my existence, if I didn't cause any scandal, the Grange would go to me upon your and Greg's deaths."

Greg Laeland came down the path toward the old well. He could just make out someone's form past the bushes. Not Jim . . . no, but then who? Sweet Christ, it was Sophie! Dammit to hell, what was she doing here? He stood rigid for a moment. Should he wait? Should he go back, forget this idiotic meeting? Wait a minute . . . that was Jim with her . . . talking? What was going on here?

He stepped forward and into their sphere, and his brow went up to discover that not only was Jim standing there in the small clearing with his mother, but he was waving a gun in her direction. "Hey, Jim . . . what is this? Put that down!" Such was his disbelief that he thought the good doctor only showing the gun for some unknown reason.

"Hello, little brother. Join us," said Jim Jakes, aiming his pistol at Greg's head. "That's a good boy . . ."

"What? Dammit, Jim . . . what is this? What the hell do you think you are doing?"

"Doing?" Jim looked at the gun. "Oh, this? It's very simple, really, isn't it, Sophie? Why don't you tell him all about my clever plan? Yes, tell my . . . *brother* all about it."

244

"Brother?" Greg turned wide eyes toward his mother. "Why does he keep calling me brother? What is he saying?"

"Greg . . . your father . . . before we were married . . . before we even met . . ."

"That's enough!" growled Jim, suddenly impatient and angry. "All you have to know is that you are both going to die . . . *now* . . . and then I am going to inherit the Grange!"

Holly paced in front of the cottage door. He wasn't home yet. Where was he? Who was he with? Stop it, stop it! This was ridiculous. Greg was right, she was asking for trouble going after Justin. Wasn't he the same arrogant, self-assured playboy that had brought her to the Grange? All he had wanted then was to have her. Well, he had had her. . . .

No. There was more to Sir Justin, and she had seen it . . . especially last night. They had shared so much of one another last night. . . . Oh, this was foolish. She was behaving like a schoolgirl with a crush . . . just a crush. No, she wasn't making him a hero . . . she was seeing him, loving him for what he was . . . wasn't she?

Go home. Don't wait here like a fool. Go back. What if he drives up with a woman in his car? Think how you will feel.

This did it for her. Immediately she ran to the wooded path and started back for the Grange. She hadn't gotten very far, however, when the sound of voices stopped her.

She moved curiously in its direction and came up short when she heard Jim Jakes's voice expound, "That's enough! All you have to know is that you are both going to die . . . *now* . . . and then I am going to inherit the Grange!"

She froze for a moment. That was Jim. Jim . . . sounding like a madman? Impossible. There was a reasonable explanation for this . . . there had to be. She took a step in Jim's direction and saw him holding a gun, and it was aimed at Sophie and Greg Laeland.

245

What should she do? No time to go get help. They coul[d] be dead by then. But why? Why was Jim doing this[?] Never mind, he was . . . that is all you have to thin[k] about now. Do something! *A rock!* She must get [a] rock . . .

One was found, and, holding it high with her hear[t] beating hard against her chest, she crept up on Jim Jakes. He heard something behind him and swun[g] partially around just in time to discover Holly bringin[g] her weapon down. He moved speedily, and it caught hi[s] shoulder. He caught her arm and simultaneously an[d] with animal ferociousness turned to aim his gun a[t] Greg, who was charging toward him. *"Back!"* he shoute[d] at Greg and shook Holly roughly. When he thought h[e] had things restored to order he allowed himself a lon[g] glance at Holly. What was she doing here? He wante[d] Holly. He had planned on having her . . . but, now [of] course, this was impossible. She would have to die a[s] well.

"Ah, Holly . . ." he said softly. "Another of Greg['s] victims. You see, the boy has gone mad. Sophie . . . sh[e] will try to stop him from killing you . . . but he will shoo[t] and kill her as well, and then in a moment of guilt an[d] shame he will put a bullet through his head. . . ."

"Jim . . ." Holly attempted to call him to reaso[n]. "Jim . . . it's not too late . . . you can stop . . ."

"No!" he shouted. "I can't stop. It's already in prog[-] ress . . . I am on my way . . ." He glanced at Sophi[e]. "Now, who shall be first?"

Sir Justin pulled into his driveway and saw the col[or] of red-gold glint in the fading sunlight as Holly van[-] ished in the thick of the woods. Holly? She had bee[n] here . . . waiting for him? He felt a rush of preposterou[s] happiness at the thought, and in a moment he wa[s] hurrying after her.

He heard her up ahead, tripping over a branc[h] clucking at herself and then suddenly she was n[o] longer on the long straight path. She had veered off. H[e] had missed seeing her go off . . . but, and he smiled t[o] himself, there was no mistaking where she had done so. She left a clear trail of broken branches and shredded shrubbery. Why? She was heading for the old well. Whatever was going on here? Voices? Yes, he heard voices. . . .

And then from a distance he saw Holly lift her arm. In her clenched hand was a rock. It happened so quickly, for in a flash she was in Jim's grip and Jim Jakes was brandishing a gun at Greg and Sophie. No time to wonder about this. He had to do something, and quickly! Stealthily, deftly, and with quiet force he brought himself into the scene, and as Jim Jakes turned and brought up his gun Sir Justin was in the air and his leg was snapping out. He caught Jakes's arm with the martial-arts movement, but Jakes managed to hold onto the gun as he went backward. He was on Holly in that moment. He had his arm around her neck, his gun pointed at her back. Everyone went rigid with fright. Justin froze.

Holly knew what she had to do. There was only one answer. Give him a little weight, unexpected weight. She cried out with fear and went limp, totally limp, apparently in a faint. Jim Jakes gasped as she slid, and he made an effort to hold her up that took some energy and put him off balance. Holly was allowed to slide to the ground. As he dropped Holly, her hand went around his ankle and she yanked as hard as she could.

Justin saw in a moment what she was at, and he was on Jim Jakes. Again he used leg motion, and this time he caught Jim Jakes soundly in the chest. The man fell back, winded. Holly was there, scooping up the gun, running out of his reach.

Justin held her tightly as she dove into his arms. He took the gun from her and leveled it at Jim Jakes's head while he spoke to Greg. "You had better go get the police." He turned then to Holly. "You okay?"

"Uh-huh . . ." she managed, but she could see Sophie was not at all feeling well. "Shall I take your aunt up to the house?"

"Sophie . . . ?" he said.

"Yes . . . yes . . . please . . . I want to get away from here," cried the woman, nearly done in by now. She looked at Jim Jakes, sitting on the earth, his head in his hands, and she wanted to cry.

Chapter Ten

Show time! The Laelands, as usual, took the majority of the rosettes and cups, as did their new instructor Holly Winslow. Their advanced and intermediate students had also made an excellent showing, which fairly ensured a good enrollment for the school's next season.

It was now time for the novice and maiden novice to do their rounds, and Holly and Lynn stood together waiting as Tracy Patterson went off to mount her horse.

So much had happened in the last few days. For one thing, Justin had returned to London with Mark Patterson the morning after Jim Jakes's arrest. Nothing had been settled between Holly and Justin. No announcement of their marriage had been discussed.

Scandal was rife in the New Forest, but Sophie had the grace to weather it. Decisions had been finally made as well. Sophie had asked Thomas to move out and her barrister was filing on her behalf for a divorce. Too much had been revealed at Joy Chen's inquest for her to ignore. His infidelities, coupled with his gambling and the forging of her name, had finally brought things to a head, and Sophie faced up to the fact that she could no longer live with such a man.

Greg had been given full management of the estate, which was running along in his hands quite nicely in spite of all the scandal.

And a letter had come from Hassan. Holly had cried as she read it, for it was apparent that her father was still angry over her dissent, but was hopeful of the future. Perhaps in time they could all be close again.

Holly and Lynn Patterson had become very close in the last few days. Holly had confided everything to her, from her strange getaway to her unusual marriage to Justin. The two women had exchanged fears, hopes, and longings, and both were pouting over the absences of their husbands.

"The thing is," said Lynn, "that he had promised me he would be here for Tracy's show." She shook her head. "I suppose I am too predictable. He knows I will be here to represent him, to make excuses to Tracy for him, to hold down the fort . . . but I plan to give him a jolt."

"And what about Justin? He knew that it is my birthday today. He didn't even call. We were supposed to talk about . . . our absurd marriage . . . about the future. He has put it off . . . and put it off . . ."

"Well then, jolt him. Come with me, Holly," said Lynn, suddenly excited. "We'll show them."

"Oh, I don't know. Are you still planning to go through with it?"

"Yep. Right after the show. Tracy goes off with friends for the next few days, and I am going off to Paradise Island. I've never done anything like this before. It's bound to shock him into a reaction . . . and at this point I am willing to settle for any kind of a reaction."

Holly laughed. "Then there is only one thing for me to do. I'll pack my things and join you!"

Lynn took up Holly's hands. "Fantastic! Oh, Holly . . . I think we are doing the right thing. I mean . . . they should have been here, they should have . . . and Justin has no right to expect you to behave like a wife. Why, he has the best of both worlds, doesn't he? You're as faithful as a wife . . . but you are only getting the status of mistress; I mean, he hasn't owned up to being married to you . . . and now he has no reason not to . . . I mean . . . his invention is public, isn't it?"

"That's right. He isn't hiding out any more. This is

249

the time I was to file for a divorce . . . but I didn't want to bring it up. I was hoping . . . he wouldn't want me to . . ."

"That's right. So off we go . . . with just enough of a message left behind so that they can find us . . . if they want to."

"Look . . . there's Tracy," said Holly, watching her student go around in perfect form.

"Thatagirl, Trace!" called her mother.

"Oh, her seat is lovely, Lynn . . . if only she will smile . . ." Holly laughed. "She looks so serious."

The judges had narrowed it down to three riders, and over and over again they were asked to canter. Right then, they had made their decisions, and Lynn screamed with delight as she watched her daughter being presented with a blue.

The casino sparkled with casual tourists out for a touch of excitement. So very different from the clubs in London, where only formal dress was permitted. Friends called out to one another merrily as they won a pot or found a one-armed bandit that gave instead of gobbled. Outside a warm breeze moved the palms and shook the flowers. Holly and Lynn, both clothed in summer knits, entered the scene. They had arrived the other night but had been too tired to do anything but collapse in their separate rooms. They had spent the day in the ocean, and now they meant to play. . . .

Holly brushed a speck off her white low-cut knit top and smoothed her tight-fitting white knit pants. When she looked up it was to find an extremely handsome roulette croupier inviting her with a smile to join his table. She looked at Lynn.

"Yes . . . oh yes," said Lynn, smiling wide at the good-looking man and taking up a seat.

Holly laughed and took up a seat opposite her. "You are a naughty girl," she teased Lynn.

"How is she naughty?" asked the croupier.

"Spin and let's find out," bantered Lynn. She was seething inside, as was Holly. By now Mark and Justin

250

should have realized they were gone . . . should have called.

The croupier began spinning, and it seemed that Lady Luck was with the girls tonight, for both Holly and Lynn began winning. It wasn't long before the table was full of players and an interested crowd had gathered around the table. Throughout, both Holly and Lynn kept up a lively flirtatious banter with the croupier.

"I shall soon be leaving on my break . . ." the dark-eyed, dark-haired, English-accented croupier informed Lynn in an aside.

"Oh no . . . you can't do that . . ."

"You . . . and your friend . . . could join me for a cup of coffee . . ." he invited and gave her a long sexy perusal.

Lynn flushed, restrained herself from giggling, and looked toward Holly. "We could . . . ?"

Justin and Mark had returned from Liverpool the morning after the horse show. Justin had dropped him off at his house and had hurried on to the Grange. It had been three days since he had seen Holly. Three days, and it seemed like an eternity. All he wanted to do was get to her. His trip with Mark had proved successful, and there was so much he wanted to tell her . . .

As he pulled into the parking lot, Greg came out of the barn, smiled, and walked toward him. What had Holly told him to say? Yes, yes, casual. He ambled over and said, "Hello, cuz . . . what's up?"

Justin passed a few friendly amenities and started out of his car. "Have you seen Holly about?"

"Holly? Why no . . . she left on holiday last night."

"What? How can she do that? Where did she go?"

"Hmmm . . . let's see . . ." said Greg, putting a hand to his mouth. "Asked for some time off . . . said something about going off with Lynn Patterson."

He calmed himself. "Oh . . . so young Tracy was with them?"

"Tracy? No . . . she is over in the ring . . . there, practicing on Waldo."

"They didn't take Tracy with them?" He felt a cold trickle of fear and irritation shoot through him.

"Er . . . no . . . I believe the child is staying with some of Lynn's friends."

"Well, where did they go?"

"Some island . . . Heaven or something," said Greg, enjoying this very much. His cousin had a look about him he had never seen before. This was all very interesting.

"Heaven? Dammit, Greg, do you mean Paradise Island?"

"That's it!"

"And which hotel . . . she must have told you a place she was staying at?"

"Well, she said something about not wanting to be found . . ." hedged Greg.

"I'll break your scrawny neck!" thundered Justin. He moved menacingly toward his younger cousin.

"Hold . . . hold . . ." Greg laughed. "They are at the Loew's . . . but don't you tell her I told you. Say you had a detective on the case . . . she really doesn't want you to know."

"Oh, doesn't she?" said Justin. His voice was low and his tone held a note of danger. He moved back into his car, went to his cottage, threw a few things in an overnight bag, and picked up the phone.

Mark Patterson had been calling everyone in the neighborhood, without success. He had discovered that Tracy was staying with some friends but that Lynn had not told them where she was. He was in a frenzy of agitation. How could she do this? Go off and leave her child, him, without a word? The phone rang, and he picked it up roughly.

"Yeah?" he said sharply.

"Hell, Mark . . . they've gone off to Paradise Island."

"They? They?" he asked impatiently.

"Holly and Lynn!"

"Damn! You mean your mistress and my wife . . ." he started. Horrified shock was freezing his body and his mind. Lynn had never gone off before, and now she was

252

with a single woman on some kind of lark? What was this?

Justin cut him off curtly. "Not my mistress, *my wife.*"

"Your wife?" Mark was puzzled. He was certain Justin had never said anything about being married. He had just assumed . . .

"Never mind that," said Justin, cutting in on his thoughts. "They have left for Paradise Island, no doubt in something of a tantrum. We know they both have reason . . ."

"Holy shit!"

"Precisely. So I'll be by for you . . . pack some things and we'll catch a flight out of Gatwick."

"Yeah," said Mark. Man, when he got a hold of Lynn . . .

"My name is Geof . . ." the good-looking, tall young croupier was saying as he came around and crooked an arm toward each of the two lovelies.

"And English," said Lynn. "Imagine coming all the way from England and finding you." There was a tease in her voice, a light in her brown eyes. Mark hadn't even called. He hadn't even called.

Holly smiled over all this, but inside she felt hurt and almost tired. Could she have been so wrong? She had been sure he would be on the phone to her by now, begging her to come back. Maybe he didn't even know she was gone; maybe he wouldn't care. . . .

Mark and Justin entered the casino in time to see their wives flanking and taking up the arms of a handsome young man, and they exchanged glances.

"You're on your own, buddy!" said Mark as he sauntered toward his target.

Justin stood back to watch, but he made certain he was in full view. When Holly turned to find Mark, she would see him standing watching.

Mark came on strong, but he was in a rage of a jealousy he thought long ago extinguished. He felt like planting the young man touching his wife's hand. He came up to Lynn, looked at the croupier, and said in a tone as hard and defiant as he felt, "The lady is with me."

Lynn sucked in breath. Holly turned, and as Justin had anticipated, she saw him. Indeed, she thought her body would break and fall in scattered pieces. Instead, she did what he did not expect. She excused herself and hurried away.

The croupier extricated himself deftly, and Lynn Patterson was left facing her husband. "Mark . . . what are you doing here?"

"You know, I haven't had any dinner yet . . . would you join me?" There was a warm smile on his lips, an invitation.

She considered him for a long moment. He had come all this way. She had wanted a little more than a dinner invitation, but it was certainly a start. She returned his smile.

Holly was weaving her way through the casino down the lobby of the Britannia, past the pool to the beach. Justin was following at a distance. He wasn't about to give chase and make a scene, but he managed to keep her in sight, and then she was running down the long stretch of sand, and he sprinted forward. A moment later he had her arm, was turning her to face him.

"Holly . . . dammit all, Holly . . . *look at me!*"

She brought up her bright aqua eyes, and they glistened with unshed tears. He had come. She should be happy. Why was she reacting so strangely? She didn't know.

"Holly . . . why?"

"Because . . . because we . . . you . . . the divorce thing has to be settled, and I thought I would get a better perspective on it from a distance, and . . ."

"And how could you just take off and leave without telling me?"

"You don't own me, Justin. I don't have to tell you anything!"

He sucked in a long gulp of air. What was she doing? Pinning him down? "Holly . . ."

"Don't. It's okay for you to just take off for any number of days and not even call . . . but you seem to feel I don't have the same rights." She shook her head. "Let me finish. I've been your mistress . . . not really your wife. Fine, as your mistress I can come and go as I please . . . just as you can."

"Holly . . . you little fool . . ."

"Stop it!" She shoved at him, for he was pulling her into his arms.

"Holly, I love you . . . love you . . . do you think I will ever let you go?"

With a long sob she dove into his chest, and her body shook with the sound of her tears. "Yes, yes, I did think you could let me go . . ."

"Well, I can't, I don't want to. I love you, Holly . . . I want you to be my wife."

She released a short shaky laugh. "I am."

And this time, she did nothing to stop him from kissing her.

A NEW DECADE OF
CREST BESTSELLERS

☐	KANE & ABEL *Jeffrey Archer*	24376	$3.75
☐	PRIVATE SECTOR *Jeff Millar*	24368	$2.95
☐	DONAHUE *Phil Donahue & Co.*	24358	$2.95
☐	DOMINO *Phyllis A. Whitney*	24350	$2.75
☐	TO CATCH A KING *Harry Patterson*	24323	$2.95
☐	AUNT ERMA'S COPE BOOK		
	Erma Bombeck	24334	$2.75
☐	THE GLOW *Brooks Stanwood*	24333	$2.75
☐	RESTORING THE AMERICAN DREAM		
	Robert J. Ringer	24314	$2.95
☐	THE LAST ENCHANTMENT		
	Mary Stewart	24207	$2.95
☐	CENTENNIAL *James A. Michener*	23494	$2.95
☐	THE COUP *John Updike*	24259	$2.95
☐	THURSDAY THE RABBI WALKED OUT		
	Harry Kemelman	24070	$2.25
☐	IN MY FATHER'S COURT		
	Isaac Bashevis Singer	24074	$2.50
☐	A WALK ACROSS AMERICA		
	Peter Jenkins	24277	$2.75
☐	WANDERINGS *Chaim Potok*	24270	$3.95
☐	DRESS GRAY *Lucian K. Truscott IV*	24158	$2.75
☐	THE STORRINGTON PAPERS		
	Dorothy Eden	24239	$2.50

Buy them at your local bookstore or use this handy coupon for ordering.

COLUMBIA BOOK SERVICE (a CBS Publications Co.)
32275 Mally Road, P.O. Box FB, Madison Heights, MI 48071

Please send me the books I have checked above. Orders for less than
books must include 75¢ for the first book and 25¢ for each additiona
book to cover postage and handling. Orders for 5 books or more postag
is FREE. Send check or money order only.

Cost $_____	Name _____
Sales tax*_____	Address _____
Postage_____	City _____
Total $_____	State _____ Zip _____

*The government requires us to collect sales tax in all states except AK
DE, MT, NH and OR.*

This offer expires 1 January 82